S0-CFS-082

CLASSROOM OF THE ELITE

NOVEL 10

MASHIMA TOMONARI

Class A's homeroom teacher. He, Chabashira, and Hoshinomiya are all old friends.

KITOU HAYATO

The best martial artist in Class A. His appearance is unusual for a first-year student.

SAKAYANAGI ARISU

The girl who reigns supreme within and controls Class A. She's willing to use whatever means necessary to win.

If she came right out and said she wanted to reconcile with her brother, then the conversation would be over right now. Manabu would walk away without a moment's hesitation. The old Suzune might well have answered that way.

"Well, what I wanted to talk to you about today is… I… Please, give me courage."

CLASSROOM OF THE ELITE
NOVEL 10

CONTENTS

CLASSROOM OF THE ELITE

NOVEL 10

STORY BY
Syougo Kinugasa

ART BY
Tomoseshunsaku

Seven Seas Entertainment

CLASSROOM OF THE ELITE VOL. 10
YOUKOSO JITSURYOKUSHIJOUSHUGI NO KYOUSHITSU E VOL. 10
© Syougo Kinugasa 2019
Art by Tomoseshunsaku
First published in Japan in 2019 by KADOKAWA CORPORATION, Tokyo.
English translation rights arranged with KADOKAWA CORPORATION, Tokyo.

No portion of this book may be reproduced or transmitted
in any form without written permission from the copyright
holders. This is a work of fiction. Names, characters, places,
and incidents are the products of the author's imagination
or are used fictitiously. Any resemblance to actual events,
locales, or persons, living or dead, is entirely coincidental.
Any information or opinions expressed by the creators of this
book belong to those individual creators and do not necessarily
reflect the views of Seven Seas Entertainment or its employees.

Seven Seas press and purchase enquiries can be sent to
Marketing Manager Lianne Sentar at press@gomanga.com.
Information regarding the distribution and purchase of
digital editions is available from Digital Manager CK Russell
at digital@gomanga.com.

Seven Seas and the Seven Seas logo are trademarks of
Seven Seas Entertainment. All rights reserved.

Follow Seven Seas Entertainment online at
sevenseasentertainment.com.

TRANSLATION: Timothy MacKenzie
COVER DESIGN: Nicky Lim
INTERIOR LAYOUT & DESIGN: Clay Gardner
COPY EDITOR: Stephanie Cohen
PROOFREADER: Meg van Huygen
LIGHT NOVEL EDITOR: Nibedita Sen
PREPRESS TECHNICIAN: Melanie Ujimori
PRINT MANAGER: Rhiannon Rasmussen-Silverstein
PRODUCTION MANAGER: Lissa Pattillo
EDITOR-IN-CHIEF: Julie Davis
ASSOCIATE PUBLISHER: Adam Arnold
PUBLISHER: Jason DeAngelis

ISBN: 978-1-64827-321-6
Printed in Canada
First Printing: March 2022
10 9 8 7 6 5 4 3 2 1

1 HIRATA YOUSUKE'S SOLILOQUY

MY FRIENDS IN MY CLASS are extremely important to me.

...Well, what I mean is, it's the *class* that's important to me. I'm well aware how bizarrely backward that statement sounds, but in order to protect my beloved friends, I will protect the class. If I can protect the class, I can protect my friends.

There are dozens of students in this class. There are as many perspectives present as there are people, and they clash over the smallest of things. But that's why I have to protect them. Before I even realized it, protecting the class had become my purpose. My challenge.

But in truth...that wasn't who I really was.

I hadn't always been the kind of person a class rallied around. If anything, I was a shadow. If I had to describe it in terms of what Class C was like now, I'd say I was a lot like Ayanokouji-kun. That's why I sometimes compare him to my old self. But I've changed.

After it happened, I suppose there was no way for me to *not* change...

When I was little, I had a really close friend. A friend who was in the same class as me all the way from kindergarten to junior high. Unbeknownst to me, that friend was being bullied. He then attempted to take his own life, and it was only by chance that he lived. He could easily have died.

That day. From that day, my destiny began to change.

I did what I could do to stop bullying...and I failed. Though we kept the class together, we did so in the wrong way. The in-fighting stopped, but so did the smiles. And now history was about to repeat itself in front of me.

I couldn't make the same mistake again. That was the one thing I was sure of. The only way I could protect the class.

That—

I saw the surprised faces of my classmates in front of me.

"Horikita... Just shut up for a second."

My words were rude, coarse, and stupid. My voice was filled with neither anger nor sadness. My classmates, Horikita-san included, looked me at strangely.

It didn't matter, though.

Now that things had gotten to this point, it didn't matter anymore.

At the end of the worst special exam, I... I...

2   THE CALM BEFORE THE STORM

WE'D FINALLY MADE IT to March. It was Monday, just a few days after the end-of-term exam, and everyone was anxious to hear the results. After all, in the unlikely event that one of us got a failing grade, that person would be expelled.

"Sensei, are you going to announce the results now?!" Ike asked enthusiastically, planted in his chair and restraining himself as best he could, even as he leaned so far forward it seemed like he might fall over.

"Don't lose your head. You'll know in just a minute."

Chabashira's movements were steady, suggesting she did this regularly. She spread out a large piece of paper that she had brought with her. The school usually made announcements digitally, via our phones or the bulletin boards, but it seemed they preferred to announce results in this manner when it came to written exams, where expulsion was possible.

"Do you feel confident you did well, Ike?"

"W-Well, I think so. I studied as hard as I possibly could and all..."

"You studied as hard as you possibly could, huh? And yet you're still feeling uneasy?"

Chabashira must have found Ike's response to be amusing rather than exasperating, because she had a slight smile on her lips. Ike's grades were generally poor, so it was only to be expected that he'd feel uneasy, no matter how hard he'd studied.

"Sudou, you're usually competing for the lowest score each time, too. How are you feeling?" she asked.

Once upon a time, Sudou would probably have been the most anxious person present. It wasn't an exaggeration to say that he'd placed last in almost every single subject in all the tests we'd taken thus far. Chabashira was expecting a response similar to Ike's, but Sudou's reply was unexpected.

"...I feel pretty confident. I didn't fail, at the very least."

"Oh?"

Although his athleticism was really all Sudou had to brag about, the look on his face and his tone seemed to imply a certain degree of confidence. Of course, I was sure he was still a little uneasy, like Ike. But the hard work he'd put in to overcome that, and the experience he'd gained along the way, allowed him to feel more confident.

What he'd gained through his repeated study sessions with Horikita wasn't the kind of temporary knowledge you got from cramming for something for one night at the very last minute. It was the kind of knowledge that was retained, slowly but surely being ingrained in his brain. Sudou's tutor, Horikita, looked confident, too.

Well, she probably didn't like that Sudou was getting a little carried away, though.

"Hm... Well, it is quite interesting how much you kids have grown. It's hard to tell exactly which of you will really make progress, but you've quite easily surpassed my expectations. Now, then. Without further delay, let me announce the results of your year-end examinations," said Chabashira.

She put everyone's test results up on the blackboard, then went to draw a red line on the paper. Anyone whose name fell below that line would be forcibly expelled from the school.

"As for your results this time..." she began.

Chabashira held the red marker in her hand. She pressed its tip against the paper and drew a straight horizontal line. It was the red line of fate. And below that line—were no names at all.

Which meant...

"Excellent work. You've all passed. These are your best results so far. I have absolutely no complaints," she added.

"Hell yeah!" shouted Ike, the first to speak.

He must have been scared to death. After all, he *had* gotten the lowest overall score in the class.

"Whew, man, that was a piece of cake though! *Ha ha ha ha*... Man, that was close!" he added, repeatedly glancing at the sight of his name directly above the red line.

"Huh. I only studied a little bit the day before and I still managed to pass, huh?" said Yamauchi, who had come in second-to-last.

"Come on, don't lie, Haruki. You were studying for dear life every day, weren't ya?"

"Was I? *Wa ha ha ha!*"

Given that both Ike and Yamauchi had managed to pass, everyone had to be pretty satisfied. Chabashira looked at them with a warm, gentle gaze. Still, these results were surprising. Ike had come in last, followed by Yamauchi, then Hondou, then Satou, and then Inogashira. Satou's name was written right above Inogashira's. Considering the kind of scores Sudou had gotten up until this point, you could say that he had made great strides.

"Over this past year, the person who has shown the most growth in terms of test scores has been you, Sudou.

It's no wonder you felt confident that you'd pass. I sincerely look forward to seeing how you improve in the future," said Chabashira, apparently sharing my feelings on the matter.

"*Heh.* Ain't nothin' to brag about," said Sudou. Despite what he said, he certainly looked pleased with himself.

On the other hand, the students whose names appeared at the top were basically the same as always. In first place was Keisei. In second was Kouenji. Keisei always exhibited a high level of academic prowess, and since he never neglected his studies, he kept his spot at the top. Kouenji, though, was a mystery. He showed no signs of studying on a regular basis, and never engaged in discussion with anyone. If he ever really put his academic abilities to use, he might even surpass Keisei's. It was even possible that he'd been occasionally slacking off here and there, depending on what was on the test, since there were some slight fluctuations in the score rankings.

In third place was Horikita. I had the impression that she struggled a little bit with English, but she'd scored high this time. While tutoring Sudou, she'd successfully brought up her own grades at the same time.

"Sensei, how about the other classes?"

"They all got through it without incident, just like you.

In terms of overall average scores, you came in third," said Chabashira.

We probably didn't even need to ask who came in first, second, and fourth.

"I suppose that if we're to overtake Class A and Class B, we'll need to raise our overall grades more." Horikita, who'd been keeping track of the test scores and rankings, didn't look too proud of the results. The students at the top had come close to hitting perfect scores, which meant that our only option was to get the students at the bottom to improve theirs.

"You did a good job helping Sudou get his grades up. I'm impressed."

"This is merely a reflection of his hard work. He pulled it off because we focused on thoroughly crushing his weaknesses."

Sudou's weakest subject was also English, like Horikita, but his scores had improved dramatically. The fact that they'd both been intensively working on their English was evident from their performance.

"I wonder if he can aim a little higher on the next test? I suppose that all depends on whether he can stay focused."

There was probably no need to worry about that. As long as Horikita was around, Sudou would continue giving it his best. He was probably beginning to get the hang of studying now. Maybe he'd even break into the top half of the class's scores someday soon.

"It seems Ike-kun and Yamauchi-kun have managed to put a little wiggle room between their score and the red line. Holding regular study sessions was the right choice. Now if only someone next to me would give it their all, perhaps our average score would go up even higher, hm?" said Horikita.

"This is as far as I go," I replied. As always, my scores were neither good nor bad. I'd placed 18th in our class this time.

"I'm not convinced. Eventually, I'm going to have you take this seriously," she answered.

"I'll do what I can to live up to your expectations."

At any rate, the fact that everyone had made it through safely was significant. Ike and Yamauchi, who'd just barely managed to squeeze by, joked around with one another in relief. Chabashira, our homeroom teacher, looked over us all with a quiet, warm gaze.

"I know this might not sound like much, but this really is a job well done. I have to give you credit for that," she told us.

Chabashira didn't often praise us, but it seemed she'd started to feel differently of late. She'd probably had a hunch that everyone was going to make it through these year-end exams safely, too.

"Yeah!"

"However, Ike, the fact that you're getting this excited is a problem, too. Special exams aside, it's only to be expected that you should be able to pass a written exam at this level. Besides, it's not as though this exam was one of the most difficult ones you'd see on a national scale."

The test certainly *had* been more difficult than the other written exams we'd taken thus far in our first year. Perhaps the school was keeping up appearances by making sure to keep tests at a level that the students could handle.

"Unfortunately, we can't keep dwelling on good news forever," announced Chabashira.

The lively and cheerful mood of the classroom immediately grew tense as she said that. A typical development.

"As I'm sure many of you may have already guessed, completing the written exam isn't the last thing you'll be doing this year. There's going to be a major special exam on March 8th, just like in previous years," she continued.

March 8th? That meant Monday of next week, huh? Even though we'd just sat through a written exam, it wasn't unreasonable for there to be a special exam as well,

THE CALM BEFORE THE STORM

since there was still a little time left in the school year. I'd heard the third-year students even had one more exam in addition to the special one.

"Well, this special exam will be the last one for this year. Let's work together and do our best, everyone. If we do that, then no one should get expelled, and we should be able to shoot for Class A," said Hirata.

Hearing those words of encouragement from Hirata, many students nodded in agreement. Chabashira watched the class with a seemingly pleasant, charming smile on her face.

"Knowing you, I think you might just be able to graduate together at the end of your third year, without anyone getting expelled. I have high hopes for you all," said Chabashira.

Despite the fact that we had a little time until homeroom ended, she dismissed us for the day after making that statement.

"I kinda get the feeling that we just got like, the highest compliment from our teacher ever. You think so?" said Ike, laughing happily with Yamauchi.

"But don't get sloppy, okay? Your final exam next week will by no means be easy," said Chabashira, giving us that casual warning before class was over.

2.1

. . . .

OUR FIRST YEAR OF SCHOOL was almost at an end.
I used the interval between morning classes to head
to the bathroom. On my way back to class, I happened
to spot two familiar faces—a second-year and third-year
student, deeply engaged in conversation. It was Student
Council President Nagumo, and Horikita Manabu, the
former president.

I thought it was probably just simple coincidence, but
Nagumo noticed me almost immediately. He beckoned
me over with a wave, and it wasn't like I could pretend
not to notice him and keep heading back to class.

"Hey, Ayanokouji. You pass the year-end exam?" he
asked, directly.

Horikita's brother, on the other hand, just looked over
at me quietly.

THE CALM BEFORE THE STORM

"I guess." He had pulled me into a meaningless conversation.

"Wow, that was brusque. I can't believe that's how you'd act in front of the student council president."

"...Is that so?" I straightened myself up a little bit. I didn't know if it would be enough to satisfy him, but figured it should be good enough.

"Well, whatever. More importantly, you've got perfect timing. There's something I've wanted to ask you," he continued.

Nagumo had a delighted look on his face, like he was happy no one else was around to hear us.

"Apparently, in order to divert attention from all the slander about Ichinose Honami, *someone* posted rumors about several students on the bulletin boards. Who in the world would do such a thing?" he asked.

He was testing me. No—I was certain he'd already seen through me. No matter how much information Nagumo had, though, I wasn't going to change my behavior.

"Who knows? I have no idea. The only thing I know for sure is that it's caused me a lot of trouble," I replied.

"Oh, now that you mention it, you were one of the students singled out, weren't you? Now, what did that post say again...?"

"School officials have already informed us not to

discuss those matters any further. I don't think even the student council president should be exempt from that." That should help me avoid prying.

"It's just as Ayanokouji says, Nagumo. Perhaps you should refrain from saying anything too carelessly."

Horikita provided covering fire, and Nagumo quickly pulled back. It didn't seem like this was a topic he particularly wanted to discuss.

"So anyway, what were you big shots talking about?" I asked.

"Oh, I was just having a little discussion with Horikita-senpai. Ain't that right?" said Nagumo.

He looked meaningfully at Horikita, who quietly nodded in response. I was curious about the spot they'd chosen to have their discussion. They were on the floor where the first-year classes were, which made me feel something was off.

"Before the first- and second-years take their exams, tomorrow will mark the beginning of the all-too-important battle to see whether or not Horikita-senpai can graduate without incident from Class A. I was asking him directly about that. You're interested too, aren't you?" said Nagumo.

Unlike the rest of the students, the third-years were expected to take one additional special exam. It made sense that that exam would be starting soon. I didn't know what Nagumo wanted me to say, but I supposed I'd just answer him honestly.

"I'm not particularly interested, no. I don't really have the leeway to worry about my upperclassmen," I replied.

Nagumo wore a somewhat dissatisfied look on seeing my lack of interest.

"Jeez, that's just cold, man. Well, I guess you're one of Horikita-senpai's favorites too, so it makes sense."

I didn't particularly remember him doting on me. In fact, I could count the number of times that we'd had contact during my first year at this school on one hand.

"Come on, you're totally getting special treatment, Ayanokouji. But it's not because you're a special student or anything. It's because you just so happen to have been placed in a special environment. Yep—it's all thanks to one of your classmates, who's been under the watchful gaze of our senpai over here."

Senpai? Looking back, I noticed the younger Horikita watching us from a distance. The fact that we'd all just happened to gather in this spot couldn't be coincidence.

"Are you the one who called her here, Nagumo?"

"Well, it's only natural for me to reach out to my senpai's little sister, isn't it? I mean, I'll be leading the younger generation next year as student council president, after all."

Apparently, he'd arranged this meeting to get both the Horikita siblings in one place. It seemed I was the only person who'd actually shown up by coincidence.

"Come over here," said Nagumo, bluntly calling Horikita's sister on over.

"...Were you the one who sent me this e-mail, President Nagumo?" asked Horikita Suzune.

"Well, not *technically*, no, but close enough, I guess. You are Horikita-senpai's little sister, right?"

"Yes... I'm Horikita Suzune."

Because her older brother was right there, Horikita shrunk back somewhat as she spoke.

"I never imagined that Horikita-senpai's little sister would be placed in Class D after enrolling here. Talk about a surprise," said Nagumo.

"What are you after, Nagumo?" said Horikita's brother, not giving his sister even a single glance.

If Nagumo had set up this meeting, then there had to be a meaning behind it. But he just shook his head, as if to say there was no reason in particular.

"I just wanted to meet up, is all. With my senpai and his little sister."

He probably did this so he could evaluate her. It was precisely because Horikita's brother sensed this that he decided to make the first move.

"I'll say this before we go any further—don't think you can get any concessions out of me by using my sister."

"*Concessions*? No way. I mean, really, do you think I'd ever try and make a move on someone who's both a cute little freshman and my senpai's little sister?"

"You'd do anything in order to win. I'm sure of it."

Nagumo didn't say anything to affirm Horikita's brother's coarse words, but he didn't deny them, either.

"Even so, you don't gotta be *that* standoffish with me, y'know? I mean, I wish you would've told me much earlier that you had a little sister. If you did, I would've invited her to the student council much earlier."

"What?"

Both Horikita siblings looked shocked to hear something so totally unexpected from Nagumo's mouth,

"I suppose if she's your little sister, I could have her take the position of student council president after I graduate, right? I think being the sister of the man who's been awarded so many honors by this school means she's more than qualified for the job," said Nagumo.

"Don't judge someone's abilities just based on their genetics. What I've done here has nothing to do with my sister."

"...Yes. I'm not qualified to be a member of the student council," said Horikita.

As if to help cover up her brother's denial, Horikita rejected Nagumo's offer to join the student council, speaking self-deprecatingly. Well, I suppose she'd reacted negatively when I'd suggested joining about the student council to her before, too.

Nagumo seemed to see something in Horikita Suzune's modest behavior. "Well, I just wanted to a chance to meet you face-to-face for today. I'll invite you again later," he said.

Whether or not Horikita Suzune actually wanted to join the student council was, in reality, an entirely separate issue. I got the sense Nagumo had said that to mean he would continue to be actively involved with Horikita Suzune in the future. He was probably doing so in order to get Horikita's brother flustered, perhaps find his weak point.

"...Well then, u-um, I—" stammered Horikita, speaking up—though it sounded like she was trying to escape from her brother, rather than from Nagumo.

"Your senpai only has a little more time left at this school. Wouldn't you like to be a bit spoiled?" asked Nagumo.

"I'm sorry. If you'll please excuse me."

Horikita Suzune, having determined that continuing this conversation would just make her brother uncomfortable, scuttled quickly toward our classroom. Her actions made it obvious how bad the siblings' relationship truly was.

"Wow, the two of you seem to have such a *wonderful* relationship, don't you, Horikita-senpai?"

"Are you satisfied now, Nagumo?" Whatever Nagumo was planning, it didn't seem like Horikita's brother was bothered at all.

"Well, if I were you, I would cherish the time I have left with my little sister a bit more," said Nagumo.

Even though he was only saying that partly to get a rise out of Horikita Manabu, it was certainly true that Horikita Suzune had come to this school because she was following after her brother, and he'd spent very little time with her so far.

"Anyway, senpai, please make your presence known to the student body by doing what you can to graduate from Class A. If, in the unlikely event that you're demoted to Class B before graduation, you won't be able to shrug it off, you know?" said Nagumo.

If that were to happen, it would be a betrayal of both the school officials' and his fellow students' hopes for him. He was probably under quite a bit of pressure... Well, no, he probably wasn't the kind of guy who'd feel something like that.

Horikita Manabu seemed to take this to mean the conversation was over. He left without saying another word.

"Oh, my. I guess this wasn't enough to get him to take me seriously, after all," mused Nagumo.

Apparently, he intended to continue obsessing over Horikita Manabu forever.

"Is competing against the former student council president that important?" I asked.

At the school camp that we'd attended not too long ago, Nagumo had proved that he would use any means necessary to win. He'd involved the entire third-year class into an attempt to attack Horikita's brother, even though they had nothing to do with him.

"Of course. Defeating Horikita-senpai is the only goal I have left to accomplish here at this school," said Nagumo.

I supposed that there were almost no avenues for a second-year and a third-year to compete directly with one another. If he really intended to do this, then he was going to have to employ some rather forceful means.

"That said...what I do depends on the contents of the exam and on Horikita-senpai."

No matter how many enemies he made in the process, Nagumo planned to settle things once and for all with Horikita's brother before he graduated. He said it depended on the contents of the exam, but I was sure he'd push to do it no matter what the test was like. He was almost out of time, after all.

"What about you, President Nagumo? Will you have any problems with the special exam next week? I can't imagine it'll be simple, even for the second-year students."

"Who can say? You're welcome to keep hoping that I'll fail," said Nagumo.

The break period was almost over. Nagumo ended our conversation there, and I returned to the classroom, where my neighbor, Horikita Suzune, looked over at me.

"Student Council President Nagumo and onii-san... What were they talking about?"

"If you're interested, then you should've just stayed until the end."

"But..."

Well, that would've been an unreasonable thing to ask, though. She became quiet and meek whenever she was around her brother, like a frightened animal.

"You're bizarre for listening to the two of them talk. A lot of people have their eye on you, don't they? Because you competed against my brother in the relay race during the sports festival?" said Horikita.

Wow, that was some nice sarcasm. That being said, it wasn't like I could predict the future. You can't make the right moves one hundred percent of the time.

"It does seem like you haven't really had the chance to connect with your brother over this past year, though."

"...Is that bad?" she asked.

Whenever I brought up Horikita's brother in conversation, her mood immediately soured. I'd probably have been better off not getting sucked into this conversation, but her curiosity about what her brother had been talking to Nagumo about, and what came of their conversation, was plain to see.

"Wouldn't it be better if you confronted him at least once before he graduates and is gone?" I asked.

"You don't know anything. There's no way my brother would ever bother meeting with me. It would be sheer stupidity for me to try and approach him, knowing how harshly he'd respond."

So she was satisfied with just enrolling in the same school and watching over him from afar, huh?

"If my brother is interested in anything, then... Well, I may not like it, but he's only interested in you," said Horikita.

That wasn't true. I almost said that out loud, but stopped myself. If I said any more right now, Horikita wouldn't believe me. More importantly, if she didn't have the courage to face him herself, then this was meaningless.

"Is that so? You might have a point."

I ended the conversation there, abruptly. I got the sense Horikita was still dissatisfied, but she didn't say anything else.

3 IN-CLASS VOTING

THE FOLLOWING DAY was Tuesday, March 2nd.

Chabashira strode into morning homeroom shortly after the bell rang. It was a sight we saw every single day, and my classmates were all relaxed. She'd announced our test results yesterday, informing us that we had all successfully passed the year-end exam. And there were still a few days left before the final special exam of the year began on March 8th. There was no reason for anyone to be nervous, so their relaxed state was only natural.

However, Chabashira had a remarkably grim look on her face as she stood at the podium. She projected a sense of tension and anxiety, and those feelings spread to the students, too.

"Um, did something happen?"

Hirata, the person always putting the harmony of

the class first, took the initiative to speak up. She didn't answer him right away, but remained silent, almost like she was reluctant to speak at all. In the past, she'd always mercilessly launched into an explanation of whatever test we were facing, no matter how harsh it was. Given that, it didn't take long at all for the students to understand that something was off about this situation.

"—There is something that I have to tell you all."

She finally opened her mouth to speak. Her expression was as stern as always, but the strain in her voice gave me the impression she was struggling as hard as she could to get the words out.

"Just as I told you yesterday, the final special exam for your first year will begin on March 8th. After you complete this special exam, you will be promoted to second-year students. That is typical of how things have worked in past years."

Chabashira turned around, picked up a piece of chalk, and extended her hand toward the blackboard.

"However, this year, things will be slightly different from previous years."

"Different?" Hirata asked, sensing that something was off.

"Even after taking your year-end final exams, not a single person has been expelled this year. Getting to this point without a single expulsion has never happened before in the history of this school."

"That just means we're really good, doesn't it?" said Ike, cutting in. I didn't think he was supposed to be celebrating, though. If Chabashira were acting like her usual self, she would probably have sternly reminded him not to get carried away.

"That's right. And the school recognizes that, too. Normally, you could say this would be something to celebrate. Even we, the faculty and staff, hope to have as many students as possible make it to graduation. However, it must be said that problems arise when things don't go according to plan."

The way she phrased that was strange. Hirata and my neighbor, Horikita, also sensed something off about her choice of words.

"You sound like something's bothering you. Like you're bothered about the fact that no one's been expelled so far."

"That's not true. But sometimes things happen that I didn't expect," she replied.

She'd said this would normally be cause for celebration, but her tone was grave. Horikita spoke up, as if trying to banish those feelings.

"What are you trying to say? That there's something wrong with us?" she asked.

But nothing we said would change whatever Chabashira was about to tell us. She wasn't free to do as she pleased. She was an employee of the school. Her only role was to convey its instructions to us.

"The school has decided that, in consideration of the fact that no one has been expelled from the first-year class—"

The words seemed to get stuck in Chabashira's throat. She struggled to get them out.

"—as a 'measure for exceptional circumstances,' a supplementary special exam will be held immediately, starting today."

Chabashira wrote today's date—Tuesday, March 2nd—on the blackboard, as well as the words "supplementary special exam."

"Wait, what? What is this all about?! Dude, *another* special exam? That's the *worst thing ever*! The school's act-ing like a whiny little kid! They didn't get their way since no one got expelled, and so they're adding this other test!" shouted Ike.

Chabashira just ignored everything he said. Students had no right to object, and in fact...maybe she was the one being forced to give us this test against her wishes. She looked much tenser than usual. She wasn't trying to scare us—it likely that the school really had decided on this test in a hurry.

"Something tells me things are a little different from the way they've been so far," Horikita muttered quietly, having realized that there was no point in fighting back.

"Only the students who pass this special exam will be able to go on to take the special exam on March 8th," said Chabashira, pausing for a moment after that brief explanation.

"Come on, I don't get this at all! I can't believe they're only giving *us* this extra special exam now!"

"Your frustration is completely understandable. This special exam is being administered although it was never previously planned for. Even though it's just one more test than what students in the past have taken, the fact that it places a burden on all of you cannot be denied. This is something that the other teachers and I are taking very seriously," said Chabashira.

The teachers were taking it seriously, huh? Which meant it was specifically the *instructors* who were taking it seriously, while the school administrators might not feel the same way. At least, that was one way to interpret her phrasing.

It was certainly true that adding special exams would be tough on the students. If it was a written exam that tested academic skill, then students would have to study harder. If it was a physical exam, they'd have to train for it in a similar fashion. Regardless of the test's contents, forcing the students to take it was harsh.

That being said, it wasn't going to go away, no matter how much we complained.

Chabashira continued speaking.

"The contents of this special exam are exceedingly simple. The dropout rate isn't high at all, either, at less than three percent per class."

A dropout rate of less than three percent. That certainly sounded low. But this supplementary special exam would certainly be unlike any written exams we'd had so far. There was no need to specifically mention the dropout rate. In fact, such an expression had never been used in any of the previous exams.

The students who noticed this felt even more suspicious. I looked over at my neighbor, who coincidentally looked over at me at the same time, causing our eyes to meet.

"What is it, Ayanokouji-kun?"

"Oh. Nothing."

"If you look at me for no reason at all, that comes off as creepy, you know?"

"...Yeah, I guess so."

I decided to just look out the window. The classroom was small enough that I could hear everything being said no matter where I was looking.

"Just what kind of test will this *be*? And what will it be testing?"

"You seem anxious, but really, there's nothing to be worried about. The supplementary special exam has absolutely nothing at all to do with your intellectual or physical ability. It's something so simple that, when the time comes, anyone can do it. That's right. It's as simple as writing your own name on your test paper. And there's only a three percent chance you'll get expelled as a result. You would agree that that's a low chance, right?" said Chabashira.

She still hadn't touched on the core issue—the actual contents of the exam.

"...The difficulty level doesn't matter. From our point of view, even three percent is scary."

"That's true. You have a point, Hirata. I do understand how that three percent scares you. However, whether or not you can reduce that risk depends on what you do in the time you have before the actual test. As I'm sure you've probably already guessed," said Chabashira.

"How was that number derived? Based on what you're saying, it sounds like it's a simple lottery. Is that it?" asked Hirata.

The odds that someone from our class would be expelled were high. Chabashira had casually thrown out the three percent figure, but the burden this exam would place on the students was greater than they could imagine. Hirata, understanding this right away, pressed Chabashira on that point.

"Please tell us. Just what kind of test will this be?"

"The title of this special exam is: 'In-Class Voting.'"

"In-Class... Voting?"

Chabashira wrote out the title of the exam on the blackboard.

"I'll now explain the rules behind this special exam. Starting today, you will have four days to evaluate your classmates. You will choose three students who you think deserve praise, and three that you think deserve criticism, and cast your votes on Saturday. That is all," she explained.

So the students would be evaluating one another? If you thought about it in simple terms, then students like Hirata and Kushida would get a lot of votes and come out on top. On the other hand, students who were considered annoying or thought to be dragging the class down would sink to the bottom. The urgency of the situation was evinced by the fact that the test was being held on a Saturday, which was originally supposed to be a day off. However, based on what Chabashira said—

"Th-That's it? That's all there is to this exam?"

"That's it. That's all there is to it. I told you, didn't I? It's a simple test."

"Wait, how do you determine pass or fail—a good score or a bad score—with a test like that?"

"I will explain that part now."

Tightening her grip on the chalk further, Chabashira continued to write.

"The core of this special exam is the number of praise votes and criticism votes each student gets as a result of the polling. The top student—in other words, the student who gets the most praise votes—will receive a special reward. This special reward will not be private points, but instead, one 'Protection Point.' This is a new system."

We hadn't heard of that kind of point before. Of course, everyone's attention was piqued.

"In the unlikely event that you are up for expulsion in the future, Protection Points will allow you to reverse that decision. Even if you fail a test, Protection Points will allow you to nullify questions you got wrong, based on the number of such points you have. However, these points cannot be transferred to others."

It was no exaggeration to say that every student in the classroom was more shocked than they'd ever been before.

"I'm sure you all understand exactly how powerful these points are. In fact, they are worth, comparatively speaking, about twenty million private points. Of course, if you are an excellent student with no fear of expulsion, then they might not be worth that much," she explained.

That probably wasn't true. No matter who you were, you would absolutely want the ability to nullify expulsion. There wasn't a student out there who wouldn't welcome having that power. This was an extravagant reward.

In fact...it was far *too* extravagant. Depending on how you used them, these Protection Points could become an incredibly dangerous weapon. And, given how extravagant the reward was, it was clear that the penalty suffered by whoever came in last would also be significant.

"So, does that mean something bad will happen to the bottom three students...?" asked an anxious Hirata.

"Not necessarily. In this case, only one student—the one who received the most criticism votes in the entire class—will be given the penalty. Other students will not be penalized, no matter how many criticism votes they receive. After all, the purpose of this supplementary special exam is to elect one student to be in the lead and one student to come in last."

"What kind of penalty is it?"

"This supplementary special exam is not like the ones you've had thus far. One aspect, in particular, is different—and it is that this test is being held to resolve the problem of a lack of dropouts. That is the purpose for which it was designed," explained Chabashira.

Yep. What the students should be concerned about was the reason why this supplementary special exam was being held in the first place. If this exam was being held because no one had been expelled so far, then—

"This special exam is, as I explained, quite easy. This is not a difficult test, irrespective of whether you have poor grades or are bad at sports. But why, then, did the school prepare such an extraordinary reward as Protection Points? Because this is an exam where it is probably impossible to advance without someone being expelled."

Chabashira turned and looked at all of us, one by one.

"That's right. The student who places at the bottom will...be expelled from this school."

If there was a vote, there would be results. If there were results, someone would place first and someone last. And the person who came last would be expelled. The outcome was inevitable. No matter how exceptional the class, or how mediocre, the results would be the same. The only difference would be the question of who.

So that's what kind of exam this is, huh?

The school, frustrated by the lack of students getting expelled, had decided to hold this supplementary exam. It was an exam that had to result in someone being kicked out—if not, there would be no point in holding it in the first place. But the person who popped up in my mind was none other than Sakayanagi's father, the board chairman. You couldn't assess everything there was to know about a person just from meeting them once, but he didn't seem like the kind of person who'd implement such an outrageous exam.

"U-Uh, I don't really get it, sensei. S-So, you're seriously saying that if someone comes in last place, then... that person is gonna get expelled?"

"That's correct. That person will be on the chopping block, so to speak. But don't worry. The class as a whole will not be penalized even if someone is expelled this time around. That's the nature of this exam," replied Chabashira.

This was clearly different from the special exams we'd seen thus far. Although the probability of expulsion varied from individual to individual, there was usually an equal chance for everyone to avoid expulsion together. This time, however, the exam was designed to ensure someone would be sacrificed. This was the "measure for exceptional circumstances" that the school had prepared.

It was precisely because they were pressing for a forced expulsion that they were dangling something like

Protection Points before us. But even so, the risk we were being made to bear was disproportionately high.

"You're probably thinking that this is outrageous. As your teacher, I think so, too. But it's been decided, and there's nothing we can do to fight it. We have no choice but to follow the rules and take this special exam," said Chabashira.

"Seriously? Really...?"

A dark cloud loomed over our class, which had only just managed to survive the year-end final exams. This weekend, one of us would be gone.

"The time you have until voting day is limited, so please allow me to continue explaining the rules. The number of praise votes and criticism votes for each student will be made public at the end of the exam, meaning the entire class's results will, too. However, information about who specifically voted for who will not be disclosed. The voting will be conducted anonymously," said Chabashira.

They had to make the voting anonymous if they were going to administer this exam. Praise votes aside, the matter of who gave who criticism votes would continue to be an issue for a long time afterward.

"Continuing on. One praise vote and one criticism vote will cancel each other out. If someone received ten criticism votes and thirty praise votes, they would effectively end up with a positive value of twenty. Regardless of whether it is praise or criticism, you cannot vote for yourself. You are also not allowed to vote for the same person more than once."

"What if we abstain...? Could we, for example, only submit praise votes?"

"No. Naturally, you cannot. You must fill in three names for praise votes and three for criticism votes. Also, even if you miss school on the day of the special exam because you are feeling ill, you will still have to cast your votes," replied Chabashira.

That meant we couldn't leave our ballots blank or abstain from voting. Several students looked deeply troubled. This exam certainly posed a serious threat for people who anticipated getting a lot of criticism votes. The students who'd made it this far by piggybacking on others' efforts would be feeling all the more pressure right now.

"...No, it's too soon to be giving in to despair," said Hirata, offering words of comfort to Ike and the others, to try and calm them down. "Sensei said that it was 'probably' impossible. That means there must be some kind of loophole."

In the tests we'd taken so far, Chabashira had chosen her words to give us hints about how to make it through.

But how would that work this time? The 'probably' in her statement seemed to imply there were a limited number of methods we could use.

"It's not easy, but there most certainly is a method you can use to avoid expulsion," said Horikita.

"Wh-What do you mean, Horikita?"

"If we choose three people to receive praise votes and three people to receive criticism votes, and as long as we can control the voting by having everyone in class band together on this, then we'd essentially cancel everything out, so the students getting only praise and the students getting only criticism would all end up with zero. If we did that, then no one would end up in last place. Am I wrong?" said Horikita.

"I-I see, that makes sense! Wow, way to go, Suzune!"

It was possible, if all our classmates cooperated. But if even just one person turned out to be a traitor, then the student targeted for betrayal would be sent down the path of expulsion. Also, there was a tempting reward waiting for whoever claimed the top spot, in the form of Protection Points. People like Kushida, who hated Horikita, might be a problem. Was it possible to compensate for that by making adjustments to the plan?

If Kushida was assigned to cast a criticism vote for Horikita, that might avert the danger, to some extent.

If the final vote totals were made known to us afterward, it would probably help identify who'd turned traitor. We couldn't afford to backstab each other on a whim.

"What Horikita said just now about controlling the vote would be meaningless," said Chabashira.

"What do you mean?"

"If no one is selected to be in first place and last place in this exam, the results will be rejected. Whether intentionally or accidentally, if the results end up showing that everyone has received a total of zero, then another vote will be held. In other words, the exam will be repeated endlessly until a decision is made on whom to expel."

The escape route that the students were desperately scrambling for had just been cut off.

"Wait, isn't that...kind of a strange rule? If we genuinely happened to end up with a total of zero after choosing who to cast our praise and criticism votes for, then we'd cast our votes the same way the second time, producing the same result. If you overrule the results by force, then you can't say those results were based on a fair evaluation," replied Horikita.

"Horikita, your reasoning is correct. If you wound up with a total of zero by coincidence, then it's true that making you cast your votes again would be contradictory. But think about this realistically. In a test where you're being asked to rank someone first and someone last, it should be *extremely unlikely* that you'd just so happen to wind up with a zero-vote total for every single person. No?"

Chabashira made a very good point in her response, too. A zero-vote result across the board wasn't happening unless the vote was intentionally set up to be that way.

"...Then, what happens if two or more people tie for first or last place?"

That outcome was quite likely.

"There will be a deciding vote. If the vote remains divided even then, and a decision cannot be reached, the school will use a special method that they've devised in order to break the tie. I cannot explain what that method is at this current time," said Chabashira.

So she'd only reveal it to us in the event the vote ended in a tie? The chances of such a deadlock were pretty low.

"There's no need to worry about that. In truth, the chances of actually getting to a tiebreaker are next to zero," added Chabashira, sharing my opinion.

"Why is that? I think it's probably enough."

"Well, that's because...where praise votes are concerned, we'll be asking you to vote for students outside your class, too."

"Outside our class?"

"You will be asked to choose one student that you deem worthy of praise from the three other classes. Naturally, each of those votes will also count as a praise vote. In other words, in the unlikely event that a student is disliked by their entire class but is liked by everyone in the other classes, it's entirely possible that they would come out with about eighty praise votes, even after subtracting the criticism votes they would get from their own class," she explained.

That was quite irregular. It meant you could theoretically secure over one hundred praise votes, which did certainly make the chances of a tie much, much lower. I supposed the big picture for this supplementary exam was now visible.

Supplementary Exam – In-Class Voting

EXAM CONTENTS:

The exam consists of a poll, wherein students in each class will each cast three praise votes and three criticism votes.

RULE 1:

Praise votes and criticism votes effectively cancel each other out. Praise Votes minus Criticism Votes = Final Result.

RULE 2:

Students cannot cast votes for themselves, regardless of whether they are praise or criticism votes.

RULE 3:

Voting multiple times for the same person, leaving the ballot blank and/or abstaining from voting, etc., are not permitted under any circumstances.

RULE 4:

The exam will be conducted repeatedly until a first place and last place have been decided. The student in last place will be expelled.

RULE 5:

Each student will also be required to cast a separate praise vote specifically for a student in one of the other three classes. This vote is mandatory.

That was all. Those were the details of the supplementary exam. There was no doubt that it was simple and straightforward, but it was also the cruelest exam we'd had so far. Someone from our class, and from each of the other classes, was going to disappear, this weekend.

But...

"Sensei, why did you say that it was 'probably' impossible? From what I'm hearing, it doesn't sound like there are any loopholes."

"That's right. There are none. However, there *are* variables at play. I'm sure this thought has crossed your minds, but things change when you use private points," she replied.

"You're saying that we can resolve an expulsion with our points?"

"Twenty million points. If you can come up with that amount, then the school will have no choice but to rescind the expulsion."

Which was precisely why she'd said "probably" before, huh? Not restricting the transfer of private points meant negotiation was a viable tactic. In other words, the ability to buy praise votes with money *was* recognized as an ability in and of itself, and you were free to go ahead and do so.

The school was basically telling us to employ what abilities we wished. The skills we'd demonstrated to those around us over the past year. The financial power that we'd accumulated through our exams. Perhaps even what you might call the power of teamwork, through our friendships.

"P-Please wait a minute. Twenty million points, that's..."

"It's impossible, even if you pooled all of Class C's points together. However, you could scrape together points from the other classes, or you ask for the up-perclassmen's charity. If you do that, then it's not an impossible amount."

It was true that we could realistically accumulate that much if we transferred points between classes or grade levels. As for gathering enough to protect one person in Class C, however—that would be difficult. The odds were high that not even Class A or Class B could gather enough points for that, even if they collected points from their peers. And even if they did manage to gather that many, it was doubtful that they'd actually use those points to protect a single student. Sacrificing all the wealth you'd accumulated so far was a considerably risky move.

"That is the only method you can use to defend your-selves. Let me just say this: it is absolutely impossible poke holes in the rules set by the school in any other way. Now, the rest is for you to assess and decide," said Chabashira, finishing her speech just as homeroom came to an end.

As our teacher disappeared from view, the students succumbed to feelings of dread.

"What do we do?! What do we do?! Dude, this is seriously the *worst* exam ever, isn't it?!"

"Will you boys shut up?!"

"The hell are you telling us to shut up for?! You're probably thinking about how you're going to give me criticism votes, aren't you?!"

The guys and girls clashed with shouts and jeers, quickly turning into a jumbled mob with both sides on their guard.

"How unsightly," sneered one male student, watching the guys and girls fighting. It was none other than Kouenji Rokusuke, the single most peculiar student in our class. "Really now, there's no use kicking and screaming now, is there?"

"And how the hell are *you*, of all people, so calm about this? Are you even aware of how much trouble you've caused the rest of the class so far?" said Sudou, pressing Kouenji for a response.

It was certainly true that Kouenji's capricious nature had complicated things for the class many times so far.

"You selfishly withdrew from both the uninhabited island test and the sports festival, remember?"

The class's eyes fell on them. The more weak-willed of them, not wanting to be expelled themselves, were currently looking for someone to be the scapegoat.

"It would appear the one who doesn't understand this situation is *you*, Red Hair-kun." Kouenji crossed his legs and laid them on top of his desk. "You seem to think that what you've developed over this past year is the key to this particular special exam."

"That's because it is!" snapped Sudou.

"No, it is not. This special exam is focused on the next two years."

Kouenji outright rejected Sudou's opinion. No—the whole class's opinion.

"Huh? What are you even talking about...?" said Sudou uncomprehendingly. He probably thought this was one of Kouenji's usual ridiculous antics.

"Don't you see? This special test is, quite literally, a special case. It's customary that a class that has a student expelled is severely penalized, no? However, no such penalty exists this time. In other words, this is an excellent opportunity to remove an unnecessary student, you see," said Kouenji.

"Well, that's all the more reason *you'd* be a target, Mr. Troublemaker!" snapped Sudou.

"No. I will not be a target."

"Huh? ...And what exactly makes you so sure of that?"

"Well, that's because I'm quite superior," declared Kouenji with unapologetic, overwhelming boldness.

Sudou flinched in the face of his unwavering confidence.

"I've *always* placed near the top of the class in written

examinations. Near the top of my entire grade level, actually. In fact, I came in second by a slim margin on the year-end final exam. Of course, if I were to really put my mind to it, getting first place would be no trouble at all. You understand that I surpass you when it comes to physical ability as well, don't you?" added Kouenji, flaunting the depth of his potential.

"Y-Yeah, and so what? It's pointless if you don't take anything seriously!"

"I agree. In that case, I will, as they say, 'turn over a new leaf.' Beginning with this exam, I will become a useful student, one who contributes to the class through the various exams and such. Don't you think that would be a rather significant boon for our class?" said Kouenji.

"Wh-Wha-... Who would even believe something like that?! I'm way more useful to the class than you are!" shouted Sudou.

He was completely justified to say so. I had no reason to believe what Kouenji had just said, and neither did any of the other students. In fact, we couldn't imagine him taking things seriously, starting with this exam. Honestly, it was likely nothing would change. If he made it through this exam, it was obvious that he'd return to leading a carefree life, doing as he pleased.

"Well then, allow me to turn the question around.

What you just said, that you are more useful than I. Is that something everyone here believes?" asked Kouenji, not addressing just Sudou, but the entire class. "Actually, I suppose it's not just Red Hair-kun. There's really no guarantee that a student who hasn't been useful thus far might become useful in the future, is there? You can make whatever claims you want, as I just did. But what you really need is hidden skill. If you don't have that, then you won't be able to convince anyone."

The notion that students without ability had to work hard to turn over a new leaf. The notion that students with ability had to work hard to turn over a new leaf. Kouenji was saying that, though those two statements sounded similar, they were actually quite different.

He seemed certain that he wasn't going to collect criticism votes and end up in last place. If anything, he seemed to be welcoming this supplementary exam with open arms. But it wasn't like he wasn't in any danger at all. Depending on how things went, he was at real risk of accruing criticism votes. For better or for worse, he was being much too blunt.

But if I were being totally honest, I agreed with Kouenji. If you considered the class as a whole, then we needed to come to a clear decision about this supplementary exam. It wasn't a popularity contest—it was a chance to single out and eliminate an unnecessary student for the whole class's sake.

The exams we'd taken thus far had probably had past instances where students who possessed some exceptional strengths also had some weaknesses, and got expelled because of those weaknesses. To put it more plainly, all we had to do was look at Sudou, the person engaged in argument with Kouenji. Though blessed with great physical prowess, his academic skills were near the bottom of the class. In fact, he'd almost gotten expelled from school once before because of his academic shortcomings.

But, with Horikita's help, Sudou had started to gradually make up for those shortcomings. As a result, he'd begun to demonstrate his value as an asset to the class.

Like Sudou, most people had both strengths and weaknesses. But there were also more than a few people who weren't blessed with strengths. They were notable only for their weaknesses, and in a bad way.

Every human being had the potential to grow. But people blossom at different times, and some people just have less room for growth in the first place. That was precisely why we need to make the most use of this test. Unfortunately, it seemed Kouenji was the only person in our class to have come to that realization.

"Oh, shut up, Kouenji, you're just spewin' a bunch of crap. I think that *you're* the unnecessary one. And nothin' is gonna change my mind."

"No matter how incompetent your closest friends might be?"

"Incompetent? ...You're seriously calling my friends incompetent? Screw you!" Sudou slammed Kouenji's desk and glared at him harshly.

"Yes, I certainly did. I suppose that's all then, hm? If you wish to decide for yourself, you are free to do so, but in that event... Well, I'm sure with them in it, our class will remain a failure. Truly defective."

Kouenji, completely unperturbed, casually combed back his hair. His repeated provocative comments had set Sudou off.

"Listen here, you little—"

"Calm down, you two. We need to talk this over calmly. Right?" said Hirata, cutting in.

How many times had Hirata intervened and played the part of mediator like this? It was a sight we'd already gotten used to seeing. However, Sudou wasn't showing any signs of cooling off.

"Whaddya mean, calm down, Hirata? I mean, you're gonna be fine, right? *You'll* never come in last," said Ike.

"Well—"

What Ike said had pierced right through Hirata. It was certainly true that Hirata had contributed to the class significantly over the past year. The words of the person who was probably in the safest position of all in this exam probably weren't going to resonate deeply with the other students.

"Well, I, I don't know what will happen to me," said Hirata, denying what Ike said. His words didn't reach Sudou.

"Hear that, Kanji? Hirata says he doesn't know what's gonna happen to him."

"No way, dude, Hirata-*sama* is the only safe one here."

Yamauchi and Ike shared wry grins that seemed to be filled more with exasperation rather than irritation. What they were saying was understandable, though. There was probably no one here who thought Hirata might be expelled. Even if he might get some criticism votes, he'd definitely get enough praise votes to be safe.

"But..."

Hirata tried to speak up several times, but the words just didn't seem to come. Besides, the special exam had only just been announced. With the class still racked with confusion, no one was ready to calmly accept what he had to say.

"Let's continue our conversation, Kouenji," said Sudou.

"I have nothing more to say to you, though," replied Kouenji.

"Yeah, well I have a boatload of things to say to you," replied Sudou, pressing Kouenji once again. He wasn't backing down. The only person who would be able to stop him now was...

"That's enough, Sudou-kun."

"Ugh..."

Horikita had spoken up, serving as the voice of authority.

"Don't get carried away just because your grades have—somewhat— improved."

"No, it's not like that, it's..."

"Quiet."

"...Okay."

She had taken complete control over Sudou with just a few words. Horikita then instructed Sudou to return to his seat and take his distance from Kouenji.

"Thank you for the help, Horikita-san."

"It wasn't a big deal. Compared to the exam, anyway," she replied.

After saying her piece, Horikita walked away from Kouenji and returned to her own seat.

"Good work on handling that," I said.

"It was an unnecessary hassle," she sighed, sitting down.

"But... this really is a troubling situation. Even though things have been uneasy so far, we've come together, and we've worked together. And despite that, they're forcing us to kick someone out. It's just... It's just a raw deal."

"A raw deal, huh?" Of course, I understood why she felt like she needed to complain.

"You don't think so?" she asked.

"Well, there were never any guarantees from the beginning. Not since we started here."

"...Yes, I suppose you're right. This exam was just a knee-jerk reaction on the school's part. I still think it's absurd, though," she replied.

"Yeah, it does seem like retaliation for the fact that no one has gotten expelled yet," I answered.

It was reasonable to feel dissatisfied by this, as Horikita did. Anyway, I couldn't stay entirely on the sidelines for this exam. Everyone in the class faced a certain risk of expulsion. In fact, as someone who was low in the class's caste system, there was a real concern that I'd get a number of criticism votes. If I wanted to avoid that, it was best to move all the pieces into place at an early stage.

"I honestly can't come to terms with this exam, but..." mumbled Horikita.

Despite the fact she was mumbling, I could sense a kind of fierce determination in her expression.

The disquieting mood continued to linger in the class-room as we carried on with our morning classes.

• •

DURING OUR LUNCH BREAK, the Ayanokouji Group held a discussion at the café while we ate.

"Ah, jeez, this is, like, the worst thing ever, isn't it? I can't believe they're gonna make use kick someone out of school. I have no idea what the school is thinking," said Haruka, letting out a big sigh while poking her straw into her drink.

Keisei was the first to respond. "I would have to agree. But for me, the most unforgivable thing of all is the fact that classmates have to fight one another. It's the complete opposite of the tests we've had so far, which have required cooperation on our part. It's mind-numbingly baffling."

"Yeah, man. No matter what kind of exams we've had so far, we've always been up against the other classes," said Akito, nodding along with what Keisei said.

"All because no one's been expelled yet... It's almost like they're just doing this out of spite or something."

Everyone had seemed anxious during our morning classes, unable to calm down as the day went on. Many students were understandably unhappy about the supplementary exam, which they felt was entirely outrageous on the school's part. Other groups of students were probably saying the same things that we were right now.

"I wonder if there really is some kinda secret trick or something to this. Yukimuu, you're a smart guy. Can't you come up with an idea or two?"

"Uh... no? I mean, Horikita's initial suggestion, about fixing the vote, is pretty much it. I think that the strategy of evenly distributing votes is the only option open to us. But, based on what Chabashira-sensei told us, that seems impossible. Though you could certainly say this supplementary exam is selfish, we can't simply ignore the rules," said Keisei.

It wasn't surprising that Keisei couldn't come up with a solution, even after giving it some serious thought. No matter how you approached this problem, it looked like our escape routes had all been cut off this time.

"I thought that the school didn't want anyone to get expelled, either. That's what I thought, anyway. But now that doesn't seem to be the case."

"...So that means the school really does want...to kick people out, huh?" said Haruka. There seemed to be a glimmer of hope in her eye, but then her expression turned grim.

"It's a good idea to not to be too optimistic this time around. We're probably going to be hit with pretty severe consequences."

Severe consequences, meaning that someone would be expelled from our class. That was the inescapable future that awaited us.

"...So that means even someone from our group might be gone this weekend," said Airi, who had been quiet for a while now. She sounded anxious, lightly shaking her head from side to side as she spoke, as if saying she really didn't want to imagine such a future.

"Keisei, there's gotta be something we can do apart from just quietly waiting for the test, right?" asked Akito, expecting to hear something that would help quell his anxiety.

Keisei, in response, nodded and looked around at each member of the group.

"You're right, Akito. There is something we can do to avoid getting expelled. So, here a suggestion. Why don't we vote as a team, and vote for each other?" said Keisei.

"By vote for each other, you mean write in each other's names for our praise votes?"

"Yeah. I mean, I can't imagine any of us are going to be leading the polls in terms of praise votes. But I think it's a good idea for us to work together, so we can avoid the unlikely scenario of being in last place."

Even with just the five of us working together, we could each get three praise votes. The important thing was that by doing so, we could negate three criticism votes.

"B-But is that really okay? Aren't we supposed to pick the people who contributed to the class...? And sensei said that it was pointless for us to try and control the vote..." said the honest Airi, sounding somewhat nervous.

"Well, a certain degree of block voting is kind of unavoidable. I'm sure that Chabashira-sensei and the other students are aware of this. Besides, even if we didn't do it, other groups certainly can and will. By voting as a group, you can coordinate your criticism votes and hit one person. In fact, we could concentrate as many as five criticism votes on a single person, with our group alone," said Keisei.

"Five votes... That's really a big deal, for this test. And if you're in a big group, it wouldn't be hard to coordinate ten or twenty votes, would it?"

"Exactly. That means that the better your standing in class, the easier this battle will be for you."

That's right. That was one of the key points of this exam. Students who ranked higher in the class caste system would have an easier time attracting votes. Highly outspoken and influential students could also gain a considerable advantage simply by organizing a group attack on a particular student.

"I agree with the idea of us covering for one another, in our group. I don't want any of us to go," I said, vouching for Keisei's idea.

"M-Me too," said Airi, speaking up shortly after in agreement.

"It's settled then," said Keisei, nodding, after recognizing that the decision was unanimous.

"Wait, hold up a second. There's something I wanna ask," said Akito. Though he had agreed with Keisei's strategy, there was apparently something bothering him. "Won't there be people out there forming groups larger than ours?"

"Of course there will. If anything, the chances of that are high," replied Keisei with a nod, naturally well aware of the danger. If he'd said we should form a large group ourselves, then I would have had to put a stop to the idea. That wouldn't be a good move, under the circumstances.

"Then, shouldn't we make our move early, too? Reach out to other kids?"

"No... Actually, I think it's best if we don't do anything to rock the boat until the exam is over. We shouldn't do anything to start trouble with anyone in class, no matter who they might be. Let's not form a larger group," said Keisei.

"So, basically... You're saying that we shouldn't do anything to make ourselves stand out, so we don't get targeted."

If you were to carelessly draw attention to yourself, you could quite easily become a target, like Sudou or Kouenji.

"Besides, it's obvious that our group isn't really equipped to pull off a strategy like that."

"Yeah, I guess."

Keisei had determined that we should avoid making a large group ourselves. Thankfully, everyone in the group, Haruka included, was convinced by his reasoning. That eliminated the possibility of one of them getting caught up in *my* strategy and losing as a result, which made me glad.

"But personally, I think that if you do get an invitation to join another group, it's all right to accept. That's a pretty important strategy, I think, so you can avoid criticism votes being focused on you."

Even though we'd all said we'd be focusing our praise votes within the Ayanokouji Group, that was still three votes per person. If you could avoid criticism votes by getting in with another group, even better.

"But won't that be kind of tough? I mean, we're a group of people who can't really do that sort of thing."

Haruka seemed to be saying that it was precisely because none of us belonged in other groups that we'd created this one. Well, Keisei had probably understood that when he suggested it.

If any of us *was* extended such an invitation, accepting it would be smart. But while accepting such an invite might be the correct answer, it was also true that there was some danger involved. If you joined up with groups left and right, you might wind up being seen as a faker—someone trying too hard to be everyone's friend—and suffer for it. Of course, you probably weren't going to find any groups that would let you in that easily.

"With just three votes, we'd definitely... Well, no, actually, we wouldn't, right...? I, um, I'm not useful to the rest of the class at all, so... so maybe everyone will use their criticism votes on me..." said Airi, concerned that she might become a target.

If everyone in class were to concentrate their criticism votes on a single person in this test, there'd be little that person that could do to defend themselves. Hirata or Kushida might be able to get enough praise votes to override the number of criticism votes, but...

No, even that wasn't certain. The essence of this exam was how many groups you could form and how many votes you could consolidate. It was best to assume that there would be very few students receiving votes based on legitimate evaluation.

"You shouldn't worry too much, Airi. You'll never make it through this if you worry too much right now."

"Y-Yeah..." Airi's expression grew darker, a sign that she still couldn't help but feel anxious. There were certainly a lot of drawbacks to having a timid personality like hers in a test like this.

"Ugh, this suuuuucks... We've gotta antagonize our own classmates and be on our guard around everyone."

"Yeah. But that's just the way this test is. Nothing we can do about it."

"You're just going to accept it? Just like that, Kiyopon?"

"I mean, it's not like I *want* to just sit back and accept it. I just think we have no choice but to," I replied.

Haruka nodded, seeming a little impressed, and quietly said, "He's really mature" to herself.

"Oh, hey, by the way. I just noticed this myself a second ago, but get a load of that," she added, pointing behind Keisei and me.

When we turned around, we saw one of the guys from Class D. He stuck out like a sore thumb in his surroundings, which made him all the more visible. That was probably how Haruka had noticed him.

"There's somethin' kinda weird about this whole situation. And there's somethin' weird going on with Ryuuen-kun too," she added.

"He was a pompous, self-appointed king, and now he's been brought low for all to see. That's all that's happened," sneered Keisei. His tone was so harsh that it made me wonder if he had a particular hatred for people like Ryuuen.

None of this was really surprising, though, considering Ryuuen's tactics and the way he'd had acted towards the other classes until now. Of course, I was also certain Ryuuen felt no regret about his current situation, and wasn't really suffering, either.

"But, I mean, this exam's gonna be *really* tough for Ryuuen-kun, won't it? Right?" asked Haruka doubtfully.

Keisei nodded in response.

"I don't think 'tough' is the word I'd use. More like hopeless, don't you think? He's been doing whatever he wants all this time. His selfishness makes it inevitable he'll get criticism votes."

Akito nodded, sharing Keisei's opinion.

"He must feel like it's all been kind of pointless, huh? I mean, since he's gonna get thrown out of the very class he'd been controlling."

"Even so, don't you think he looks kind of calm? He's just sitting there all alone, reading a book... If I were in his shoes, I'd probably be crying my eyes out..." Airi looked at Haruka, sounding confused

"But don't you think he'd be *that* kind of guy?" said Haruka. "Y'know, the kind who's too stubborn to give up? Besides, in this exam, there's really no point in fighting if you're all alone and someone everyone hates. He probably plans to tough it out, standing tall to the bitter end. Don't you think?"

Her assessment didn't seem wrong. But the truth was that if Ryuuen didn't do anything, chances were high that he'd get expelled.

"Miyacchi, go over there and talk to Ryuuen-kun. Ask him how he's feeling now."

"It's not like I can just waltz up and ask him..."

Despite his calm demeanor, there was no changing the fact that Ryuuen still concealed sharp fangs. You had to wonder what the repercussions of carelessly bantering with him might be.

"Stop starin' at him so much," said Akito.

"Okaaay," replied Haruka, responding to Akito's warning by tossing her hands up in the air.

"Anyway, back to talking about Class C. How do you

think we should take what Kouenji said?" said Akito, directing his question at Keisei.

Keisei must have been thinking about that too, because he replied almost immediately.

"You mean the stuff about people being skilled enough to stick around? He has a point, I suppose. But even so, I think that Kouenji, in particular, is an unnecessary student. He'd always getting the class all riled up. To be honest, he's terrifying."

Keisei disliked taking risks. If you looked at things from his perspective, I supposed Kouenji was precisely the kind of person you couldn't plan for.

"Besides... Well, this might come off as a little cruel, but my heart doesn't exactly ache for Kouenji. He's probably going to be one of the easiest people to write in a criticism vote for. What about you guys?" he asked.

"I suppose you might be right. If we do have to pick a name, then I guess it's better to have someone in mind that we won't hesitate to vote for when the time comes."

"Um... But even though Kouenji-kun is a rather strange person, he always gets amazing test scores, doesn't he? I think he contributes to the class far more than I do," said Airi, speaking up in defense of Kouenji while clearly still feeling anxious herself. "Whenever the test results get announced, I always think, 'Wow, Keisei-kun and Kouenji-kun are really amazing...'"

"Come on, that's not good, Airi. If you don't come to a decision at a time like this, you're only going to make yourself suffer later, y'know?"

"I know that, but..." Even so, Airi seemed to feel a strong resistance to the idea of just voting someone out.

"Well, at any rate, I think that Kouenji-kun is our pick. Can we all agree on that?" said Haruka.

"I have no objections," replied Akito.

Haruka looked over towards Keisei, asking him, "Is this a good plan?" with her eyes.

"For the time being, yeah. Since we have to pick three people anyway, we can just change our votes depending on the situation," said Keisei.

So, the members of the Ayanokouji Group had, at least tentatively, had decided to use their criticism votes on Kouenji. Our opinions on the matter varied—some thought we needed Kouenji, and some disagreed. In my opinion, Kouenji was risky. His capricious whims could have a major negative impact on the class.

But... there was no doubt that he was talented enough to overcome that issue. If Kouenji ever tackled a test or assignment in full seriousness, he could achieve almost anything. Even though I hadn't seen the full extent of his abilities yet, I was certain he had the skills to do so.

"Well, I don't hate him or anything but... Well, for better or worse, Kouenji is an unknown quantity."

That seemed to be partly why Akito was convinced he should use his criticism vote on Kouenji. Kouenji just stuck out, compared to everyone else. Or rather, he was someone you just couldn't get the measure of, even with all the talk surrounding him.

"Other than that... there's Ike-kun, Yamauchi-kun, and Sudou-kun. Those three seem like the main targets for criticism votes, don't they?"

"Yeah. I'd say that those three and Kouenji are very likely candidates for expulsion right now. But I can't imagine they'll sit around quietly and wait for exam day. I'm sure they'll probably try to form a large group to collect praise votes and avoid as many criticism votes as possible."

"It's not like we're in the clear ourselves by any means."

That was right. The test had already begun. This was a battle to make allies while simultaneously establishing a common enemy.

"Wow. With the discussion we're having right now... it's hard to imagine everyone in class was all buddy-buddy just until this morning." Akito let out a frustrated sigh as he thought about what laid ahead. "I'm just sick of it."

Haruka must have thought of something, because she looked over at Ryuuen once again. "There are still several candidates for expulsion left. Maybe it would be best if everyone had a chance to avoid getting expelled."

It was precisely because Haruka understood Class C's current state that she knew how difficult of a situation that Ryuuen, in Class D, was in. It didn't matter what kind of person you were. If everyone was out to get you, there was nothing you could do.

"Hey, Miyacchi, Yukimuu. If you were in Ryuuen-kun's position, what would you do?" she asked.

"It probably wouldn't matter. I mean, if the entire class is against you, there's no point in even struggling. If it were me, I'd just give up," said Akito, expressing that he'd just throw in the towel right away.

Keisei gave Haruka's question some serious thought, but after a while, he simply shook his head.

"Nothing."

"Nothing, huh? What if he, like, threatened everyone in class or something?"

"That'd just have the opposite effect."

If anything, there were probably several students who were expecting Ryuuen to do just that. Anyone Ryuuen threatened would probably have no reservations about using their criticism votes on him.

"Well, in that case, what about getting praise votes by yielding to the other classes?" asked Haruka.

"If Ryuuen asked you, would you use your praise votes on him?" asked Keisei.

"Huh? No, I doubt it."

"There you have it," answered Keisei with a nod. "I'm sure most people would come to the same conclusion, since they know what Ryuuen's like. There can't be a lot of oddballs out there who'd want to help a guy like that."

"Okay, what if he like, bribed his classmates to buy votes or something?" asked Haruka.

"Even if Ryuuen's saved up quite a few points, I can't imagine he'll have enough to buy a lot of votes. He hasn't just made a lot of enemies—he's earned the reputation of being a really troublesome opponent. I don't see his classmates selling him their votes for cheap," said Keisei.

"But doesn't he have a chance to get praise votes from the other classes then?"

"I don't think so. As someone from another class, don't you feel like it'd be easier to fight Class D with Ryuuen gone?" asked Keisei.

"Ah... Yeah, you might be right about that. It was scary, not knowing what he'd do next."

That was exactly why Ryuuen was in this predicament. He'd become nothing but a burden, dragging down the rest of Class D. He might have dared to try collect praise votes and prevent his expulsion, but since even the other classes saw him as a hostile and troublesome foe, many people wanted him gone. There was little benefit to anyone, whether in or outside his class, in deliberately keeping someone who might present a future threat around.

Some students might be wondering what the future would hold. Some might even believe Ryuuen would become their class's savior. But it was safe to say, based on what we could see, that such students were few and far between.

Even if he did get multiple students to make deals with him to use their praise votes on each other, it would be very difficult to verify if they'd actually held up their end of the bargain. As long as the votes were anonymous, and at least one praise vote actually went through, anyone could lie and say they'd kept their word. In the unlikely event that Ryuuen wanted to dispute the matter, claiming he'd been wrong, it would be too late—he'd already have been expelled. Of course, before you could even get that far, the question still remained of who would even actually want to form a contract with Ryuuen by choice.

"So, he's totally screwed then, huh?"

"My guess is that he's doing his best to stay calm. I don't think he wants to get expelled, but getting all flustered and desperate would just look lame."

"Yeah, I suppose that's true... I guess that would be disgraceful for someone who used to be a king."

It was a shame, but Ryuuen's expulsion was a certainty. Of course, if he intended to fight for his life, then the story might turn out differently. But...

Well, no matter how much we argued, we probably weren't going to come up with any answers. Ryuuen's thoughts on this situation were something only he knew.

"In that case, why don't we see for ourselves?" said a voice close to my ear.

It was Horikita. She had a plastic bag in hand, from which peeked the sandwich she was having for lunch.

"See? See what?" asked Akito, confused by her choice of words, or perhaps sensing something was off.

"What Ryuuen-kun is thinking about right now. What's going through his head. The only way to know for sure is to talk to him," said Horikita.

"I wouldn't. It'd be like kicking a hornet's nest."

Nobody wanted to approach Ryuuen.

"Well, all right then. Never mind," said Horikita.

"There's no point in getting involved with Ryuuen now. He's got nothing to do with us in this exam."

"I suppose so. It's true that he has nothing to do with us. But he might be useful to me," said Horikita. She paused for a brief moment, then, perhaps because I wasn't getting up to join her, walked off by herself.

"What did she mean? Might be useful to her...?"

Keisei and Akito shook their heads, unable to understand.

"Hey, uh, isn't this kinda bad? Don't you think Horikita-san might be in danger?" asked Haruka.

"I think so too... Kiyotaka-kun," said Airi.

"...Yeah. I'll check it out."

I didn't think anything would happen, but it would probably be best if she had someone with her, just in case. For better or for worse, Horikita was the sort of person not to mince words. Akito got up to join me, but I stopped him from coming along, then followed after Horikita.

"What are you going to talk with Ryuuen about?" I asked.

"I thought he might be able to give me a useful hint."

A useful hint? I couldn't see what Horikita was expecting to get from Ryuuen. But seeing her take action like this, I guessed she had something in mind.

"Did Sakura-san and the others ask you to watch out for me?"

"Yeah."

"I knew it."

Horikita's pace didn't slow as we had that brief exchange. Soon after, we arrived at where Ryuuen sat. He had to have noticed us, but his eyes stayed focused on the book in his hands. Based on what I could see from the pages it was opened to, it was some kind of literary novel.

"You're awfully relaxed, Ryuuen-kun," said Horikita.

"Oh, look who it is. Suzune, eh? And you got your little tagalong with you, it looks like."

He suddenly closed the book with a *klop*. I could tell by the sticker that it was from the library. It went without saying of course, that when he said 'little tagalong', he meant me.

Ryuuen briefly glanced at me, but then turned away. He focused his gaze in Horikita's direction.

"And what do you want with me?" he asked.

I wondered why Horikita was willing to take the risk of making contact with Ryuuen at all.

"I'll cut to the chase. What do you intend to do in this special exam?" she asked.

"There's nothing I really can do, so I'm not going to do anything," he replied.

"So, you're saying that...you're prepared to accept expulsion?"

If he left things as they were right now, Ryuuen's expulsion was, needless to say, inevitable.

"I'm a good target for my class. In an exam where you gotta kick someone out, no one wants to deal with the resentment of the person getting kicked to the curb. But I'm a special case," said Ryuuen.

He reopened his book and looked back down, perhaps because he felt that this conversation wasn't worth it. Apparently, he was serious about leaving school. About accepting being kicked out.

"I'm sure people will be casting criticism votes for you. I'm sure many students may feel guilty for doing so, but comparatively speaking, voting for you will be far less of an emotional burden on them than voting for other students. If you do intend to accept your expulsion, then I won't say anything...and I suppose it won't just be me. I'm sure there are many people in Class B and Class A who wish to see you gone. For better or for worse, you've gone too far, and there's no one who will offer their hand to you," said Horikita, hitting Ryuuen with the truth.

The truth hits harder when you're already aware of it. But the truth wouldn't hurt Ryuuen at all. He understood and accepted it wholeheartedly.

"You're probably right. Class D doesn't stand a chance of winning after I'm gone. As my enemy, the best and

most reasonable decision would be for you to crush me right here and now," said Ryuuen.

Rather than taking it in a negative way though, he seemed to react positively.

"You have quite a high opinion of yourself. That is very like you, Ryuuen-kun. But even so, you got demoted to Class D because you lacked skill as a leader. Isn't that right?" said Horikita.

"Heh heh. Certainly."

Class D had been a dictatorship ruled by Ryuuen's iron fist. Now that the system had collapsed and they'd been demoted to into last place, they were losing their chance to bounce back. However, Ryuuen's plans had never been bound by class rankings in the first place. Whether you were in Class D or in Class A, if you had enough private points, you could turn things around and win.

Which was exactly why he wasn't upset by being criticized for Class D's demotion. Being in Class A might have its advantages, but they weren't worth much. Ryuuen's strategy went beyond that. It was an interesting battle tactic, but it also had a few flaws. He was keeping his classmates in check with force, rather than seeking their understanding. He'd been looking so far ahead that he lost sight of his own two feet. That was what led to his defeat and current situation.

"It seems like you and I will never understand one another, no matter how much we talk," said Horikita.

"Seems that way. Happy?" said Ryuuen.

Despite listening to the whole conversation, I still couldn't see what Horikita wanted to learn.

"Well, today might be the last time I'll get to speak with you, so may I ask you just one more question?" asked Horikita.

Apparently, she was getting to the point now. What was she hoping to hear that could serve as a useful hint?

"You're in a more hopeless situation than anyone than now. If you were to try and tackle this exam seriously... would you be able to make it through without getting expelled?"

Horikita gave him a sharp look as she asked him that question. It was like she was telling him to look her in the eye and give her an answer. So that was why she'd wanted to talk to Ryuuen, despite having no need to get involved with him. She wanted to ask him how he could survive this almost totally inescapable situation, where there was a ninety-nine percent chance he'd get expelled.

"That's a stupid question. Obviously, I could," replied Ryuuen, without a moment's delay. He seemed to be confident in his belief that he could survive if he wanted to. As he stared back at Horikita, I saw no hesitation in his eyes at all.

"Even if you're bluffing, that's still impressive. I can sense nothing but confidence coming from you," said Horikita.

"Satisfied now? Or perhaps you want me to teach you my secret plan to survive?"

"No need. You and I are in different positions."

"Yeah, I suppose so."

"Thank you. I feel that my resolve has been strengthened a little, thanks to you."

"Your resolve?" asked Ryuuen.

Horikita nodded.

"Someone will most certainly be expelled in this supplementary exam. That is a fate that we cannot escape. In that case, we need to make the right decision about whom to expel. Do you understand the weight of the words I'm saying to you right now?" she said.

Ryuuen smiled, not responding with a yes or no. "Your efforts might make the rest of your class push you away," he said.

"If that happens, I suppose it just means that I'm not that qualified after all."

"Wow, that's weak. All I'm hearin' is bluffing."

"Tch..."

Even though Horikita had remained calm, Ryuuen saw through her composed façade. No—rather than seeing through it, I should say he'd reached out and broken it.

"You're trying to gain some self-confidence by talking to me... But your confidence, your resolve, it's all still just for show."

Horikita was getting a bit agitated at his words, beginning to heat up.

"It's the cutting someone out that's the only hard part of this, you know," Ryuuen added.

"...I can do it. I've shown no mercy to any student who has held the class back, ever since I enrolled here," replied Horikita.

"Nah, you can't."

"What do you... What do you even know about me?" snapped Horikita.

"I've had plenty of time to observe you over the past year. I know practically everything about you. Besides, I can see the weakness hiding behind the words coming out of your mouth," said Ryuuen.

Horikita didn't stand a chance of winning this game of words. The way she'd so carelessly, sloppily said, "I feel that my resolve has been strengthened a little, thanks to you." The brief silence before she opened her mouth to say,

"I can do it." Ryuuen was quick to notice the things that others would pay no attention to. Horikita had shown him her weakness without even realizing it. Ryuuen was the one controlling the flow of the conversation.

"You're already trapped in dull, uneventful complacency. It's your class. There's absolutely no way you could be cold enough to make a hard choice now. The people who can are the people like me, who have no lingering affection for their class, or like Sakayanagi, who see their classmates as nothing more than pawns," said Ryuuen.

The kinds of relationships you now had with your classmates, after making friends in class, were entirely unlike the ones you'd had before you made any friends. Certainly, Horikita wouldn't have hesitated to do something of the sort when she first started at this school. She'd even been okay with expelling Sudou, who'd failed a test. But could she kick Sudou out now? If you asked that question in earnest, the answer was that she absolutely could not. Relationships were always changing.

"You talk a big game, but you really don't have a plan to get out of this after all, don't you?" said Horikita.

"Why do you think that?" asked Ryuuen.

"Did you really lose against your classmates? Or did you get beaten by someone outside your class...?" said Horikita, briefly glancing at me for just a minute before immediately looking back at Ryuuen. "At any rate, you're just going to silently accept that you've lost and let yourself get expelled, huh?"

She was trying to provoke him. But Ryuuen just quietly listened.

"It's like a reward for Ishizaki, the guy who beat me. That's why I'm just gonna quietly accept it. It's an opportunity that the rest of Class D shouldn't miss out on. And of course, that includes you, too. You shouldn't let this chance go," he said with a smile, before looking back down at his book once again.

"...I suppose so. Well then, I'll have to keep an eye on my friends in Class C to make sure that they don't waste their praise votes on you, even if it's just by mistake. Of course, even if I didn't do anything, it's not like they'd vote for you anyway," said Horikita.

She left and I followed after her. Ryuuen's gaze remained directed at his book, not bothering to look back at us.

Horikita seemed both calm and angry as she walked away.

"He is just absolutely, completely full of hot air. A total liar. There's nothing he can do at all, but even so, he's just trying to make himself look good, like a show-off. No matter how much he struggles, it's not going to stop him from getting expelled," said Horikita.

"I dunno about that. Maybe he really does have some way to get out of it," I replied.

"It's impossible. No matter how you look at the situation, there's no way Ryuuen-kun can avoid expulsion. Even if he apologized right now and tried acting like an actual, decent human being, it wouldn't change the number of criticism votes he'll undoubtedly be getting. And it won't give him more praise votes, either."

"Yeah, I guess a straightforward strategy like that wouldn't work."

"But it would be pointless if he tried bribing others or resorting to threats, either. You were saying the same thing earlier, weren't you?" answered Horikita.

Yeah, that's true. I guess she'd heard us.

"Or perhaps you can see what Ryuuen-kun's thinking? About how he can get out of being expelled?"

"Nope, I can't at all," I answered.

I tried crunching the numbers and running the variables in my head, but still couldn't see any reliable method for Ryuuen to survive in his current situation. There was a necessary part of the puzzle that he was lacking, which he'd need if he was going to survive.

"Then there you have it," said Horikita.

She left the café, still looking like she was in a sour mood. I turned around and looked over at Ryuuen for a brief moment. What would have happened if Ryuuen and I had crossed paths earlier...?

"No, that's just pointless speculation. Especially at this point in time."

There wasn't any point in giving any further thought to a student who was going to be leaving. I decided to stop thinking about it and return to my group.

3.2

THAT NIGHT, I got a phone call from Kei. It was mostly about the special exam.

"Hey, so, for this exam, what should I be doing, anyway?" asked Kei.

"You've already started to form a group, right? With the people around you?"

"Yeah, I've got a few people. There's seven girls in my group."

Kei gave the names of the six other girls in her group. They were the girls that she was usually hanging around with.

"Everyone's pretty scared of getting expelled, after all. And well... to be completely honest with you, I have no idea how many people hate me," said Kei.

"I guess it wouldn't be strange if you got some criticism votes," I replied.

"Hey, uh, shouldn't you *not* be saying something like that? Even if it's just a lie?" snapped Kei. She sounded angry.

"It's best to keep a low profile for now, so you don't draw any negative attention to yourself. If you stand out too much in a bad way, it could make you a candidate for expulsion," I reasoned.

"Got it. I'll make sure I don't do anything to make people mad," replied Kei.

"That's good. Actually, the fact that you've broken up with Hirata might actually work in your favor, Kei."

"Huh?"

"Hirata is really popular with the girls. If you were still going out with him, then some of the students in class might have been planning...to force you out of the picture and break you up themselves, by getting you expelled," I reasoned.

"Whoa, *that's* a scary thought. But it makes sense..."

It was precisely because the vote was anonymous that some people could make some pretty bold moves.

"...You should be good though, right? I mean, you don't really stand out. And your grades are pretty average, too," said Kei.

In the eyes of many of my classmates, there wasn't really anything praiseworthy about me. Nor was there anything to criticize, either.

"Sometimes not standing out is a good thing," I told her.

"But don't you think that you might get a vote from Sudou-kun? I mean in the sense that he'd be eliminating a rival, as someone vying for Horikita-san. Though that might just be a selfish assumption on Sudou-kun's part, I guess," said Kei.

"You might be right."

As long as we each had to write down the names of three people, everyone was probably going to get a criticism vote or two. It wasn't really worth worrying about now.

"But those three idiots and Kouenji-kun are probably the ones in the most trouble in our class right now, right?" asked Kei. Apparently, her group had had a similar discussion to ours.

"They are definitely the most likely picks, but even so, we don't really know what's going to happen. Still, Kouenji isn't really in a good place."

"He isn't the kind of person who would try to form a group to control votes, I suppose," she reasoned.

"Yeah."

Ike, Yamauchi, and Sudou were clearly going to form a group to try and support one another. Kouenji, on the other hand, was completely isolated and helpless. He also made enemies quite easily, thanks to his bullish attitude. And he'd had an explosive argument with Sudou right in front of everyone on the day the exam was announced. That had to have hurt his chances.

"So, what are you going to do? Who are you going to use your criticism votes on?" asked Kei.

"Still haven't really thought about it. But basically, I plan on picking the people that won't be useful to the class in the future."

"That's a level-headed approach. That's very you, Kiyotaka."

Considering someone would be getting expelled, it was the only way I could make a decision.

"Oh, but... you're not thinking about people like me, are you?" said Kei.

"You are an important part of the class. There's no way I would," I replied.

"I-I see. Well, that's obvious." She sounded a little bit embarrassed and surprised.

"If you do happen to notice anything—students being ostracized, or anyone starting to sound like a solid candidate for expulsion—contact me. It's hard for me to get that kind of information," I told her.

"Okay."

I ended the call with Kei.

I'd said that I'd be picking people that weren't useful to the class moving forward, but that was, at best, just my personal opinion. As long as I wasn't actively involved in the class, I had no plans to get deeply invested in manipulating the vote. In the end, a lot of groups were going to be clashing with one another in this test, and I intended to calmly accept whatever the results of that might be. Of course, it'd be a different story if I was the one under fire.

Still, as Kei had said earlier, the likelihood of Ike, Yamauchi, or Sudou being expelled was high. Then there was Kouenji. And if you turned your attention to the girls, you could probably say that the people with poor grades, like Inogashira, Satou, and Airi, weren't in the clear.

However, the fact that groups were still continuing to form meant that votes were probably going to be thrown around for reasons other than grades. Loners like Kouenji and timid people with few friends like Airi would probably be easy targets.

"I wonder what will happen?" I asked myself aloud.

I decided to keep an eye on how the votes were being allocated and prepare for unforeseen circumstances, while continuing to gather what information I could.

4

THE DIFFICULTY
OF SAVING

WHEN I WOKE the next morning, I decided to check my phone. Sure enough, the Ayanokouji Group had been chatting away at great length while I was asleep. I suppose the supplementary special exam had only just been announced yesterday, so it wasn't surprising that the conversation revolved around that.

"They're really letting their anxiety drive them up the wall, huh?" I said to myself.

It was plain to see from the chat that Airi in particular was worried. It would be extremely troublesome if someone from our group did become the rest of the class's target. While I was uncertain about how much it would involve me, it would be difficult to deal with.

Though I was planning on laying groundwork focused on Hirata and Kei, there were no guarantees. Even if you practically threatened someone, or made a deal with them, people could still change who they were giving their criticism votes to at the very last minute. There was no ironclad method of avoiding expulsion if criticism votes were concentrated on you. Everyone would be at a certain degree of risk.

As I scrolled through the messages in the chat, I noticed that Keisei had made a rather interesting suggestion. I started reading from the beginning of his message.

Keisei: *"How about we have one person from the group go to school early for the next three days, starting tomorrow, to gather info?"*

Akito: *"Since our group's pretty small, that's probably a good idea. I'm on board with Keisei's suggestion."*

Haruka: *"Yeah, that's probs a good plan. I am pretty curious about what people are talking about."*

Airi: *"I agree."*

Haruka: *"Well, I'm heading out early tomorrow anyway, so lemme handle it."*

Everyone had come to a unanimous decision. They'd mentioned my name in the chat, but then decided to go ahead and get my approval after the fact, since I'd been too slow to read the messages in time.

"I see," I said to myself.

While I couldn't imagine information would fall into our laps that easily, it was better than doing nothing. It was a pretty easy strategy to pull off, and it might give us results. Given the fact that these messages were from yesterday, Haruka was probably already in the classroom around now. Judging from what was said in the conversation, I assumed the other members of the group were going to head to school early on other days, so it'd probably be fine even if I did nothing.

The vote was coming up in three days. That meant we should have a solid idea of who to focus our criticism votes on by today at the latest. In the meantime, though, it would be a lucky break for the Ayanokouji Group if we could secure some information in the mornings.

While I waited for Kei to report back on the girls' movements, I decided I would try and get some information about the guys from either Hirata, or Horikita, who was using Sudou. It was important to know as much as I could at this early stage.

4.1

. . . .

T HAT SAID—you really did get used to things with time. Before I even realized it, I'd spent an entire year in this dorm.

"It doesn't feel like time is passing the way it used to," I said to myself.

How you perceive the passage of time depends on whether or not you're having fun. When I'd first encountered that concept, long ago, I honestly didn't understand it at all. Before I started high school, the passage of time felt rigid. Not a single second was out of place.

But now, things felt different. Obviously, the days were still passing at the same speed that they had been in years past. And yet, the thought that I'd be graduating in just two years made me feel like time really had gone by in a flash. It was odd.

"Good morning, Ayanokouji-kun!"

I heard Ichinose call out to me from behind. Perhaps she tended to head out of the dorm around the same time as me in the mornings.

I turned and responded to her. "Oh, hey. Morning, Ichinose."

But for some reason, Ichinose stiffened up a little bit in that instant.

"Hm?"

She didn't get any closer. She just stood there, completely still, her hand still up in the air after waving to me.

"What's up?" I asked.

When I said that, Ichinose finally started to approach, as if she had just been released from a spell—though her movements were still somewhat stiff.

"Oh well, uh, it sure is cold today, huh?" she said.

"Yeah," I replied. Whenever we spoke, you could see our breath form white clouds in the air.

"Do you have plans to walk to school with anyone?" asked Ichinose.

"Nope, not at all. I usually walk by myself in the mornings."

"Oh, in that case... Do you mind if I come with you?"

There probably wasn't a single person out there, guy or girl, who would turn Ichinose down if she asked them that question. I nodded, accepting her offer.

"........."

"........."

Whenever it was just the two of us, Ichinose was usually be the one to strike up conversation. But now, we were both totally silent. Ichinose was walking slightly behind me, and the only sounds we could hear were our footsteps.

I decided to try talking about the exam. "This upcoming exam's gotta be pretty tough for your class, huh, Ichinose?" I asked.

Compared to the other classes, Class B was overwhelmingly unified, with solid teamwork and a strong sense of camaraderie. It had to be extremely distressing for them to have to choose one of their own to remove.

"Ah... Well, yeah. You're right about that. I think this is probably the most difficult exam we've had so far," said Ichinose.

"Yeah," I replied.

Ichinose's downcast expression made that point abundantly clear. Only she, the person that the rest of her class rallied around, was absolutely, positively safe. Her situation wasn't quite like Hirata or Kushida's, either. She was probably the only student guaranteed to pass this exam.

That was precisely why it was difficult for her to decide who to cut from the class. It might be best if she stayed on the sidelines for this one, not getting involved in discussing either praise or criticism votes. If was possible she intended that to be her strategy, but...

"Even if this is a really tricky exam, I have to do something, don't I?" she said.

"You're probably right."

"...Yeah. I think I have to do something," said Ichinose, now walking beside me.

I saw a faint smile on her profile.

"Wait, you're not...thinking of dropping out yourself, are you, Ichinose?" I asked.

"Huh? Oh, no way. I would never say something like that, y'know?"

Though she denied it, I could see in her eyes that she was a little upset. She looked like she was prepared to make that choice if it came to it.

"Just for the record, I'm sure that your classmates wouldn't use their criticism votes on you so easily," I told her.

"I didn't say I was going to drop out, but if that's what you think Ayanokouji-kun...you might have a point."

"It's written all over your face. You're an open book."

"R-Really?" replied Ichinose, flustered and trying to confirm if what I said was true.

Was that a natural response? Or was it intentional? It seemed more the former.

"*Sigh*... Well, please just keep this between us, okay?" she asked.

"Are you willing to sacrifice yourself to save someone else?"

"Well, not exactly. I think it's more like...I have to fight and face the risks myself."

Fight and face the risks herself, huh? In other words, she had no intention of taking the easy way out and staying on the sidelines.

"I don't get it. Is this like you offering some kind of tribute to the student who's going to get expelled?" I asked.

Even though a parting tribute from Ichinose was a lot better than one from anyone else, it still probably wasn't any student's ideal outcome. I couldn't exactly imagine someone just leaving the school with a smile on their face.

"I can't really talk any further right now. This is something that I don't want other people to hear, and besides, you're a student of Class C, Ayanokouji-kun. No matter what kind of exam it is, there are some times where we can't really collaborate, y'know?" said Ichinose.

"Yeah, that's certainly true."

At best, all we could really do was discuss praise votes with one another. A praise vote from Ichinose would give you a slight advantage in the test. That being said, Ichinose wasn't the kind of student who really needed praise votes herself, in the first place. I doubted she'd sell her vote for points or anything, either.

And so, I wasn't going to make any suggestions. Even if I did buy her vote, it wouldn't really be anything more than a good luck charm.

"Still, I have to say, the school really is terrible, isn't it? I mean, forcing someone to get expelled? Even if you manage to get praise votes from kids in other classes, someone's going to have to get kicked out in the end," said Ichinose.

None of us were exactly welcoming this exam with open arms. Someone was going to be forced out just as our first year came to an end.

"Are you going to be okay, Ayanokouji-kun?" asked Ichinose.

"Well, I'm not so sure about that... I mean, I'm not really that essential of a student in my class," I replied.

"Well, if you're all right with me helping, I might able to do something," said Ichinose.

"Meaning what?"

"Well, since I have a praise vote to use for someone from another class, I could use it on you, Ayanokouji-kun."

She'd brought up the topic of praise votes—which I had decided not to mention, earlier—of her own accord.

"It's just one vote, so it might not be worth very much, but..." she added.

"I'm really grateful for the offer, but I have to decline. I think your vote would be wasted on someone like me," I told her.

"That's not true. If anything, it's probably the most appropriate use of a vote in this exam. You're supposed to use a vote to praise someone from another class. So, yes, I think you're definitely the one who deserves it, Ayanokouji-kun, since you're the one who saved me," said Ichinose.

What she'd just said was difficult for me to respond to. "All right. Well then, if the time comes, I might ask you for help," I told her.

"Okay. I'll keep that in mind," she replied with a smile.

"God morning, Honami," someone called out to Ichinose from behind us.

"Good morning to you, Asahina-senpai," said Ichinose.

"You look as bright as ever today. Wait a minute, aren't you two from separate classes? You must get along quite well, hm?" said Asahina.

"Uh, well, yes. He's a good friend..." said Ichinose, somewhat bashfully, with a smile on her face.

"Oh? A friend, hm?"

Ichinose could have answered in a more normal manner... it would probably have been less misleading.

"Well, anyway, I'd like to borrow Ayanokouji-kun for a little bit. Is that okay?" asked Asahina, approaching the two of us as if hoping that Ichinose would keep going so that she could talk to me alone.

"Okay. Well then, Ayanokouji-kun, I'll be heading off," said Ichinose. Showing no signs of displeasure, she bowed and did just as Asahina had asked.

"Sorry, Honami. See you later."

"Oh no, no problem. See you later!"

I didn't sense anything odd from their short conversation. If anything, it seemed like the two of them had a solid upperclassman and underclassman relationship.

"She's a good girl, isn't she? Cute. Bright. Even the second-years have nothing bad to say about Honami," said Asahina.

"Yeah. I think Ichinose's really popular with both the first-year guys and girls, too."

"Maybe you're the one who's won her heart though," said Asahina. It seemed Ichinose's somewhat odd behavior moments ago hadn't been lost on her.

"Nah, there's no way."

Putting aside the matter of Ichinose, who was in my grade level, I wanted to keep my conversation with Asahina as brief as possible. If I was seen with someone under Nagumo's control, then people would probably get the wrong idea. If she had something she wanted to talk to me about, I'd prefer she get right to it.

"If you have some business with me, I'd like to hear it," I told her.

"Wow, you're all business, huh? Well, whatevs. You and Honami were chatting away so happily, so I just wanted to run something by you real quick," said Asahina.

She'd been smiling cheerfully this whole time. But now, the smile disappeared from her face.

"I heard about the test you freshman are about to take. Someone's gonna be forced out of school, right?" she asked.

"Yeah, seems that way." It seemed the test had already become a topic of conversation among the second-years.

"You know how Honami's the kind of person who puts friends first, right? Or like, how her personality won't let her simply accept someone from Class B being expelled?" asked Asahina.

"Yeah, you're right about that. People aren't talking about it, but I think they're concerned about what's gonna happen with Class B." I chose my words to be bland and nondescript, while still conveying my thoughts clearly.

"Then, how do you think Honami is gonna tackle this exam?" asked Asahina, looking at me with prying eyes.

It seemed she was testing me, perhaps trying to get something out of me, rather than simply asking out of curiosity. Would giving her an absurd, roundabout answer be counterproductive, then?

"Assuming that she's operating with the goal of preventing anyone from getting expelled, then... Well, Class B has saved up a considerable number of private points. So she just has to gather the rest of the points she needs to save the person about to be expelled. Something like that, right?" I asked.

"Ding ding ding. Well, I guess that's really the only possible answer, huh?"

If you began with the assumption that she wasn't going to let anyone get expelled, then I supposed anyone would arrive at this conclusion. But this wasn't something just anyone could pull off. Coming up with twenty million points was extremely difficult.

"And it looks like she went to Miyabi to ask him for help. When she did, do you know how he responded?" asked Asahina.

"I'm guessing he agreed to help almost immediately?" I replied.

"...Correct."

Based on what had happened so far, it didn't seem like things could have gone any other way.

"Let me just get this out of the way. There's no way he'd just lend her private points that easily, is there?" I asked.

No matter how many private points Class B already had, the amount they were lacking must be significant. They had to be millions of points short.

"*Totally* not. I mean, if it were tens of thousands of points, then that would be a different story. In that case, there'd be room for consideration. But no one can just give away *millions* of points," said Asahina, without hesitation. "The third-year students and us second-years have gotta be prepared for the special exams ahead. And since we never know 'til the very last minute whether or not private points will come into play, it's not like we can afford to hand them over to freshmen."

All true. That was precisely why Chabashira talked about it the way she did. You might manage to get a few paltry points out of the upperclassmen, but it was almost certainly impossible to get them to hand over tens or hundreds of thousands of points. Sure, you could offer to pay them back with interest, but that was hardly attractive to a third-year who was about to graduate. Even if you got a second-year student to lend you some points, it still seemed impossible to secure such a large sum.

"I guess that if there's anyone out there who could handle something like this, it would probably be Student Council President Nagumo," I reasoned.

"He has saved up quite a bit."

"So what happened, then?"

Based on what I'd heard so far, I could already imagine what she was about to say. Even so, the fact that Ichinose had seemed anxious indicated Nagumo's help came with strings attached.

"Come on, don't be in such a rush. I'm just in the same class as the guy, is all, so I've got my doubts about him thoughtlessly handing out such a huge sum to a junior. I mean, Honami is super cute, right? There's absolutely no way she's going to get expelled in this exam. You think so too, right?" said Asahina.

"Yeah, for sure. This is probably a strategy she came up with to stop someone other than herself from getting expelled."

"Yeah, that's why I really don't want her to borrow points from Miyabi. Sure, that's partly 'cause I'm thinking of my own class, but also... Well, more than anything else, it's because I feel sorry for Honami," said Asahina.

"Is there a harsh condition attached to the deal? Like, is the interest rate very high or something?" I asked.

"His condition for lending Honami the money is... He wants her to enter into a relationship with him," said Asahina.

"I see."

This was pretty typical Nagumo. Asking her to date him in exchange for lending her points, huh? Normally, that would be a dealbreaker. You'd expect someone to reject such a condition at once immediately. But Nagumo had to know there was a possibility that Ichinose would accept if for the sake of protecting her class.

"Is it really okay? For you to be telling me all this, I mean," I asked.

"I already told you, didn't I? It's for my own class's sake. If Miyabi lends all those points to a first-year, the rest of us might suffer for it. And Honami will really suffer too, in exchange for protecting her friends. That doesn't sound good to me at all," said Asahina.

"You might be right about that. But why come to me? I'm in Class C. We're competing with Ichinose."

"I don't know. I just figured you'd be able to do something about this."

"You're giving me too much credit. There's no way I could afford to make up for Class B's lack of points."

It would be a different story if I could personally raise enough points to help, rather than having her rely on Nagumo. But that was out of the question.

"Yeah, I guess. You guys are rivals, after all," she answered.

Helping out a rival class would be incredibly foolish when we were supposed to be grateful our rivals were being impacted at all, even if it was just the loss of one student. Besides, a plan that involved gathering millions of points would require *everyone* in Class C to come together. It was absolutely impossible.

"I can't do anything," I told her.

"Don't worry about it. I won't hold a grudge or anything, even if you can't. I suppose it was just wishful thinking on my part. But despite all that, I think you'll take your chances still," said Asahina, lightly slapping me on the back. "Anyhow, that's all I was gonna say. The rest is up to you."

Having said that, she headed toward the school, showing no sign of stopping and turning around. Based on her words and mannerisms, I didn't get the sense she was lying.

"Making a deal with Nagumo, huh?"

It didn't seem like Ichinose...but it was the kind of strategy Ichinose would come up with. If she really did this, she might be able to prevent any casualties in her class. A class that was united and had a huge sum saved up was precisely the kind of class for whom such a strategy was a viable option.

But based on what Asahina had said it, it sounded like entering into a relationship with Nagumo would be a hard pill for Ichinose swallow. If the relationship thing didn't worry her, then the smart thing to do would have been to just go ahead and get the private points from Nagumo before he changed his mind. I supposed it was difficult to make such a snap judgment when it came to being in a relationship with someone of the opposite sex, though.

If I'd been in a position to help out, I would have gladly done so. But the issue was money. Class B was probably short by four or five million points. That was well beyond the scope of what I could help with. It would be more economical for her to just let one of her friends go. But how would Ichinose weigh her options when she put the condition of dating Nagumo on the scales...?

"Considering her personality..." I muttered to myself.

It wasn't difficult to imagine what was going to happen.

4.2

• •

THIS EXAM was difficult to discuss in class. There was a bad feeling hanging in the air in the classroom, and it felt like everyone was on pins and needles.

"Morning, Kiyopon."

"Morning."

Haruka and I exchanged greetings as I got to my seat. The students who were already in class seemed listless. Clearly, having to decide who to use their criticism votes on was getting in the way of maintaining normal relationships, and it would probably continue to be like this until the special exam ended. In fact, it would probably continue to be like this even *after* the exam ended.

"Sure feels like there's a dark cloud over our heads, huh?" Haruka texted me privately.

"Anything unusual happen?" I replied.

"Nothing yet. But everyone's really on their guard, dontcha think?"

You had no idea who might be listening in when you were in the classroom. I doubted anyone would be so careless as to say the names of the people they were voting for out loud.

"Here's hoping we get results tomorrow."

"Yeah."

After that brief conversation with Haruka, I put my phone away. We were going to remain inconspicuous and just wait for the storm to pass by. That is, if our classmates would allow us to be that naïve.

4.3

• •

WHEN LUNCHTIME came around, I decided to head on over to the library. I didn't mind spending time with the Ayanokouji Group, but it was important to get some alone time, too. Besides, there were other students in the library who liked books as much as me.

And lo and behold—one such student, Shiina Hiyori, was in the library yet again today.

I randomly pulled a book from the shelf, sat down, and started reading it to see if I wanted to check it out and take it back to my dorm with me. Shortly afterward, someone called over to me.

"Hello, Ayanokouji-kun."

Since lunch had just started, and there were only a few people in the library, it seemed she'd noticed me almost immediately. She was holding a book in a similar genre to the one I was looking at.

"I see you're quite the bookworm, as always," I replied.

"This really is such a wonderful place."

After asking for my permission, Hiyori sat down beside me. The two of us quietly read our books. Naturally, students who loved the library had no need of excessive conversation. The act of reading a book could be called a form of conversation, anyway.

Roughly thirty minutes went by. We continued to read without saying a word until the lunch break ended.

"I suppose it's time to head back," I said aloud.

"Yes, I suppose so," replied Hiyori.

Once we looked up to check the time, though, we decided to delay leaving the library.

"Oh, Hiyori, there's something I wanted to ask you."

"What is it?" She looked up at me with a puzzled look on her face, unsure of what I was going to ask her.

"I want to know what's going on with Ryuuen," I told her.

"What's going on with Ryuuen-kun...? To be completely honest, things aren't looking good."

"So he is the top candidate for expulsion, then?"

"Yes. Nearly everyone in class has agreed to use their criticism votes on Ryuuen-kun."

"Has Ryuuen himself accepted that decision?"

"I think he must have. To tell you the truth, Ryuuen-kun has been coming to the library after class quite often of late. I've gotten to talk to him a bit as a result, so I think I have a fairly good idea of what's going on."

So, the book he'd been reading in the café *was* from the library. It made sense that he'd made contact with Hiyori. Coming here had been the right decision.

"So, what do you think about all this, Hiyori?" I asked.

"Well, it's sad, but we can't change the fact that someone will be expelled in this exam. I'm willing to accept the reality that someone, myself included, might be leaving our class. But I do think that if Class D intends to aim for the top, we might need Ryuuen-kun..." said Hiyori.

I was sure she had conflicting feelings about Ryuuen, but that meant she recognized his abilities. Thinking back, it didn't seem like Ryuuen had treated Hiyori too badly, either.

"Sorry for asking you about this. I mean, about how things are going in Class D—" I said, stopping myself suddenly. "No, actually, I probably don't want Ryuuen to get expelled either."

There had been no need for me to come here myself today. But I wanted to know what was going on with Ryuuen, so I did just that.

"I think the more friends you have around, the better," said Hiyori.

"...I suppose you're right," I replied. This felt a little strange. Ryuuen and I were just supposed to be enemies.

"Um..."

"What is it?"

"I, um, well, I suppose it might not be my place to say this, but..." said Hiyori hesitantly. Even so, she continued speaking. "Please don't drop out of school, okay, Ayanokouji-kun...? I really don't want to lose any other dear friends."

"I'll be careful."

I returned to my classroom, feeling grateful for Hiyori's concern.

4.4

THE BAD FEELING still lingered in the air after classes had ended. Whether she sensed it or not, my neighbor, Horikita, quietly started collecting her things to head back to the dorms, as usual.

It would be hard to get through this exam alone. It would be normal to want to have as many allies as possible. But Horikita showed no signs of doing so. Viewed in the most optimistic light possible, the only praise vote she was guaranteed was from Sudou. But then...

I remembered her confronting Ryuuen the other day. Taking into account what she wanted and what she seemed to be lacking helped me see what kind of strategy she had in mind. Apparently, she was trying to get through this exam using a different method than everyone else. It wasn't going to be an easy road, but if she could make it work, the results would be ideal.

I supposed the strategy I was envisioning might be the same as Horikita's. If that was the case, I'd let her be the one responsible for it. I looked at my classmates, imagining how Horikita might see them.

"It's unusual that you haven't come to me for advice yet. Do you have a good handle on this exam?" I asked Horikita. Though it had only been a single day, I wanted to see if there was any change in her.

"Even if I did come to you for advice, you wouldn't give me a straight answer," she replied.

"You're certainly right about that." It seemed she was beginning to understand that about me.

"Besides...this isn't exactly the kind of exam where you can simply go to your classmates and ask for help," said Horikita.

"A lot of the other students are sticking to the idea of forming groups and gathering praise votes," I replied.

"If people want to do that, they're welcome to do so," said Horikita. She finished gathering her belongings and rose from her seat.

"In that case, what are you planning on doing?" I asked.

"What I can," she replied, leaving the classroom after uttering just those few words.

I couldn't help but feel just a bit curious, so I followed after her.

"What?" snapped Horikita, evidently displeased. She scowled at me.

"I'm interested to see what it is you're going to do," I told her.

"You usually don't get involved with me. Why are you trying to now?"

Why? Put simply, it was because I had high hopes for the strategy Horikita was trying to pull off. If she could make it happen, then I wanted to support her as much as possible. But I wasn't going to tell her that right here and now.

"You haven't joined any groups yet, right? If you find yourself in a pinch, I can help," I told her.

"That's exactly what I'm talking about. So you *are* concerned about my situation, hm? Are you saying that if I asked you to help, you'd let me join your group?" asked Horikita.

"It wouldn't be a bother for us to take in more people."

"While I appreciate the offer, I have to decline. You aren't the person I'm looking for right now."

I suppose that meant she'd already made up her mind. It seemed like her resources were still scarce, though, leaving her in a position where she was being driven by her anxiety. I'm sure I wasn't the right "fit" for what she needed.

"You really are..." said Horikita, glaring at me even harsher than before.

"What is it?" I asked.

"Anyway, just leave me alone," she snapped.

I nodded and stopped in my tracks. Even if I tried pursuing, I'd probably just make her even angrier. After watching Horikita walk off, I stared out the hallway window.

"I guess I'll just head on back," I muttered to myself.

"...Hey, do you have a minute, Ayanokouji-kun?"

Hirata walked up to me, apparently having been just passing by. I wondered if he was following me. Judging by the timing of his arrival, he might have been waiting for Horikita and me to part ways.

"If you're okay with it, would you mind coming with me for a little while after class today? I wanted to talk to you," said Hirata.

It was unusual for Hirata to approach me this way. I had no particular reason to turn him down, so I accepted his offer with a nod. When I did so, he let out a sigh of relief. After spending the entire day in such a strained, tense environment, Hirata seemed like he was the most physically exhausted person in our class. Of course, I could tell this had something to do with the exam.

"Okay then, how about we meet at 4:30 at the... yeah, at the south entrance of Keyaki Mall?" he asked.

"Sure."

And that was all we said about that. It seemed this was something Hirata didn't want to talk about in the hallway, where students were constantly passing through on their way back to the dorms or their respective clubs.

I'd been planning on meeting up with Keisei and the others after class, so I let them know I'd be late. Hirata seemed to be busy chatting with his friends when class ended, so I decided to head over to Keyaki Mall ahead of him.

4.5

● ●

AFTER LEAVING THE CLASSROOM, I headed down to the school entrance. On my way there, I bumped into Sakayanagi Arisu from first-year Class A. Beside her was Kamuro.

"Ayanokouji..."

Kamuro stiffened, clearly on alert. However, Sakayanagi didn't react at all. Her movements were relaxed and calm. The contrast between the two was quite amusing to me.

"My, my, this is quite a coincidence, Ayanokouji-kun."

"Looks that way. What do you want with Class C?" I asked.

It seemed to me like Sakayanagi and Kamuro were making their way over to Class C. But rather than answer me directly, Sakayanagi just chuckled and dodged the question. "Where are you headed now, hm?" she asked instead.

"I'm planning to meet a friend at Keyaki Mall in half an hour."

"I see. My, you are enjoying your life as a student here to the fullest, aren't you? If it isn't too much of a bother, would you mind giving me a few minutes of your time?" asked Sakayanagi.

She took out her phone and checked the time. Had she come here to meet me? No, that was unlikely.

It was still only 4:10 right now. Even if it took several minutes to reach Keyaki Mall, I still had about 10 minutes or more to spare.

"Is it okay if we stand and talk?" I asked.

"Yes. However, I would think we might draw attention if we talk here. Would you mind relocating somewhere nearby?"

"No worries."

I also wanted to avoid attracting attention as much as possible. If I were with a classmate, this wouldn't be an issue, but Sakayanagi was the sort of person who drew the eye whether or not she wanted to. She was well aware of this herself, which was why we moved to a less populated place. I matched her slow pace, taking our time as we made our way through the school building.

"At any rate... Ayanokouji-kun, Masumi-san, don't you think that this supplementary exam is absolutely outrageous? Forcing someone out of school just because there haven't been any dropouts as of yet? It's strange to think that the school administrators would come up with such an exam, when you think about it rationally," said Sakayanagi.

"Yeah. Mashima-sensei's normally so calm and composed, but even he seems pretty shaken up," said Kamuro.

So it wasn't just Chabashira. The other teachers weren't thrilled about this supplementary exam, either.

"There is a reason for that," said Sakayanagi.

"What, you know something about it?" asked Kamuro.

"Well, this is a personal matter that I am ashamed to speak of, but my father was suspended from his position the other day," said Sakayanagi.

"Wait, suspended...? If I remember right, he's the director, right? Your father?" asked Kamuro, pressing her for more information. She must have known who Sakayanagi's father was.

"I was unable to ascertain the details, but I heard a number of unsavory *things* had come up regarding my father. The father I know is not the sort of person who would sully his hands with such things. Of course, I cannot rule out the possibility that I, his daughter, was simply unaware of such things... But, well, it's possible someone might be scheming to bring my father down," said Sakayanagi.

The words seemed meant for Kamuro's ears. But in reality, they were probably directed at me. If Sakayanagi's father really was innocent, then it wouldn't be strange if *that* man was involved. The impression I'd gotten of Sakayanagi's father might not have been inaccurate after all.

"That being said, it that has absolutely nothing to do with students like us. It's nothing more than idle chatter." It sounded like Sakayanagi didn't see her father's suspension from office as something worth exploring further.

"But does that have anything to do with this exam?" asked Kamuro.

"Can't you see this...hastily prepared exam being meant to get a certain someone expelled?" said Sakayanagi.

"Someone...?"

Kamuro glanced over at me for a moment, then immediately looked back to Sakayanagi.

"I've been trying not to worry about this so far, but why do you have your eye on Ayanokouji?" she asked as she walked beside Sakayanagi.

"Oh? So, so you haven't been worried about it until now?"

"...Yeah. There's no way I'd have been thinking about that."

Kamuro denied whatever Sakayanagi was trying to

imply, but the look on Sakayanagi's face suggested that she already knew everything. However, rather than keep pressing, she simply answered Kamuro's question.

"It's because I've known him for a long time. Is that not a convincing enough reason?" said Sakayanagi.

Though Kamuro sounded concerned, Sakayanagi's tone was casual and nonchalant. Considering the fact that she hadn't revealed much of anything to Kamuro before, it was a fairly revealing answer. I could also see it as her trying to gauge my reaction. If I were to thoughtlessly start panicking and interrupt Sakayanagi's conversation, it would be the same as showing weakness.

To be honest, I didn't really care, though.

"So you're saying that you just happened to reunite at this school? Sounds like the chances of that happening are pretty slim, though."

"Yes. The chances really are quite slim. Don't you agree, Ayanokouji-kun?"

"Yeah, probably."

While we hadn't actually ever met before starting here, the way Sakayanagi phrased it was technically true. It was just that our relationship was one-sided. She knew about the old me.

"So, what, you're supposed to be really tough? Sorry, but you really don't look it, at all."

Kamuro cut right to the chase, just as Sakayanagi had done. In that sense, these two might really be similar.

"My, you've really become rather direct, haven't you? I don't think you've ever posed a question to me so frankly before," said Sakayanagi.

It seemed Kamuro had gotten some ideas, thanks to the many times she and I had made direct contact with one another. Perhaps that had caused something like an uncontrollable curiosity to well up within Sakayanagi, too.

"Anyone would think the same. You've never been fixated on anyone like this ever before," said Kamuro.

"I thought you were an indifferent person who didn't care to meddle in other people's affairs. That was why I didn't hesitate to ask you to keep an eye on Ayanokouji-kun, but... Well, I suppose you really are quite troublesome, aren't you?" said Sakayanagi.

She sounded exasperated, but also pleased. I'd thought she wanted to gauge my reactions, but it was possible that she was saying these mean-spirited things because it was *Kamuro's* reactions that amused her.

As we talked, we'd arrived at our destination.

"No one will bother us if we talk here, I believe," said Sakayanagi. It certainly was quiet here. We were in the special building after class, so it made sense. "Now then,

Masumi-san. I am terribly sorry, but please head on back to the dormitory."

"...Oh, okay."

Apparently, she'd brought Kamuro along simply to have someone to talk to along the way, ultimately deciding to send her back without revealing much more about me. Kamuro must have understood that, because she headed back down the stairs without putting up a fight.

"Was that okay to do?" I asked.

"Yes. It would inconvenience you if I carelessly revealed something about you, wouldn't it?"

"Nah, not really."

Showing any sign of weakness would just give her an opening. I wasn't going to deliberately give Sakayanagi any unnecessary information.

"I suppose you've identified me as your enemy, in a manner of speaking. I have decided to accept that," said Sakayanagi. What my reasons might have been for doing so, of course, meant nothing to her.

"So, what do you want to talk to me about so badly that you'd send Kamuro back?" I asked, urging her to cut to the chase. We'd wasted a lot of time getting here, and I didn't have long before my meeting with Hirata.

"It's about the promise we made, Ayanokouji-kun."

"Yeah. I agreed to face off against you in the next special exam, which means this coming one."

"Yes, that's exactly it. However...if you're all right with it, Ayanokouji-kun, I would like to save our confrontation for another time. This exam is not a competition with the other classes, but rather, designed to screen and eliminate one of our allies. The only way we can influence the other classes is via praise votes, leaving no way to attack them. So... would you mind if we were to postpone our contest until next time?"

In other words, she was saying that this special exam didn't count, since it wasn't a situation where we could compete with one another.

"Are you willing to accept?" asked Sakayanagi.

"Whatever you decide is fine," I replied, agreeing to her request without any resistance.

Since I had so easily accepted her offer, Sakayanagi politely thanked me for it.

"Thank you very much. I'd been thinking about what I might do if you said something like, 'An exam is an exam.' Now I can concentrate on Class A's internal affairs without worry. However..."

"However?"

"Well, because we have this truce, I've decided to tell you a little something as a show of faith. I will not do anything to impede you in this test, Ayanokouji-kun. Of course, that means I will not be giving you a criticism vote," said Sakayanagi, promising me that she would hold herself back. "Also, in the unlikely event that I somehow become involved in Class C's affairs in a way that negatively impacts your results, Ayanokouji-kun... Well, if that happens, I'm willing to pay a price. You may even go so far as to refuse to compete with me in the next test."

"If people focus their criticism votes on me in this test, there won't be a next time, though," I replied. I'd just get expelled. End of story. Hooray.

"You are certainly right about that. At any rate, please, be at ease. That is all that I wished to say," said Sakayanagi.

She was being almost excessively polite, but I supposed she considered this necessary to gain my trust.

"You might end up being sloppily betrayed by one of your own minions before your battle with me even begins," I told her.

"Heh heh heh. Oh my, you must be joking."

Most of the students in Class A belonged to Sakayanagi's faction. So she was confident they weren't going to try to get rid of their leader, huh?

"I decided who would be expelled the moment that this exam was announced," said Sakayanagi.

"You decided who to remove immediately, huh?

Sounds like the right decision." You could say that was a move she could make precisely *because* she had true, complete power over her class. "So, when do you plan to tell your classmates who it'll be?"

"I already informed them quite some time ago. Had I waited until the very last minute to notify the class who would be removed, it would only make everyone quite anxious. Telling them right away makes things easier on them. Wouldn't you agree?" said Sakayanagi.

Well, it was probably unbearable for the student who was going to be expelled. However, there were no signs at all that Class A had fallen into chaos.

"Do you happen to know who I've chosen?" asked Sakayanagi.

"Dunno. I haven't the slightest clue, really," I told her. In truth, I had a pretty clear idea.

"Katsuragi Kouhei-kun."

"Is that a reasonable choice?"

"He's the former leader of Class A, who stood in opposition to me in the past. There's no need for two people at the top of an organization, after all," said Sakayanagi.

Katsuragi was a calm and composed guy. He'd probably realized he was going to be sacrificed as soon as the details of the test were announced. So he'd accepted it without a fight, huh?

There were some students who continued to idolize Katsuragi, like Yahiko, but they were outnumbered.

"I know he opposed you pretty early on, but I thought he'd stepped aside," I replied.

As far as skill went, Katsuragi was near the top, even among the students in Class A. I would have thought he'd be too valuable to discard, but it seemed that from Sakayanagi's point of view, he was unnecessary.

"More than a few of my friends dislike him. They cannot agree with his conservative way of thinking. I think it would raise morale if he were to make an exit," said Sakayanagi.

It seemed the trade-off of boosting morale at the cost of losing a powerful asset was her goal.

"Are you sure it's okay for you to tell me this? About who your target is?"

"It's not as though you'll be making some dodgy dealings behind my back to protect him. Right, Ayanokouji-kun?" said Sakayanagi.

It wasn't like I could do anything that was worth that kind of effort, anyway.

"What do you intend to do in Class C?" asked Sakayanagi.

"Dunno. I'm not getting involved. I just plan on letting my classmates decide."

"So it's merely a question of whether it's an unlikable student or an unskilled one who will be removed?" She seemed to enjoy the thought. "As for Class D, the only person that comes to mind is Ryuuen-kun. There's no need to even think about it."

I couldn't argue with that. Class A, in particular, stood to gain nothing from helping Ryuuen. I was sure they wanted him to be expelled, even if it meant breaking the contract he had with Katsuragi.

"But I can't quite picture what Class B will do. The question of who will be expelled from that close-knit class is the most exciting thing to come out of this exam. Or will Ichinose-san come up with some kind of interesting plan?"

"Sorry, but it's about time for me to get going," I told her.

She was free to indulge in all the delusional fantasies she wanted, but I'd prefer if she did it on her own time, alone.

"I see. I suppose we'll end our conversation here for now. The next special exam begins next week, after all."

She struck the ground with her cane with a *crack*. Sakayanagi directed her gaze at the security cameras in the hallway for a brief instant. The movement of her eyes was so subtle that I wouldn't have noticed if I weren't paying close attention. I was unable to determine if it was a random glance or an intentional one, though.

"Well then, let's have our match during the final special exam of our first year of school, just as planned. It's a promise."

I gave her a slight nod and then left.

4.6

THERE WEREN'T MANY STORES you could meet up at after class. Usually, people gathered at the café in Keyaki Mall. But today was different.

"Thanks for coming today."

"No big deal. I wanted to talk to you too, Hirata."

"I'm glad to hear that. How about we take a little walk first?"

We met up at the southern entrance, and Hirata started moving right away, as if trying to scope out our surroundings.

"Sorry, Ayanokouji-kun. Do you mind if we change our plans a little?" he asked.

"Change how?"

"Could we talk in my room instead? I think I'd feel more relaxed if we did that."

"I don't mind. That's fine by me."

"Thank you!"

Apparently, it seemed the mall wasn't the best place for us to meet right now. I was guessing he didn't want other people to hear what he was going to talk about.

As we walked back to the dorm, we made casual conversation. "Our first year is already almost over. How do you think your first year went, Ayanokouji-kun?" asked Hirata.

I looked up at the sky, letting out a sigh. "Between the uninhabited island and the camp school, I'd say it was a pretty turbulent."

"Yeah. It was certainly tough. But I had fun. Thinking back to when I started here...I think I've managed to build some real trust among my classmates," said Hirata.

"Yeah. I think so too."

I wasn't going to deny the truth of that. There were more than a few people in class who hated each other, of course, but I supposed there was some truth to the expression "the enemy of my enemy is my friend." While we were forced to cooperate with each other, we had gradually begun to form what you might call bonds.

"To be honest... Everything was fine before this exam came along," said Hirata. There was a shadow over his smiling face.

"So that's what you wanted to talk about, huh?"

"Yeah. Sorry, Ayanokouji-kun. I know that you really don't want to talk about it."

I'd never really taken an active role, irrespective of the nature of the exam—though Horikita, ignoring my personality, would forcefully demand I cooperate each time an exam came around. Interestingly enough, it was the exact opposite this time. Horikita wasn't asking for my help, but Hirata was.

I supposed Horikita had grown as of late. Maybe she'd come to accept that I wasn't going to cooperate, since the frequency of her requests had begun to decrease.

"I just can't seem to come up with a way to tackle this exam. No matter how hard I think about it, no matter how many times I try to put a plan together, nothing works," said Hirata.

"No matter how many times...?"

I looked closer, noticing dark circles under his eyes. I was guessing he'd spent so much time thinking about the exam last night that it had cost him sleep.

"That sounds hard," I said. "In this exam, the more you think about your class, the more you suffer for it."

"Huh...?" said Hirata.

"Oh, nothing. Don't worry."

If I carelessly let something slip, Hirata would just sink

deeper into despair. The best plan for now was probably to leave things be.

"I-If there's there some way to save our class, please tell me," Hirata said.

Apparently, my reaction just now had given him the mistaken impression that I had some kind of idea to share with him.

"Do you think it's actually impossible to save up twenty million private points?" I asked.

"I've tried running calculations, but I just can't find any way to get to that number. I even talked about it with the seniors in my club. But they have their own special exams coming up," replied Hirata.

"So they can't spare any points to help out?"

"Yeah..."

Potential methods to save our class from suffering any casualties were very limited.

"Sorry, I just can't think of anything else. If I do think of something, I'll definitely let you know, Hirata," I told him.

"I see... Okay, thank you," Hirata said, trying his hardest to put on a smile.

That was the best answer I could give him at the moment. This special exam was both extremely difficult and extremely simple. If you shifted your viewpoint a little, the path ahead was clear. Of course, Hirata couldn't see things that way.

Namely, he couldn't see that this was a test designed *only to discard an unnecessary student.*

The moment we heard the rules of the exam, Kouenji and I understood the goal being outlined. Of course, there was no way of knowing *who* would be expelled. All you had to do was make sure it wasn't *you*. However, Hirata wasn't the kind of person who could think that way. He'd never be able to make up his mind about that question of *who*. It was like he was stuck in a maze, unable to see the exit.

"Ayanokouji-kun, do you think it's okay even if someone gets expelled?" asked Hirata.

"It would be great if we make it through this without anyone getting expelled, of course. But I think that's going to be difficult."

"...Yeah, you're right, of course. But there must be some way to—"

"Hirata, you haven't been sleeping well at night precisely because you know that's true, right?" I said, interrupting him.

"That's..."

We both fell silent as we approached the dormitory entrance, partly because we could see several students chatting away in the lobby. However, the main problem lay elsewhere. Our eyes met those of a certain someone sitting on a sofa in the lobby.

"Well, well, look what we have here. If it isn't Hirata Boy and Ayanokouji Boy. What a strange coincidence this is," said Kouenji.

"Hey, Kouenji-kun. Are you waiting for someone?" asked Hirata.

It seemed he'd guessed as much based on the fact that Kouenji's gaze fell on us as soon as we entered the building.

"If I did have plans to meet with someone, would you be concerned?" he asked, answering Hirata's question with one of his own.

"I suppose I might think it's unusual," replied Hirata.

"I don't dislike honest people. But unfortunately, no, I am not waiting for anyone."

Although he had answered Hirata's question, he didn't say what he *was* doing here. Kouenji wasn't the kind of person who'd usually hang around in a place like this.

"Let's go," said Hirata.

He walked over to the elevator and extended his hand to press the button. Just as he went to do so, Kouenji called out from behind us.

"You'd best do everything you can to muster your wits and get through this exam," said Kouenji.

Hirata's finger stopped just a hair's breadth from the button.

"...You never change, do you, Kouenji-kun?" he said, sounding a little bit bothered by Kouenji's attitude.

"This isn't an exam worth changing for," replied Kouenji.

"Is that so?"

It was rare to see Hirata to get worked up. He turned to look at Kouenji, but remained calm and collected, rather than glare at him.

"You say this isn't the kind of exam worth changing for, but I have to wonder if you're actually the one who most needs to change. I'm worried, Kouenji. I've been thinking that...our classmates might make an example of you. And if that happens... Well, that worries me," said Hirata.

That was Hirata's way of both showing concern and expressing a mild threat. His words conveyed a powerful desire for cooperation. He was probably hoping that Kouenji would match the feeling, if only a little.

"Such worries are needless. Besides, you are the class leader, are you not? Isn't it your job to take care of such things?" Kouenji had absolutely no intention of changing his stance. He was going to sit back and do nothing until the very end.

"There are things I can't do, you know. I might not be able to live up to your expectations," said Hirata.

"Oh no, I don't think that's true."

Despite Hirata's lack of confidence, Kouenji just kept heaping more expectations on him. I couldn't tell if he really meant what he was saying, though.

Kouenji stood up, walked on over, and then lightly patted Hirata on the shoulder.

"Even though I'm sure you'll spend time tending your friends' wounds, I trust you'll handle disposing of the unwanted garbage," said Kouenji.

The moment he said those words, Hirata firmly pressed the call elevator button.

"...Let's go, Ayanokouji-kun."

"Okay."

Hirata's tone, which had sounded amicable until that point, now contained slight hints of anger. Apparently, he couldn't help but feel irritated by Kouenji implying some of our classmates were garbage. As soon as the elevator doors closed, he opened his mouth to speak.

"*Sigh*... I'm sorry. I was acting a little out of character back there."

"Don't worry about it. Kouenji's excuses are a problem."

Hirata forced a smile, and slightly lowered his head.

"So, what he said got to you too, huh?" he said. "...I

understand it's not realistic to hope no one will ever get expelled. I gave up on that idea long ago, despite everything I've been saying out loud."

The elevator arrived at Hirata's floor and we got off.

"Please, come in."

"Pardon the intrusion."

This was the first time I'd been inside Hirata's room. It was decorated in similar fashion to my own, which was to say that it was simple. There was a pleasant scent in the air, like some kind of air freshener. It was a bit glum, a bit bland, but neat and orderly, like Hirata himself.

"Please sit. Would you care for some coffee or something?"

"Sure, if it's not a bother."

"It's not a bother at all. I asked you over, after all," said Hirata.

I was usually the one who had guests over, so this was something of a new experience for me.

"So, picking up where we left off..." Hirata addressed me over his shoulder as he prepared the coffee. "I wonder if there's really no way to save everyone in class?"

"I dunno. Maybe it's just that I can't think of anything."

I gave him the same kind of answer I did earlier. Even though he knew the truth, Hirata was still looking for some path to salvation. I'd hoped my answer would make him feel better, but it seemed to have had the opposite effect.

"If you can't come up with anything, I can't imagine that anyone else will," said Hirata.

"You're giving me way too much credit." When did Hirata develop such a high opinion of me?

"Ever since that matter with Karuizawa-san, I've considered you the most reliable person in our class," said Hirata, as if he had just read my mind.

"I'm sorry to say this, but I'm really not."

The coffee finished brewing and he handed me a cup.

"It's the truth. Though you are quite humble, so I figured you wouldn't admit that yourself," said Hirata.

It would be a waste of time to argue. No matter how I tried to deny it, Hirata wouldn't listen. It seemed smarter to just change the subject.

Hirata had guessed what I was thinking. "This test requires someone to be expelled. But that's not something I can deal with, no matter how hard I try to understand. There's no one in my class that I would be okay with losing," he said.

"I understand your concern, but we have no other choice. We just have to wait for the answer to come next week."

"An answer, huh? Ayanokouji-kun... Is there anyone

in particular that you think should be expelled?" asked Hirata, looking at me intently.

While I could see kindness in his eyes, there was something else hidden there, too.

"Not really."

My words could be interpreted as cowardly neutral, but they were honest. There were a few students whom I wanted to stay, but no one I would specifically name as a candidate for expulsion. Our classmates would talk to each other and choose someone for expulsion based on the results of those discussions. That was how it was going to be.

"No matter who ends up going, we just have to accept it," I added.

"That's a very pragmatic approach. You're much more qualified to be the leader of the class than I am," said Hirata.

He'd taken the initiative to lead the class so far, but the words now coming out of his mouth sounded timid and weak. He was stuck, unable to move forward.

"What should I do next? What's the best way for me to tackle this exam?" he asked.

It wasn't my place to give advice, but Hirata had often tried to help others. I wanted to do something to help him, but...

"Well, I don't want you to just take my word for it, but I'll tell you what I think," I told him.

"Yes, please do."

"Okay, let's set aside idealistic thoughts about saving everyone for a moment. Hirata, you've been agonizing over the question 'Who should we get rid of?' for some time now. But you haven't been able to come up with an answer."

What I was saying was hard for him to swallow. Even so, Hirata seemed to agree with what I was saying, as he nodded in the end.

"In that case, why not try the opposite approach? Rather than 'Who should get rid of?' why not ask yourself 'Who should we keep around?'" I continued.

"Who should we keep around...? Well everyone, of course—"

"Rank everyone in class by priority. Arrange everyone in class, yourself included, from top to bottom. Of course, there might be multiple students whom you'd give the same level of priority. Even so, you should try to arrange them into a ranking, anyway. You can base this on whether you personally like them, or on whether they've contributed to the class," I added.

By creating such a ranking, you'd wind up with someone at the top and someone at the bottom.

"That's... but..."

Yep, it was a simple solution. But Hirata wasn't going to do it. His heart was set on saving everyone. The idea of trying to rank people was probably anathema to him.

"If I do rank people, though, what I come up with won't be the same as what a classmate would," said Hirata, still making excuses, still trying to flee. If things continued this way, he'd be heading into the special exam completely defenseless.

"That's okay. I think you should start by coming to your own conclusions," I replied.

This was probably the only advice I could give Hirata for now. What he would do with it was entirely up to him.

Grateful for the coffee he'd made me, I took a sip. It was a little more acidic than what I was used to. Perhaps he used a different brand than I did.

"I see. Okay. You might be right about that. Lately, I've just been filled with this desire to run away from everything," said Hirata.

He'd heard me out and was doing his best to understand what I'd said. I doubted he could absorb it right away. It probably didn't sit well with him, making him feel sick to his stomach. Still, he held it in, doing his best to swallow what I'd just said.

"*Sigh*... Okay. Thank you for this," he said, managing to squeeze out words of gratitude. It seemed our conversation had reached a stopping point for now.

"Hey, can I ask you a personal question? It might be a little insensitive," I said, deciding to change topics from the exam by asking about something that had me curious.

"Hm? What is it?"

"Has anyone told you they have a crush on you since you and Karuizawa broke up?"

"Wow, that's an unexpected question. I never imagined you'd ask me something like that, Ayanokouji-kun."

There was a mix of surprise and bewilderment on Hirata's face. I was interested in whether or not he had a romantic partner because of a conversation I'd had with Mii-chan, a classmate of ours. She'd come to me before the year-end exam, asking for advice because she had a crush on Hirata, and I was wondering if anything had happened between them.

"Well, I won't say who, but...yes, there was someone," said Hirata.

That meant girls had already started telling Hirata about their feelings for him. I wasn't going to ask whether or not Mii-chan was the one who'd approached him, but wow, popular guys really were amazing. They didn't even have to do anything for girls to fawn over them.

Well, maybe it was just the way Hirata behaved all the time that made that happen? It wasn't like he ever slacked off.

"Are you dating this person?"

"Oh, no way. I'm not planning on dating anyone right now," said Hirata, quite flatly.

"Is there someone you like or something?" If he was holding out for his true love, then I could understand that.

"I think dating someone is just too much for me right now. I'm not qualified," said Hirata.

"If *you're* not qualified, Hirata, then dating would be just a pipe dream for someone like me." Besides, you didn't need "qualifications" when it came to romance.

"I'm just not good enough for something like that," said Hirata.

The more capable someone was, the humbler they were. The more incompetent they were, the more arrogant.

In the end, the conversation ended without Hirata and me delving deeper into anything.

4.7

• •

"Sorry for calling you over at such a late hour, Ichinose."
I'd invited her to my room around 11 o'clock at night. It would have been perfectly understandable if she'd declined my request out of caution, but Ichinose didn't seem to resist the idea at all.

"Oh no, it's perfectly fine. But I have to say, it's pretty unusual for you to call me, Ayanokouji-kun."

"Well, that's because there's something I really wanted to talk to you about, Ichinose. Oh, and please feel free to sit down on the bed for now, if you like. The floor's probably pretty cold," I told her.

She thanked me with a smile and then sat down on my bed.

"I kind of feel like my heart's going to beat out of my chest..." Ichinose muttered to herself quietly.

THE DIFFICULTY OF SAVING

"Huh?"

"Oh, uh, it's nothing. Anyway, why didn't we just talk this over on the phone?"

Why, huh? As I brought some water to a boil in the kettle, I grabbed some white cups.

"Well, there's a lot I couldn't really convey too well over the phone. For example, there's something I wanted to confirm with you directly," I told her.

"I see."

"I won't beat around the bush. What are you planning to do for this exam?" I asked.

"So, this is about our conversation this morning, huh? Well, I've been...considering how to come up with a way to get through this exam without anyone getting expelled," said Ichinose.

"Have you come up with any solid ideas?" I asked, as I turned around.

Of course, that question was merely a kind formality. We both already knew quite well that the only option was to spend the twenty million points.

"Unfortunately, no, I still haven't come up with any-thing... There isn't much time left, so I'm kind of starting to panic," said Ichinose.

Neither her words nor behavior gave the impression she was hiding anything. This was how she really felt.

That said, I remembered being very impressed with Ichinose's surprisingly good poker face back during the exam on the cruise ship.

"I was thinking that you might have gone to President Nagumo for help or something," I told her.

"Help?"

What I'd just said might have made someone panic if they weren't ready for it, but Ichinose seemed the same as always. What I was about to say next, however, was probably going to get past her poker face. After the water in the kettle came to a boil, I poured a cup of cocoa and handed it to Ichinose.

"Thank you," she said.

"This supplementary exam is different from what we've had so far. We can't make it through without some-one being forced out of school. However, there is one sole path out of that: saving up twenty million points. No matter how many points Class B has saved up al-ready, there's no way you've accumulated twenty million. Which makes the cooperation of a third party absolutely essential," I told her.

Ichinose's gaze shifted down to her cocoa. She blew on it gently to cool it down.

"I see. Asahina-senpai already knew that, too. But I didn't think she'd talked to you about it, Ayanokouji-kun."

Since she'd guessed how I'd found out right away, she must have come to the conclusion that she couldn't hide anything.

"In that case, I'm guessing you also heard about the condition he has in exchange for lending me the number of points we need?" asked Ichinose.

I gave her a gentle nod. Ichinose had a pained smile on her face.

"It really is stupid, isn't it? In a lot of ways," she said.

The idea of lending out points in exchange for entering into a relationship. The fact that she was seriously considering his condition. That was probably what she meant by a "lot of ways."

"In case you were wondering, Nagumo-senpai forbade me from telling anyone about the deal. He said that if word got out, he'd just act like it never happened. But if Asahina-senpai is the one who told you, then I suppose it's okay," said Ichinose.

"I wouldn't worry about that part," I told her.

"But this doesn't concern you, does it, Ayanokouji-kun...?"

"That's true." This was Class B's problem. This was Ichinose's decision. "How many points are you short?"

"A little over four million, give or take," said Ichinose.

So by starting a relationship with Nagumo, she'd

make up those four million points and no one would get expelled.

"That's one hell of a deal," I told her.

"Yeah. It'd be impossible for someone like me to both go out with Nagumo-senpai and borrow points from him. When you think about it, I suppose it's natural that he'd ask for something in return," said Ichinose.

As I listened to her speak, I started to understand what was going through her head. There was absolutely no way she'd let someone from Class B get expelled. To keep that from happening, she was prepared to sacrifice herself.

"It's probably the only way I can save everyone in Class B," she added.

"I see..."

No matter what I said to Ichinose right now, there was no way I could help her. Realistically speaking, private points were the only solution to her problem. And four million points wasn't a sum I could come up with, even if I were in her position right now.

"Are you... worried about me, by any chance?" she asked.

"It might be a bit presumptuous, but yeah."

"Oh no, not at all. Actually, it makes me really happy." Despite saying that, there was still a dark cloud hanging over her. Ichinose slowly brought the cocoa to her mouth now that it had cooled down slightly. "But I really do think I might be in trouble... Honestly, if I hadn't talked to you, Ayanokouji-kun, I might have been able to make a decision more readily. What do you think, Ayanokouji-kun?"

"About the deal?"

"Yeah. What does it look like I'm trying to do here, from your point of view?" she asked, her eyes meeting mine.

I answered her directly. "I think this is a tactic that only you could use to prevent anyone in your class from getting expelled, Ichinose. The option of saving up enough private points is available to you because you have a connection with President Nagumo thanks to being on the student council. This—the option of getting to twenty million points by accepting his condition—is a valid choice."

"And you're not going to hold me in contempt for it?" she asked.

"No, there's no need for that. But to be honest, I can't really determine if spending twenty million points to save a classmate is worth it."

"...I see." Ichinose took another slow sip of her cocoa, still looking me in the eyes. "Hey, Ayanokouji-kun."

"Hm?"

"Ayanokouji-kun... Maybe you're actually a really amazing person?"

Hearing her call me amazing left me a little bewildered. All I did was tell her what I'd heard from Asahina.

"What makes you think I'm an amazing person? Sorry, it's just something I don't see myself as at all."

"If that's true, it just makes you even more amazing. After all, Ayanokouji-kun, you..." Ichinose stopped in the middle of her sentence.

"What's up?" I asked.

"Oh, nothing. It's all right."

It was almost as if even *she* didn't even understand what she wanted to say. It was like her mouth was moving ahead of her thoughts.

"...What is this, I wonder...?" muttered Ichinose quietly, seeming to direct the question at herself.

Even though I'd been a bit forceful in arranging this meeting, I was glad I'd invited her over. I was once again cognizant of the fact that, no matter what, Ichinose would act in Class B's best interests. She would probably agonize over this for a long time, then come to a decision.

A decision about whether or not to begin a relationship with Nagumo Miyabi.

5 OLDER BROTHER AND YOUNGER SISTER

IT WAS THE MORNING of the third day since the supplementary exam had been announced. The vote would be held on Saturday, the day after tomorrow. Far too soon, one of our friends were going to be expelled from school.

As I opened the front door of my room, I felt the cold air wash over me. I stepped out into the hallway and made my way down to the first-floor lobby. As I was going down, I noticed Sudou headed down as well, via the stairs.

"Using the stairs, huh?"

"Yeah. I was thinking I'd get a little workout, even if it's not much," he replied.

Sudou was probably trying to live his student life to the fullest right now, between his club activities and his studies. And so, the two of us headed off to school together, side by side.

"I might be dumb and have a short fuse, but I've been makin' lots of progress. That's why I definitely don't wanna get expelled," said Sudou. He seemed to be monologuing, rather than making conversation with me. "Would you think it was wrong if I said that I wouldn't care if people resented me, as long as I got to stay here at this school?"

"No, I think that's the right approach, honestly. I think it's the people with a strong desire to stay who are going to make it through this test."

"Yeah."

When we made it to school and entered the classroom, I sensed something off. Sudou, on the other hand, went over to his seat without noticing anything. The atmosphere had changed, and frankly, I wasn't *that* oblivious. The moment I set foot in Class C, I sensed something was different from the other day.

Everything looked normal, at first glance. It seemed like a typical day. Yep. People were chatting away like normal and I could hear friendly conversations. But that was exactly what felt so out of place. Just yesterday, everyone had had their guard up. Our classmates were all supposed to be keeping each other in check.

And yet, despite that, there was this bizarre sense of unity.

"Good morning, Ayanokouji-kun," said Hirata, calling over to me.

"Morning." After giving him that brief reply, I looked Hirata over.

"Hm? What's up?" he asked.

I wondered if he really hadn't noticed anything, or if he was just pretending. Hirata looked into my eyes with the same expression he always had.

"Oh, it's nothing," I replied.

"Really? Well, all right then. I hope today goes well," he answered.

After Hirata and I finished greeting each other, he headed over to the girls who'd been calling for him. However, the feeling of something being out of place began to fade both as time passed and the number of students in the room increased. The conclusion I came to was that a large group of people had probably formed for the sake of getting through this exam. Additionally, they were starting to come to a consensus not about who to protect, but about who to kick out.

There were eleven students in the classroom. Even if I put Hirata aside, that left ten people. And if those ten people all conspired to use their criticism votes together on someone, their target would be in serious danger.

I spotted Ike and Yamauchi among the guys in that group. There were also some girls in the group who had little if any connection whatsoever to either of them.

It was possible that everyone here was conspiring together. What struck me as odd was that some of the girls in the group belonged to Kei's circle. Kei hadn't reported anything about this to me.

"Morning."

Not long after, Horikita arrived at school. Although her behavior was the same as always, she did take a look around the room.

"...Did something happen?" she asked.

"You feel it too, huh?" I asked.

"Yes. Something feels a little off. If you're concerned about it though, why not go speak with the people in question?"

"I'll pass. It's best to just let sleeping dogs lie, after all."

If nothing else, this warranted proceeding with caution. I sent a message to Keisei, who had gotten to school earlier that morning.

Me: *"Did anything unusual happen?"*

Keisei: *"I don't know. But I do feel like there's something different in the air today, for some reason."*

Though uncertain, he did seem to have picked up on something unusual.

I texted him exactly what I thought. *"Some people might have formed a large group. Our classmates seem strangely calm."*

After he got my message, he looked around the room, and then at me.

"Yeah, you seem to be right about that," he texted back. *"The dark cloud that hung over the class the other day is totally gone. Good work picking up on that."*

"I don't have many friends, so I'm alert to changes in my surroundings."

"If a group of ten people or more has formed, it's possible they've talked about who they're going to kick out, right?"

"Whoever they go after is going to be in trouble, for sure."

"I have to wonder who's in this group... Are we going to be okay?"

I could feel Keisei's anxiousness through his message. As the group's numbers swelled, students who weren't even that close to its members would naturally begin to want to join. Directing the actions of such a group wouldn't be that easy.

At any rate, since more students were showing up in the classroom, I decided to stop texting. I could continue this conversation during lunch or after class.

5.1

LUNCHTIME FOUND ME chatting with the Ayanokouji Group. Well, I say chatting, but we were really discussing the supplementary exam. Naturally, the first topic that came up was the change in the air in the classroom that morning. Since Keisei was the one who came to class early today, he began telling the rest of us that there were signs a large group had formed.

"...I see, I see. Yeah, you might be right about that. It definitely seemed like people were way more chipper than they were yesterday," said Haruka.

"But it's still just...speculation, at this point, right?" asked Airi.

"Yeah. There's no proof a large group has formed, and even if they have, it doesn't seem they've necessarily narrowed down their target to just one person," said Keisei.

In the end, this was all we could infer based on what we'd seen this morning.

"So, should we have one of us do some digging, for the time being?"

"I'm not so sure. If we end up picking the wrong person for the job, then the group's leader might find out someone's snooping. And if that happens, there's a chance someone from our group would wind up being targeted." That in and of itself was something Keisei wanted to avoid.

"There's probably a reason we weren't invited to join."

If someone were to make a large group, then it would be okay for them to ask anyone to join in, except for the person that they were specifically targeting. The ideal development would be to have 39 people corner the solitary person. However, that wasn't that likely to become reality.

"What if one of us is...close to whoever it is they're targeting, or something?" guessed Haruka, quietly scanning her eyes over the group. "...Or what if...one of *us* is the target?"

"S-Stop it, Haruka-chan...!" said Airi.

She seemed to be getting a little too anxious, but honestly, this wasn't exactly a laughing matter.

"People probably started trying to form a group on the very first day. From there, they've been working to expand that group with people they can trust. The signs just became more obvious now, on the third day," said Keisei.

He was probably on the mark. The group's apparent growth was too much for a single day's work. I was guessing they'd made their move the very day the supplementary exam was announced.

"If they're still planning on bringing more people into the fold, they might make contact with one of us sometime today."

"What do we do if they talk about targeting one of us, though? I mean, what if they come to us and threaten to have one of us expelled if we don't cooperate with them... What then?" said Akito, unintentionally posing a significant, challenging question.

"Isn't it obvious? We've already decided we're going to prioritize our own group, right?" said Haruka.

"But what if you end up being the one targeted as a result, Haruka?" he asked in return.

"That's... But I don't think I want to stay in school badly enough to make me betray my friends. If they did say something like that, I'd probably go and complain about it to the school," replied Haruka, recoiling a little bit, though she still managed to answer Akito's question.

"I'm the same. I'd never want to betray my friends," said Airi, nodding forcefully, despite her anxiousness.

"What about you, Keisei?" asked Akito.

After a brief silence, Keisei gave his honest thoughts on the matter.

"...Fundamentally speaking, I share Haruka and Airi's opinion. But things are never that simple. If you actually do wind up being targeted in this exam, there's probably no way out. Saying things like 'I'm okay with getting expelled in exchange for defending my friends' might sound better, but...it'll still be really painful."

"That's... What do you think, Kiyopon?" asked Haruka.

Everyone's eyes fell on me. I should try guide their thoughts to a certain degree to bring them into accord.

"I'm against Haruka's approach—that is, complaining about it," I said.

"Wait, does that mean you'd betray your friends and join the large group?" she snapped back.

"No, cooperating with the group to try get one of your friends expelled is completely out of the question. However, I think it's better to pretend to play along on the surface. I don't think being uncooperative or speaking out sharply would be a good idea," I told her.

You had to make sure you didn't let your emotions get the better of you.

"By making it seem like we're cooperating with them, we can find out how many criticism votes they have and who they're planning to invite into the group next. We need that kind of information. Am I wrong?"

"...No, you've certainly got a point," replied Haruka.

She'd gotten really heated, but now started to calm back down. If you got worked up and pushed people away when they tried to talk to you, then you'd lose the chance to get any information out of them. At that point, you wouldn't even know who they were targeting.

"Even if you pretend to be one of them, since the vote is anonymous, they won't be able to know exactly who anyone actually used their criticism votes on," I added. In other words, we could obscure what was really going on.

"Yeah, I guess it would probably be in our group's best interest to do things that way," said Haruka.

I nodded.

"Besides, if their group has been quietly expanding since day one and has a fair number of people in it by day three, it's possible that the mastermind who brought them all together is pretty clever. They've been taking bold action, but also treading carefully. More importantly, they haven't let anything slip that would identify the person they're targeting for expulsion. And it seems both Hirata and Horikita haven't noticed this big group's existence," I added.

Horikita might have had some suspicions, but Hirata

seemed not to have noticed anything at all. It wouldn't have been strange if word of the group's existence had gotten out, but they'd kept things under tight wraps, even at such a critical moment.

"I suppose the reason why Hirata hasn't really joined a particular group is because he takes a very neutral stance with everyone. If they just thoughtlessly approached him and asked him to join their group, then he might not only refuse, but try and break up their group," I reasoned.

"So you're saying that the person who started this group has thought of all that, huh?"

"You're amazing, Kiyotaka-kun! It's awesome that you've figured out so much!" said Airi, clapping her hands happily, congratulating me.

"You're certainly right about that. I wasn't the one who noticed the abnormality this morning. Kiyotaka was," said Keisei.

"I already told you, didn't I? When you're on your own for a long time, you can't help but unintentionally pick up on extraneous details. Besides, it's not like this group's existence is official. We're still speaking in hypotheticals."

We were just talking through theories right now. There was no proof any of it was actually for real.

"I suppose it's probably best to be on our guard, though."

"Everything we've been talking about has been so dark and depressing, jeez. Can't we talk about something a little lighter?" said Akito with a sigh, while fiddling with his phone.

Everyone shook their heads.

"It's not like we can really talk about anything else right now. It's hard to just sit back and enjoy ourselves when we're being confronted with the fact that one of our classmates is going away, and soon."

No matter how much we continued to plan together as a group, our anxieties would continue to burn in the back of our minds.

"Still, when I think about that, I... I am really worried..." said Airi.

"Come on, you're still talking about that, Airi? You'll definitely be fine!" said Haruka, lightly patting Airi on the head, telling her not to stress.

"But..."

"If anything, I suspect I'm the one the girls in our class hate, anyway," said Haruka.

"Yeah, you're probably right," said Akito, nodding in agreement.

Haruka shot him an intense glare.

"What? You said it yourself, didn't you?" he shot back.

"It's fine if *I* say it, but do you seriously think I'd like hearing that from someone else?" she snapped.

"...I guess."

In the face of that unassailable argument, Akito just gave in. Seeing this, Airi's self-confidence seemed to shrink even further.

"You're cute though, Haruka-chan. And you've got a good sense of humor, and you're smart, and..."

"No, no, wait... Come on, at the very least, you shouldn't be saying that first part to me," said Haruka, sounding exasperated, but still trying to console Airi anyway.

"There's probably no need for you girls to worry, though. I think there are way more targets among the guys," said Keisei, trying to reassure the two of them.

"Yeah, the guys are the ones in serious trouble right now. So there's no point in getting super scared about it," said Akito.

"Yeah, I suppose you're right. Compared to the girls, the guys are definitely... Hey, wait a sec, isn't that Hirata-kun?" said Haruka, sounding somewhat unsure.

The rest of us followed her line of sight. There, indeed, was a lone figure walking listlessly by. It was Hirata. He normally stood straight and tall, and always had a smile on his face. But looking at him now, you couldn't call him cheerful by any stretch of the imagination.

"I wonder if he really is worried about this test after all."

"Semes like it. He almost looks like a different person."

The two of them watched Hirata walk off, sounding worried about him.

"Wow, even though he doesn't have to worry at all about getting expelled himself. That guy is just carrying too much on his shoulders."

"Someone *will* get expelled, though. That much is unavoidable."

They looked at Hirata with pity in their eyes. As I was listening to the conversation, I got a message. One I couldn't ignore, apparently.

"Sorry, I gotta go meet someone," I announced.

"Who are you meeting?" asked Haruka with interest, looking at me with curiosity-laden eyes.

Airi looked at me too, though her eyes showed anxiousness.

"Horikita. It's probably about the test."

"Ah, 'kay," replied Haruka, losing all interest, as if she had come to realize something on hearing my response. She was probably remembering the incident with Horikita and Ryuuen the other day.

I said bye to the group and left the café.

5.2

. . . .

OUR MEETING LOCATION was a rest area along a path that seemed an odd choice for a lunch break. Spring and autumn aside, no one really liked to go all the way out here at this time of year.

"Sorry for the trouble, calling you out to meet like this."

"Not a big deal. I'm the one who is sorry, having to make you wait out in the cold weather."

"I don't mind."

I was meeting with Horikita—but not the younger sister, Suzune. I was meeting with the older brother, Manabu.

"...Hello."

Tachibana bowed her head to me, gently. They weren't on the student council anymore, but Tachibana still continued to accompany Horikita, waiting at his side. It went without saying that what they had seemed to go beyond a simple hierarchical boss-subordinate relationship.

In the past, Tachibana had been a bit harsh to me, but she seemed somewhat mild-mannered today. I wondered if it was because she was still reeling from nearly getting expelled after being caught in Nagumo's trap.

"It seems like a new supplementary special exam has begun," said Horikita.

"Word travels fast, I see. Well, the test will be over pretty soon."

"Some first-year students have already approached third-years to talk about it. But I doubt there's anyone in our grade who can help out in a concrete way."

"So, there're no upperclassmen who'd lend out private points?"

"It would be difficult, I imagine. Special exams are held each year, but generally speaking, the formats are rotated every three years or so. This is done in order to prevent currently enrolled students from leaking information about the tests," said Horikita.

That was exactly what I'd imagined. I supposed it was an obvious conclusion, though.

"The number of private points we possess will determine loss or victory in the special exams we third-years will face. We can't afford to give points to our juniors," said Horikita.

I see. I was betting that was the reason Tachibana didn't look so well right about now. Her class had had to pay up twenty million points because of her mistake. If those points were basically the war funds needed to get through the special exams, it was all the more understandable why she looked green in the gills.

"I'm sorry. If I'd only handled myself better, I..."

Compelled by her feelings of remorse, Tachibana bowed deeply toward Horikita.

"There's no need for that." Horikita rebuked her. I wonder how many times she had apologized to him.

"O-Oh, o-okay..."

"Any word from your sister?" I asked.

"Suzune will not come to me," he replied.

"This special exam isn't like anything we've ever had before. Horikita needs someone who can give her advice."

She was struggling right now, which was why she'd made contact with Ryuuen. In the end, though, she got shut down.

"In that case, can't you fulfill that role?" asked Horikita.

"That's an impossible ask. Your sister and I are just different kinds of people."

"Are you saying she and I are the same kind?"

"At the very least, a lot more similar than me."

"........."

There was a brief silence.

"She's probably going to be compelled to make some tough choices about how to fight this battle. You're the only who can guide her," I told Horikita.

"Even if that's true, this is something she'll have to decide for herself."

That was certainly true. He wasn't going to compel her to make a decision. Ultimately, it was up to Horikita Suzune to choose her own path.

"Okay then, what did you call me out here for?" I asked.

I doubted either of us really wanted to be having a long conversation out here in the cold. Since Horikita didn't really enjoy talking about his sister, I thought I'd change the topic.

"It's about Nagumo. I wanted to ask you if you've noticed any unusual activity going on," said Horikita.

"Is this something you felt like we specifically needed to meet up in person to discuss?"

"Actually, I was the one who asked for it," said Tachibana.

I'd found out why the meeting had been set for this location, albeit in a way I didn't expect.

"It's because I wanted to know the reason you've been acknowledged," said Tachibana.

I could see the feelings of frustration welling up in her eyes. Perhaps Horikita Manabu had taken this opportunity to meet because he thought it would help Tachibana grow.

"I've been acknowledged? I've probably only ever been rude to Horikita, though," I replied.

"I know that," she snapped. Having her give me such a clear, immediate answer honestly stung a little. "But...I've decided to try and broaden my horizons. You might have ability worth recognizing, that I just can't see."

"So? What is your impression of Ayanokouji now that you're seeing him again?" asked Horikita.

"Honestly, I don't have the slightest clue."

"I know what you mean," said Horikita.

What kind of conversation was this? Maybe because of the strange, relaxed atmosphere, Horikita let out a small chuckle. "Unfortunately, we probably won't understand Ayanokouji's true worth until after we graduate," he said.

"No. Nothing's going to change, even after you graduate," I replied.

"Well, I think you're right about that," said Tachibana.

Really? They'd had me meet them out here in the cold for *this*? I supposed it spoke to how wounded Tachibana was.

"Nagumo is obsessed with you. He probably wants nothing to do with me, right? Given that, it might be a good idea for you to engage him directly yourself," I told them.

This wasn't really something I should be demanding of a guy who was about to graduate from Class A. Regardless, Nagumo was definitely going to pick a fight. In fact, he might already have made his move.

"...Nagumo-kun has been in close contact with third-year Class B lately. I think he's giving them his total support, just like he did at the training camp."

He might have presented them with the idea of knocking Horikita's brother down to Class B. All for the sake of his goal to defeat Horikita Manabu.

"The nonsense never stops. I just want to live in peace," I said.

"If you first-years are to have any peace in the future, we can't leave the Nagumo problem unresolved," answered Horikita.

Horikita was convinced that something terrible was going to happen next year. Once the person Nagumo was obsessed with defeating was gone, Nagumo might go on a rampage and do whatever he pleased. Horikita was implying that we'd be in big trouble if we didn't take action now.

"I intend to do whatever I can," I told him.

At least for the moment, that was the answer I had for him.

5.3

· ·

WHEN I STEPPED OUT of the shower that evening, I saw I had several missed calls from Kei. It must have been something urgent, considering that each call was about a minute apart. As I'd just barely finished drying my hair, I picked up my phone, thinking that I'd go ahead and call Kei back. But she called me again right then, so I just answered her call instead.

"Hello?"

"Ah, I finally got through...!" she huffed.

"You sound really flustered."

"Well, of course I am...! Something really awful is about to happen, Kiyotaka!"

"Something awful?"

"I don't know who's putting this together, but...it sounds like everyone's gonna vote you out of school," said Kei.

"Is that so?" I asked.

"W-Wait a second, did you already know?"

"No, this is the first I'm hearing of it. I just had a vague understanding that someone was probably being targeted." I hadn't known until now that it was me.

"Why are you so calm about this?" asked Kei.

"Do you know how many people are going to vote against me?" I asked.

"Not sure... But I get the feeling about half the class is on board with the idea. Also, it sounds like they're threatening people that they'll get targeted too if they tell you about what's going on, Kiyotaka," said Kei.

On top of setting someone up to get expelled, they were going around making threats like that, huh? It seemed the majority of the class had fallen in line, then. Even if I got praise votes from the Ayanokouji Group and another from Kei, it'd be just a drop in the bucket.

"Are you okay with telling me this? It sounds like you could get targeted yourself," I told her.

Of course, that would only happen if I went around blabbing that I'd heard about the situation from Kei. I didn't know who was behind this, but they'd handled things well. Although targeting a specific person for expulsion was a simple strategy, actually securing all those votes wasn't easy. Anyone who proclaimed their desire to get a specific person expelled stood the risk of being seen as "evil" by others. If a student with a strong sense of justice, or someone close to the target, heard about it, there was a possibility that the ringleader would actually wind up being the one expelled. People were resistant to the idea of passing judgment on a friend, but not as resistant to the idea of passing judgment on evil.

That was precisely why even relatively sharp-tongued people like Haruka and Akito hadn't taken the initiative to ask us to eliminate someone. At most, people would try to come up with candidates through group discussion, and then everyone in the group would vote in line with each other.

The ringleader targeting me in this case wasn't afraid of the risk of being expelled themselves.

"You've got to do something. I mean, you *can* do something about this, can't you?" asked Kei.

"I'm not sure. If half the class really is against me, then that's a troubling development," I told her.

Even if I did manage to get a total of ten praise votes myself, that didn't necessarily mean I was out of the woods. The people conspiring together in the large group would obviously use their praise votes on their own friends. I was facing a significantly high risk of expulsion.

"Thanks for letting me know about this."

"Yeah, you're welcome, but... Seriously, what are you gonna do?"

"I'll have to think about that," I replied.

"Look, you might seem like you're perfect, but you're lacking in some areas too, y'know. If I wasn't around, you might have gotten expelled without even knowing it was coming," said Kei.

"That's why I have you," I told her. "For times like these."

"I-I see..."

It was precisely because I had talented people on my side—people with access to information I couldn't get myself—that I'd been able to learn about my impending expulsion like this.

"I'll contact you again," I told her.

"Okay, gotcha."

I ended the call. I'd wanted to talk about March 8th coming up next week, but decided to hold off on that for now. First, I needed to find out why I was being targeted.

"All right, then..."

As I clutched my phone, I started slowly thinking the situation through. The question of who I would contact was going to be a big part of how things would move forward. I needed to exclude the ringleader targeting me, and any of their cronies, of course. Still, with that being said, talking to someone completely useless wasn't going to make my situation any better either.

"Okay, in that case..."

I pulled up someone's name in my contact list and called them right away, without notifying them that I was going to call. First, I needed to finish something that needed to be done. A few moments later, the call connected.

"What?" asked Horikita Manabu, his tone of voice the same as ever.

"I need to talk to you about the supplementary special exam. It's pretty serious."

"Wait just a moment."

I waited for about ten seconds. I could hear the sound of running water on the other end of the line.

"I was just washing the dishes. I didn't think that was something you wanted to talk about over speakerphone."

"Sorry for the bother."

"From the sounds of it, something happened. Something not good."

We'd just met up this afternoon. He was probably guessing something had happened because I hadn't mention it when we spoke earlier.

"There's been some activity in my class. A large group was formed, and they've picked a specific person they're going to get expelled," I explained.

"Considering the nature exam, the formation of a large group was inevitable. Who is being targeted?" he asked, likely thinking of his younger sister.

"Me."

"That's not a very funny joke."

"It's not a joke. Right now, about half the class has agreed to use their criticism votes on me."

"Really?"

"I'm in a really tight spot right now. That's why I thought I'd talk to you about it."

"Are you saying that even you can't do anything about this test?"

"To put it plainly, yeah. That's exactly it." Though, to be precise, I was talking to him right now *because* I was trying to do something.

"What do you want from me? I don't think I can really do anything to help you with this exam," said Horikita.

"There's just one thing I want you to do," I replied.

I made Horikita Manabu a proposal. Whether he accepted or rejected my offer would affect how I dealt with this problem going forward.

"...I see. So that's what this is."

"This shouldn't be a bad thing for you, either. You can use this case as a reason," I told him.

"That's certainly true. I wouldn't have talked to you if that weren't the case."

"You don't need to demonstrate your authority as the former student council president. And you don't need to help me directly, either."

Surely a student like Horikita Manabu would be able to understand what I was getting at without me explicitly stating anything.

"You were probably planning to use this strategy regardless of whether you were targeted by your class or not," said Horikita.

"Yeah. I was planning on contacting you anyway. I would've happily told you about this earlier today, but..."

"But Tachibana was there, right?"

Of course, I knew she wasn't the kind of person who'd go around spilling the beans. Still, I'd held back just in case.

"Okay, so what kind of tight spot are you talking about? You've never been in a tight spot to begin with."

"That all depends on tomorrow. Without your help, I'd have to make some pretty heavy-handed moves. And you know as well as I do that it's not a great idea for me to take center stage, right?" I replied.

"...All right. We'll make a move tomorrow."

"Thanks. I'll contact you when I identify who the mastermind is."

I ended my call with Horikita's brother and plugged my phone in to charge.

"First things first."

I'd originally intended to implement a certain strategy for this exam. A necessary action, to remove an unnecessary student. If I was being targeted myself, however, that meant I needed to improve this strategy's accuracy.

The next person I called was Kushida.

"Good evening, Ayanokouji-kun. I was wondering if you might call me today," said Kushida.

"I assume you already have a grasp of the situation, then?"

"Yes. Seems like you're in quite a pickle right now."

So, the news that I was a candidate for expulsion had already reached Kushida's ears, huh?

"You're not going to say you wanted me to tell you about this because we're cooperating with one another, are you? If I'd had leaked any information about this, I might have become the next target... You understand, right?" said Kushida.

Of course, that probably wasn't the real reason she didn't tell me.

"So, who did you hear about it from? That you're being targeted?" asked Kushida. She was clearly interested in finding out who'd told me about my planned expulsion.

"They were anonymous."

"Hmm. Well then, tell me one thing. What did this anonymous person tell you?"

What did they tell me, huh? I remained silent, not giving her an answer.

"You're quite clever, aren't you, Ayanokouji-kun? You're probably thinking that you can't be careless with what you say."

"Sorry, but I'm completely failing to see what you're getting at. What do you want to know?" I asked her.

"For instance, did this person tell you who the mastermind is? Or how many votes they've gotten?" asked Kushida.

So that was what she wanted to know, hm? If, for instance, she'd told Kei that half of the students would be voting for me, but had told other students that one-third would be voting for me...that would be enough information for her to narrow things down and determine Kei was the one who tipped me off.

"It seems like we're both trying to get a read on each other's intentions, doesn't it?" said Kushida.

"Don't tell me that you're the mastermind, Kushida. Are you?"

"Oh no, I couldn't possibly be the one. I hold a completely neutral position in the class. I'm the epitome of peace. Don't you agree?"

But even if she wasn't the mastermind, it seemed she was close to whoever it was. I moved onto something else.

"I suppose so. If you were the mastermind, I'd expect you to make Horikita your target," I told her.

"Ah ha ha, yes, I suppose you're right. Judging from the fact that you went ahead and contacted me anyway, despite knowing the risk, you must be in quite a bit of trouble... So, what would you like from me?"

"I want to know who the mastermind is."

"Even though there's nothing you can do once you find out?"

Kushida was always analyzing the situations, adapting herself to the needs of the moment. It wouldn't be difficult to bring her over to my side.

"Please tell me," I told her.

"My, you're quite direct, Ayanokouji-kun. But I can't betray my friends, so... Well, you know," replied Kushida, adding a devilish little chuckle, which I could clearly hear over the phone. "Well, I suppose it would be more accurate to say that... I couldn't tell you even if I wanted to."

"And that means?"

"I'm sorry to be the bearer of bad news, but unfortunately, I'm the only one who knows the mastermind's identity," she replied.

"...So that's it."

"It sounds like you understand, Ayanokouji-kun."

The mastermind, having selected me out of everyone in class to be expelled, chose Kushida to be their confidant right away. From there, they used Kushida to expand their reach by recruiting people who weren't close to me. It would be hard for people to turn down Kushida, who was highly trusted by her classmates.

"Well, this is you we're talking, Ayanokouji-kun. I'm sure you can find out who the mastermind is sooner or later, right? It doesn't really change anything, even if I don't tell you now. Don't you agree?" said Kushida.

"No. If I don't hear it from you, I'm in for a tougher time. I'm sure whoever this is wants to keep their role hidden. That's probably the exact reason why they entrusted everything to you, right?" I replied.

"You certainly are frank."

"Well, this is you we're talking, Kushida. I'm sure you've already guessed what I'm thinking."

My strategy of trying to get Kushida to tell me the mastermind's identity had been a success—and at the same time, also a failure.

"I'm surprised that you're going along with this. Even though it means you're complicit in getting someone expelled," I added.

"I suppose so. It's a difficult situation, even for me.

After all, if I refused them, they'd think I wasn't willing to help them, wouldn't then? It would spell trouble for me if talk got around that I turned down someone who came to me for help," said Kushida.

That was entirely possible.

"So I've had to make a rather difficult decision. I don't want you to get expelled, Ayanokouji-kun, but I also cannot betray the trust of a student who came to me for help. That's the way it is. On top of that, they gave me the impression they understand a little bit about my weakness. And then, word started to spread about how anyone who betrayed them would end up being their target," said Kushida.

Kushida might have been able to remain neutral, even in that position. The fact that she'd deliberately decided to cooperate with them was worrisome. It was probably partly to protect herself. If she'd turned them down, she might have been blocked from joining the mastermind's group, or suffered the blowback of their resentment. Instead, even though there was some risk involved, she became central to the group and took up a position as one of the people controlling it. That story checked out.

Kushida was entirely self-absorbed. Self-importance was her thing. She liked being worshipped and flattered by others, and she liked dominating people in turn. She was the kind of person who took pleasure in dealing with people inferior to her.

"So, you understand the situation I've been put in, right? I can't help you even if I wanted to," repeated Kushida.

If the mastermind's identity became public, it would mean Kushida's failure. They had manipulated her quite cleverly.

"I suppose I can't force anything out of you, then. Sorry for calling you in the middle of the night," I told her.

"Oh? You're giving up so easily?"

"I don't want to cause trouble for you. It doesn't seem like I can count on your help this time."

"Do you think that you can find out who the mastermind is without my help?" she asked.

"Not sure. I'm not feeling too confident about it."

I backed down. By doing so, I was inviting Kushida to take a step forward. If she didn't respond to that invitation, then that would be that. Either way, the mastermind's identity had nothing at all to do with my strategy. Knowing it would just make things a little easier, was all.

"Hm, what should I do?" said Kushida.

She wasn't backing down. It seemed like she was at a standstill. No, wait—she was taking a step forward, all on her own.

"Ayanokouji-kun, we're friends. So, I guess I'll tell you."

So, I stopped backing down myself.

"...Why did you change your mind?" I asked.

"I suppose it's because I want to see how you'll handle this situation, Ayanokouji-kun. That being said, if this ends up hurting me, I won't forgive you. Okay?"

"I know what kind of people I can make enemies of and what kind not to."

"I'm glad to hear that."

I had a feeling she was smiling.

"Yamauchi-kun," said Kushida.

She gave me the name of the possible mastermind. I specifically say *possible,* because I still had no evidence to determine whether or not that was actually true.

"I see. Yamauchi, huh?"

"You don't sound surprised."

"He's a likely candidate for expulsion himself. It's not surprising that he'd take the initiative to make a move himself."

"...Satisfied?" she asked, like she was testing me.

"Now that I've heard who the mastermind is, something doesn't quite add up. There's no way a student like you would be stupid enough to be manipulated by someone like Yamauchi. I'm sure you could have easily taken control of the conversation and turned down his request for help. It has to be pretty risky, going to the trouble of protecting the mastermind while playing ringleader," I told her.

"I wonder why didn't I turn him down, then?" said Kushida.

"Maybe because Yamauchi isn't the real mastermind. Maybe because you realized that it was the student pulling his strings."

Kushida had sounded like she was having fun, so far. But now her tone of voice dropped and grew serious.

"So you know that much."

"Sakayanagi came to visit our class before. Maybe that has something to do with it?"

Before the year-end final written exams, Sakayanagi had visited Class C—to see Yamauchi. It had been something of a hot topic for the class. Leaving aside my direct connection with Sakayanagi, I presented Kushida with some other evidence that she might find convincing.

"It really was quite the surprise when she visited our class, wasn't it? But yes, you're exactly right. It seems Sakayanagi-san from Class A is the one pulling Yamauchi's strings. I really wanted to avoid making her my enemy," said Kushida.

"How did you know Sakayanagi was the one behind this? Did Yamauchi tell you?" I asked.

"No, Yamauchi-kun has been desperately trying to hide it at all costs. But you know the extent of my information network, don't you? I found out from someone in Class A. They told me she was manipulating Yamauchi-kun and trying to do something to Class C," said Kushida.

Everything was proceeding almost too perfectly. Considering what had happened, I was guessing Yamauchi going to Kushida was also something that Sakayanagi had instructed him to do, most likely. Hashimoto from Class A had some doubts about the extent of my relationship with Kei. If he'd wanted a group to be formed without my knowledge, I would have expected him to advise Sakayanagi to make sure that Kei was left out of it.

If that had been the case, they shouldn't have brought Kei into the group until the very end. If they'd done that, it would probably have taken me longer to notice I was being targeted.

"So is it a coincidence that you're being targeted by Sakayanagi-san, Ayanokouji-kun? Or is this intentional?" asked Kushida.

"No clue. I've never really had much contact with her. Maybe I'm just being targeted as a student who doesn't stand out."

"I see. I suppose that makes sense. Other than Horikita-san, Sudou-kun, Satou-san, Yukimura-kun and the other people in that group you hang out with, there's probably no one willing to take the risk of telling you what's going on," said Kushida.

Still, Sakayanagi being the mastermind was rather odd. Why did she deliberately come up to me and ask me to postpone our match until the next exam, then? Was she so eager to destroy me that she was willing to stab me in the back and break her promise? If she was going to make a move against me now, then she'd have to be prepared for the fact that I wasn't going to compete against her in the next special exam.

Having Yamauchi gather criticism votes against me absolutely went against what we had promised. The only way this made sense was if what she'd promised me was a lie. She'd made it seem like she was going to postpone our competition until next time, while actually laying a trap for me. But...

No. That wasn't it. As far as I could tell, Sakayanagi wasn't the type of person who would be satisfied with something like that. But then what should I make of this mess?

"Thanks, Kushida."

"I hope you get through this without getting expelled."

After ending the call, I tossed the phone on my bed.

"Well, no matter what they're scheming, it doesn't change what I'm going to do," I said to myself.

Now that I knew the mastermind's identity, all that remained for me to do was tell Horikita Manabu and have him work it out.

6 GOOD AND EVIL

THE MOMENT I SET FOOT in the classroom the next morning, many pairs of eyes fell on me all at once. But those students quickly looked away from me, in all directions. Then several gazes fell upon me once again, from all over the room. This process began to repeat itself, over and over again.

I was going to be expelled. The reality was that they had already begun taking action to get me expelled. This was precisely what I had sensed just yesterday—the feeling that something was out of place.

Akito, Keisei, and the rest of the Ayanokouji Group seemed no different today, though. The four of them weren't such incredibly gifted actors that I wouldn't be able to notice anything out of place about them. Since they were in the same group as me, I was sure the mastermind had naturally made sure no information was leaked to them. Of course, I didn't intend to make the four of them worry about me. If I carelessly let something slip, then Kei's involvement in my situation could be brought to light. I had no choice but to deal with this myself.

"Good morning, Ayanokouji-kun."

"Oh. Morning."

Horikita, who had just arrived, didn't seem to notice anything either.

"Sup."

Apparently, Sudou must have tagged along with her, since his greeting came at almost the exact same time.

"Just so you are aware, this is a coincidence," said Horikita.

"I didn't ask," I replied.

For some reason, Sudou had his nose in the air, looking proud as he headed toward his seat. He probably had nothing to do with my current situation. Sure, he might want me expelled, but if he did go along with what Yamauchi was planning, then it would greatly impact Horikita's opinion of him. Besides, he wasn't a skilled enough actor to put up a good poker face.

"...By the way," said Horikita in a quiet voice, once it was just the two of us.

"What?"

"What did you do?" she asked.

"Is it just me, or am I missing something? Can you explain whatever it is you're talking about?"

"Regarding me. What did you do?" she asked.

That was a rather abstract question.

"I don't know what you're trying to say, but I'm not doing anything. I don't exactly have enough free time to worry about you."

"You don't have the time to worry about me? What do you mean?" she replied.

"Look, don't worry about it," I told her.

Class was just about to begin. Considering how Horikita was acting, she probably hadn't gotten in touch with her brother yet. It seemed like the action was going to happen this afternoon.

6.1

I T WAS LUNCHTIME on Friday. The test was happening tomorrow. I, Horikita Suzune, thought back on what happened last night.

Just as I'd been thinking it was time to go to bed, I'd received a text message. I remember feeling like my heart was going to jump out of my chest when I saw the sender's name. It was a message from my brother. He had written one single sentence.

"Do you have any regrets?"

He'd sent me just that one question. I read his message over and over, thinking deeply, thrown completely for a loop.

What should I do? This was a once-in-a-lifetime opportunity that had just fallen into my lap. If I let this chance slip away... Then the next time I'd be able to hear my brother's voice would be his graduation ceremony.

After making up my mind, I wrote a message back to him.

"Would you be willing to speak with me?"

Even though all I had to do after typing that message was hit send, my fingers felt heavy. I couldn't press the button.

"Ah..."

I took a deep breath and hit the send button. All that was remained was to wait for my brother's response. Just as I began to be consumed by anxiety, wondering if he'd actually respond, I heard from him. In the form of a phone call.

If anything, I felt relieved. I was glad that he called. It saved me from having to watch my hands shake while I texted back.

"...It's me. Suzune," I said aloud.

"You said you wanted to talk?" he asked.

"Yes..."

"What did you want to talk about?"

"...Um, well, why did you send me a message like that...?" I asked.

"Is that really important right now? Is that what you wanted to talk to me about on the phone?" he asked in return.

"N-No, that's not it." I had a feeling that he was about to end the call, so I frantically denied it, trying to stop him from hanging up. "Actually, if you're okay with it, would you...mind meeting me, in person?"

"In person?"

"Y-Yes."

"When you enrolled in this school and rejected my proposal that you drop out, our relationship was over. You do understand that, don't you?" he asked.

That was the harsh reality of the situation. I couldn't help but think that he had called me like this only on a whim. That was how distant my brother and I were now.

Honestly, I wanted to talk to my brother about lots of things. About everything that had happened. About everything that was going to happen. But...my brother would never ask me about those things.

"There's something I want to ask you in person," I told him.

My brother went silent. I slowly continued speaking.

"This will be the last time... I will not involve myself with you ever again," I told him.

That was the only thing I could offer him.

"I see. Very well."

That was the conversation that I had last night.

I was now on my way to meet with my brother. We had decided to meet in the special building to avoid being seen by anyone else, since no one usually went there.

When I arrived at my destination, I saw he was already there.

6.2

"**S**ORRY TO HAVE kept you waiting..." said Suzune.

Manabu just stood there quietly. From Suzune's point of view, her brother hadn't changed at all. He was still the goal that she'd been chasing all this time.

"I wonder how long it's been since we've talked like this. Just the two of us."

"...If we're not counting that time right after enrollment, then it's been about three years," said Suzune.

"That sounds about right. So, it's been that long, hm?" said Manabu.

He thought back to when Suzune was in her first year of junior high. When Suzune had decided that she would enroll in the Tokyo Metropolitan Advanced Nurturing School, he'd pushed her away. At the time, he'd never thought his little sister would follow the same path as him. But now here she was, standing before him.

"You said you wanted to talk to me. I'm listening."

If she came right out and said she wanted to reconcile with her brother, then the conversation would be over right now. Manabu would walk away without a moment's hesitation. The old Suzune might well have answered that way.

"It's about the supplementary special exam. I'm sure you already know what the first-years are dealing with," said Suzune.

"Yes. Classes are being forced to expel students in this exam."

"That's correct."

"And?" Manabu urged her to keep speaking.

Suzune, who had been speaking relatively eloquently and easily thus far, stammered a bit.

"If you're asking about my personal balance of private points, then I need to tell you that I used nearly all of them during the school camp. If that's what you're after, then you're wasting both our time."

"That's not it. I'm not asking you...for that kind of support," said Suzune.

She steeled herself, as if trying to cut through the hesitation she was feeling.

"Well, what I wanted to talk to you about today is... I... Please, give me courage."

Having managed to get that out, she continued speaking.

"I want to face this exam head-on. Other people are forming groups and trying to control the vote in order to keep themselves from getting expelled. But I'm sure that they'll come to regret that down the road. That's why, I... I want to stand up to them," said Suzune.

Manabu just looked silently back at her, meeting her eyes as she spoke. As he listened, he thought back to what Ayanokouji had said yesterday. What his little sister was trying to do was not the easy path. But she was trying to do something with her own two hands—something that others couldn't do. And so, to bolster her resolve, she'd come to meet with her brother.

"Do you have time now?" he asked.

"I didn't really have any plans after this..."

"I see."

Suzune was a little taken aback by her brother's unexpected question.

"Then, before we get into the specifics of your situation, I'd like to ask you something. How's school been for you?" he asked.

"Huh?"

"Has it been fun?"

"Uh, well... O-Okay," said Suzune, obviously thrown off. She hadn't been expecting to be asked a question like that. "I-I'm sorry, but well, uh..."

Even though she seemed unable to answer the question, Manabu didn't scold her for it.

"Well, if the question is...whether or not I'm having fun, then, I honestly don't know. But it's not boring," said Suzune.

"Is that so?"

Suzune couldn't begin to understand the intent behind of Manabu's question. After all, it had been such a long time since she'd had a normal conversation with her brother.

"It seems as though you've conquered one of your weaknesses," said Manabu.

"One of my...weaknesses?" asked Suzune.

"That's right. You were so focused on yourself that you couldn't see what was going on around you. Now that you've broadened your horizons, you've managed to break free of spending your days in boredom," said Manabu.

"Somehow, you don't...sound like yourself," said Suzune.

The Manabu that Suzune knew was a serious, dedicated person, someone who never let others see him smile. Someone who never stopped trying to improve himself. She'd never thought he might conceive of school as something to be enjoyed.

"You've only ever seen me as a number. You were fixated on getting high scores on tests," said Manabu.

"That's because... Well, that's because to me, you've always been the goal I'm chasing."

Suzune had said that her brother was her goal many, many times now. And every time Manabu heard her say that, he got a stern look on his face.

"Your goal, huh?" said Manabu.

"...I know. It's absolutely impossible for me to catch up to you. But even so, I think that trying my hardest to get as close to you as I possibly can shouldn't be a bad thing," said Suzune.

Even though she was ashamed of her own arrogance, she still wanted her brother to see just how hard she was trying to catch up to him. Manabu didn't respond to her feelings, but instead, quietly closed his eyes.

"What does Ayanokouji look like, in your eyes?"

"...What does he look like to me?" she repeated.

"Just tell me your honest thoughts about him," said Manabu.

"I don't like him. I don't like the fact that he's capable enough to be acknowledged by you, but doesn't even attempt to make use of his abilities. However, I do think of him as someone that I want to catch up to and surpass someday," said Suzune.

"Unfortunately, you are not going to catch up to Ayanokouji," said Manabu.

"Tch..."

"But there's absolutely no need for you to catch up to him. It's fine if you just grow in your own way."

"In my own way..."

Manabu moved a little closer to his little sister. If Suzune closed the distance a little more, then they'd be close enough to touch one another. However, she was unable to take that step.

"Are you scared?"

"...Yes, I am..." replied Suzune.

Ever since she was little, she'd been unable to close that distance. The short distance between them was hopelessly far.

"To close the distance, you need to take that step forward," said Manabu.

"But what can I... How can I close this distance?"

"You're inexperienced. But I'll help you find the answer. So, talk. What are you planning to ask of your class?"

Suzune nodded, and after carefully choosing her words, slowly began to speak.

6.3

I T WAS THE DAY before the vote, and class had ended for the day. Tomorrow, each class would be deciding who would get expelled, and that person's seat would be empty. Even though everyone was anxious, deep down, there was a sense of relief, since they believed that they would be okay.

That was right. Because someone had been chosen to be the sacrifice.

Ayanokouji Kiyotaka was going to be expelled.

Half of the students in class were on board with that plan. Many of my classmates were probably feeling some degree of guilt about it right now, but that guilt was a small price to pay if it meant saving themselves. Those feelings would fade over time. A year from now, they'd only remember that I'd once been a student in their class.

I wasn't going to hold a grudge against them for it, of

course. Everyone was desperately racking their brains to figure out a way to avoid getting expelled. I just happened to be the one who got targeted, is all.

Yamauchi had successfully drawn Kushida into his plan by appealing to her emotions, and talked her into voting for his sake, out of sympathy. Then, Kushida approached others to request they vote as Yamauchi wanted. Since Kushida was trusted by her friends, who'd confided their secrets to her, they couldn't turn her down.

Yamauchi's strategy wasn't a bad one. As the mastermind, he'd taken some risks, and handled things well. It was just a shame that he'd targeted me. If his goal was to avoid getting expelled, then he should have gone after Ike or Sudou, who weren't capable of fighting back. Well, since Sakayanagi was the one pulling his strings from the shadows, I supposed that was impossible.

Regardless, since it seemed I was about to get kicked out, I had no choice but to make sure someone else got kicked out instead. But this time, I wasn't going to be the one to make it happen. I was just a student who didn't stand out. A student who was being targeted by Yamauchi. I wasn't the kind of student who could defuse a situation like this. Someone else was going to be responsible for doing so.

The expression of the girl sitting next to me was much, much different from what I had expected. She had a completely different aura about her. It was almost as if she'd been touched by something magical.

"All right then, homeroom is done for the day. Tomorrow is Saturday, but it's also exam day. Don't oversleep," said Chabashira.

And with that, the school day was at an end. In that moment, everyone started to get ready to head on back to their dorm rooms. A moment of complete silence.

Okay... Make your move, Horikita. As you are now, you should be able to do it.

My neighbor pushed back her chair and stood up.

"Excuse me, could I have a minute of your time?" asked Horikita, raising her voice to call out to every student in the classroom.

Naturally, that got everyone's attention, making them wonder what was going on.

"I'm sorry, everyone. But I'd like to ask that you all wait here for a little while longer," said Horikita.

Even Chabashira stopped in her tracks. Perhaps she was also curious about what Horikita was up to.

"What's up, Horikita-san?" replied Hirata, responding before anyone else. He was, after all, more sensitive than anyone else when it came to changes in our class.

"There's something I need to talk to you all about, regarding tomorrow's special exam."

"Regarding tomorrow's exam?"

"O-Oh hey, uh. I've got plans to go hang out with Kanji after class, so, y'know."

"Th-that's right."

Yamauchi and Ike spoke up, trying to signal that they didn't have the time for this.

"You two seem awfully relaxed. Making plans to go out even though someone might get expelled tomorrow?" replied Horikita. When her gaze fell upon Yamauchi, he averted his eyes in a panic.

"That's... Well, that's 'cause it's like, you know, we can't really do anything about it, so we might as well just prepare ourselves," he said.

"That's right. That's quite an admirable mindset. Unfortunately, not everyone is as admirable as you. What I'm about to say is meaningless unless everyone in class stays. Will you help me out?" asked Horikita.

"What in the heck are you talking about?" asked Yamauchi.

"It's about tomorrow's test. About who will be expelled. I'd like to have a serious discussion about this."

Horikita walked up to the front of the class and stood at the podium, taking up a position where she could scan the room and see everyone's faces.

"About who will be expelled...? Huh? The heck?"

Yamauchi began speaking noticeably faster than usual. It was probably an unconscious expression of his own guilt, as well as a hint that something was off.

"I've been doing a lot of thinking over these past few days. Who should remain? Who should be expelled? How should we arrive at our answer? And today, I was able to come to a clear decision. So please, allow me to go over it with you right here," said Horikita.

"Please wait a minute, Horikita-san." The person who stopped Horikita wasn't Yamauchi, but Hirata. "No one in our class should be expelled."

"Is that true? Isn't it possible that there might be someone who should be expelled?"

"B-But, that..."

"Ever since we've been informed of this test, I've had some significant concerns. Even though we should be evaluating the students in our class and using the results of our discussion to determine who will be getting expelled, the school hasn't even left us time to do so. That means this is just going to turn into a battle where people will form groups to try and control the vote. As a result, there's a danger that excellent students who should remain in our class may be expelled. This can't even be called an 'exam,' really," said Horikita.

The first person to look impressed by what Horikita said was Chabashira. Then, Kouenji spoke up.

"I have no idea what has happened to you, but it's almost as though you're a completely different person. Still, I must say, what you're saying is quite on point," said Kouenji, clapping. "Let's hear it, then. What would you like to do?"

"Well, originally, we should have had a discussion and narrowed down the list of candidates for expulsion. But realistically speaking, I understand that would be quite difficult to do now. So, that's why... I would like to name someone who should be expelled," said Horikita.

"W-Wait just a minute, Horikita-san," stammered Hirata.

"I'm sorry, but I'm speaking right now. I'll provide a proper explanation of the reasoning behind my nomination later." Horikita continued pushing the conversation forward, wasting no time.

"No, this is not okay. I am completely against doing something that would throw everyone into chaos," said Hirata, holding his ground. He had his own way of doing things.

"She's at least got the right to speak, man. Raise your objections after she's done," Sudou interjected, trying to get Hirata to stop interfering.

"Yes, yes, it's just as Red Hair-kun says. This is cutting into my valuable afterschool time, and it will just be a further waste of my time if you continue to be an obstruction," said Kouenji, speaking up in support of Horikita. He was interested in this discussion, too.

"B-But..." stammered Hirata.

Taking advantage of the opportunity to take the floor, Horikita opened her mouth to speak once more.

"For this special exam... I have decided that Yamauchi Haruki-kun ought to be expelled," she said.

With all of her classmates' eyes on her, Horikita clearly uttered the name of the student she was nominating out loud. A number of students had become potential targets for criticism votes through secret conversations, so far. However, Horikita was the first to directly and publicly nominate someone whom we should vote on.

Why had no one else done so, you might ask? The reason was, of course, that whoever did so would naturally earn the resentment of whoever they nominated. Above all else though, if the student failed in their attempt to sway the vote, it was highly likely that they would become a target themselves.

"Wh-Why me, Horikita?!" shouted Yamauchi.

Naturally, the first person to object to this was none

other than Yamauchi, growing frantic. If Horikita's outburst went unchallenged, he'd be a target for criticism.

"There's a very good reason behind it. First of all, your contributions to the class over the past year have been extremely few," said Horikita.

"Th-That's not true though! I've always done better than Ken on tests!" shouted Yamauchi.

"He outscored you this time, though," said Horikita.

"But come on, that's just been this one time!"

"Okay, let's say for the sake of argument that your academic performance is superior to Sudou-kun's. That's fine. Even so, you are far behind him in terms of physical prowess," said Horikita.

"Okay, then shouldn't Kanji be in the running too?! He's at the bottom of the barrel!" shouted Yamauchi.

It was only to be expected that he'd fight back this desperately. Any student would become desperate if they were singled out like this.

"That's true. I'm sure there are a certain number of students who are on a similar level. You are correct on that point," said Horikita.

"S-see? Come on guys, seriously? Nominating me? Give me a break..." huffed Yamauchi.

"But even if we compare you to the rest of them, you're still a half-step behind. If we evaluate everyone's value to the class based on the attitude you've shown in class so far, number of days you've been tardy or absent, as well as strengths and weaknesses, you would be at the bottom of the list. Ike-kun is next in line after you, followed by Sudou-kun," said Horikita.

"I-I'm a candidate for expulsion too?!" said Sudou, panicking.

"You've certainly improved both academically and mentally of late. That much is true. However, that doesn't undo the number of times you've been a burden to the class. Does it?"

"...No. You're right," said Sudou.

Confronted with the truth, he accepted it plainly. Ike also wore a serious look on his face, having accepted it as well.

"Come on, you're just saying whatever the hell you feel like right now! I'm gettin' pissed, dude! Come on, you are too, right? Kanji? Ken?!"

Yamauchi tried to bring the other two students who were nominated as candidates for expulsion to his side, but they just didn't have the wherewithal to argue with Horikita.

"Plus, I mean, come on, I'm kinda cute and all, right? Not like a *certain* problem child, like Kouenji, who cuts class even during special exams!" shouted Yamauchi.

"It is true that Kouenji-kun has some major work to do regarding his behavioral issues. However, he did understand the importance of this discussion. And in terms of skill, the difference between you two is so vast that we can't even begin to compare. At the very least, he is not a student who should be expelled in this exam," said Horikita.

Kouenji crossed his arms, a satisfied, audacious smile on his face.

"Well, I ain't buyin' it! No! I ain't buyin' this at all!"

"Then shall I tell you exactly why you were specifically chosen out of everyone?" said Horikita, calmly zeroing in on him as he continued to throw a tantrum.

"E-exactly why?" stammered Yamauchi.

The strange aura emanating from Horikita made him flinch for a moment.

"There's definitely something you feel guilty about. Something you haven't told anyone about, where this exam is concerned. Am I wrong?" asked Horikita.

Yamauchi was overpowered by Horikita's confident words.

"I don't got anything to feel guilty about..." he muttered.

"If you don't feel like saying it yourself, I'll go ahead and say it for you. You were using Kushida-san as a mediator to bring several students over to your cause, all for the sake of getting Ayanokouji-kun expelled. Weren't you?"

"Huh?!"

The classroom exploded into noise. Even though half of the students in class knew the vote was being manipulated, they wouldn't have known that Yamauchi was the one behind it.

"You were trying to get Ayanokouji-kun expelled...?" said Hirata.

He was the person who looked the most shocked, apart from the Ayanokouji Group. There was no way that Hirata, who always remained neutral in class and was close to everyone, would have gone along with this.

"Yes. That is the undeniable truth. Isn't that right, everyone?"

Kushida had approached many students at the request of Yamauchi, the mastermind. They didn't make eye contact now, but they were clearly upset if they knew what was going on. This was enough to make Hirata understand that half of the students in class were part of Yamauchi's group.

"Still... everyone seems much calmer than I had imagined..."

"Your plan started with a small group. Then it steadily expanded outward. If you could concentrate the majority of criticism votes on someone, then that person would most definitely get expelled. Isn't that right?" said Horikita.

"I-It wasn't me!" Yamauchi denied it, but didn't go on to explain further.

"Okay, who was behind it, then?" asked Horikita.

"I-I dunno, man! It's just, well... I was just told to put my criticism vote in for Ayanokouji!" shouted Yamauchi.

Lying out of desperation typically didn't end well.

"If you don't know, then why don't you tell me who told you to cast your criticism vote for Ayanokouji-kun?" asked Horikita.

"That's, uh... well..."

"You heard it from someone else, right? Then you have to know who told you," said Horikita.

Yamauchi raked his eyes around the room, looking as though he was on the verge of a breakdown.

"...Kanji! I heard it from Kanji! Right?!" He threw out the name of his closest friend.

"Huh? Wait, what? I didn't!" Naturally, Ike denied it.

"Is that true, Ike-kun?" asked Horikita.

"No, no, no, really, I didn't! I..." stammered Ike.

He was at a loss for words. I supposed that was understandable, though. The person who'd approached him was none other than Kushida. There was no way he could just sell her out.

"Judging by the fact that you can't seem to give an answer, I trust that means you are the mastermind, just as Yamauchi-kun says?" asked Horikita.

"No, no, I'm not! It's, uh... Well, it's just, that Kikyou-chan came to me asking for help... She said that there was someone in trouble and to cast my criticism vote for Ayanokouji," said Ike.

Now Ike had passed the buck over to Kushida. Of course, there was no way Kushida was just going to sit there and take this situation lying down. She feared the idea of being targeted for criticism votes more than anyone else here, after all.

"Really? You're the mastermind, Kushida-san? I can't believe it," said Horikita.

Horikita was going to go down the list, one by one, until she arrived at the answer. In a situation like this, where one specific person was being targeted, it didn't even matter if she didn't know who the mastermind was. The truth would eventually come out if she just continued to confront each person one by one.

"I... Well, someone came to me asking for my help... I couldn't just refuse them..." said Kushida.

"And who is this someone?" asked Horikita.

Even though Yamauchi had gone so far as to throw someone else under the bus to save his own skin, it came back around to bite him. Still panicking, he tried frantically to pass the blame once more.

"Y-Yeah! I got asked by Kikyou-chan! She asked me to help get Ayanokouji expelled!" shouted Yamauchi.

There was no telling when this chain reaction, which started with a single lie, was going to end.

"M...Me?!" said Kushida.

"Yeah, I'm sure everyone heard it from Kikyou-chan, right? Right? Right?" said Yamauchi.

It was certainly true that Kushida had been entrusted with the role of mediator and go-between. But there was something that many of our classmates knew for certain, and it was that Kushida Kikyou was a student who did things for the sake of her friends. She wasn't a person who was out to get anyone or put anyone in a tight spot. There was a difference in the amount of trust that Kushida and Yamauchi had earned from those around them.

"I-I can't believe you'd say something so awful, Yamauchi-kun... You came to me asking for help, and even though I really didn't want to abandon Ayanokouji-kun, you... So, I tried my best despite that, and still..." said Kushida in anguish, burying her face in her desk.

That was probably all our classmates could have pictured in the first place—a vision of Yamauchi coming to Kushida, practically begging her for her help.

Yamauchi's situation was rapidly worsening. I was sure he'd felt bad for Kushida, of course, but he had to avoid being the target of criticism votes. The absolute worst-case scenario for him would be getting expelled from school.

"...Kushida-san."

Horikita called out to Kushida, who was still hiding her face. Everyone probably thought that she was going to offer her a few words of comfort.

"You made a big mistake, too," she said, reprimanding Kushida with a firm tone. "You probably have the same level of influence in our class as Hirata-kun and Karuizawa-san, and—no, actually, you probably have even more influence than they do. If you call for students to use their criticism votes on someone, many people will follow you."

"B-But, I would never... I just wanted to help Yamauchi-kun..." stammered Kushida.

"Enough with the sophistry. You're not that stupid. You should have been able to see from the very beginning what would happen if you helped Yamauchi."

As Horikita continued to criticize her, Kushida stood up, crying.

"I hadn't thought that far ahead! It's just, well, I couldn't just leave Yamauchi-kun while he was in trouble... while he was suffering... I just wanted to do *something*...!"

"No, you did see that far ahead. You knew what was going to happen and you just ignored the problem," said Horikita.

"I..."

Horikita was grilling Kushida almost too harshly, causing her to recoil. Even if Kushida wanted to snap back at her, she couldn't. It was simply impossible for her to remove her angelic mask right here and right now, and Horikita had to know that.

"You made an error in judgment in this instance. You should have done something at an earlier stage," said Horikita.

"But I... What am I supposed to do...?"

"Use this as an opportunity to reflect, and try to take actions that will benefit the class in the future," concluded Horikita, disinterested in listening to Kushida's excuses. "That being said, the undeniable truth of the matter is that Yamauchi-kun is the main offender."

She turned her attention away from Kushida, whom she'd temporarily excoriated, and locked on to Yamauchi once again.

"W-Wait a second, Horikita. I already told you, it wasn't me..." said Yamauchi.

"My, my, this is *quite* an interesting discussion, I must say. Though I suppose the act of trying to get someone else expelled isn't all that odd. This exam, all attempts at niceties aside, is really just a battle for survival for those at the bottom of the barrel, after all. Or is there a particular reason why he's the one being condemned with such fervor?" announced Kouenji.

Apparently, he intended to remain perfectly neutral to the very end. However, everything he'd just said lead right into Horikita's next pronouncement.

"You're right. The act of forming a group and trying to force someone out, while certainly not the most admirable, can be thought as necessary for survival—if that were all there was to it, that is."

"Oh?" replied Kouenji.

"Yamauchi-kun. You haven't been trying to get Ayanokouji-kun expelled just for the sake of protecting yourself," said Horikita.

"W-Wait! Look, I'm telling you, I'm not the guy!"

"How unsightly. Everyone in this classroom already believes this is your handiwork," said Kouenji, before turning to Horikita. "So then, let's hear it. Why did he target Ayanokouji Boy?"

Horikita nodded her head in response.

"He—that is, Yamauchi-kun—was working with Sakayanagi-san behind the scenes. He's been acting on her orders," she said.

The truth of what Yamauchi did was exposed for all to hear.

"My, now that is *quite* curious. One of our own with connections to Class A? How unsettling," said Kouenji.

There was probably a reason why Kouenji was really sinking his teeth into Yamauchi like this. Being a target for expulsion himself, he was probably trying to piggyback on what Horikita was doing for safety's sake. And what she was doing was trying to bring the unnecessary student out into the open and put them on trial before the whole class. Even if Yamauchi hadn't been working with Sakayanagi and hadn't targeted anyone in particular in this exam, there was still no changing the fact that he was the most unnecessary student in our class.

Things would probably have turned out like this in the end, regardless. However, it was safe to say that it was thanks to Sakayanagi inviting Yamauchi to work with her that we'd been able to skip a fair number of steps in the process of capturing him.

"Hey, Haruki, were you really working with Sakayanagi-chan? Like, what the hell, man..."

Not only had Yamauchi been hiding that he was the mastermind behind this, but now his connection with Class A had been brought to light as well. Even Ike couldn't stay calm about this.

"Th-this is total bullshit! Come on, where's your proof?!" shouted Yamauchi.

"In that case, may I see your phone right now? You should have Sakayanagi-san registered in your Contacts," said Horikita.

"But that's... that's because we're friends! That's nothing weird about that!" Yamauchi protested.

It wouldn't be strange for them to really be friends. However, Ike and the others now remembered that Sakayanagi had blatantly made contact with Yamauchi out in the open. Horikita had probably asked to see Yamauchi's phone precisely because it would remind everyone of that.

"Dude, are you seriously working with Sakayanagi-chan?" said Ike. Yamauchi's best friend's words were filled with scorn.

"L-Look, come on, I already said... I mean, like hell I'd join up with Class A! I'd never betray my friends! I have *no* clue what you're talkin' about! Cut me a break already, jeez...!" shouted Yamauchi, at his wits' end, pretending to be the victim.

"No. You must have been instructed by her to rally the students in our class and get them to target Ayanokouji-kun. She is significantly cleverer than you are. She gave you precise instructions on how to get Ayanokouji-kun expelled."

"N-No! No, NO!"

"I'm sure there was something else she mentioned that made Yamauchi-kun more than willing to cooperate. For example, perhaps she said something about a relationship?" said Horikita.

"Ugh!"

Bullseye.

Yamauchi reached a new level of agitation after Horikita pointed out the truth that he'd wanted to keep hidden, Horikita had probably figured that last part out through complete guesswork. But given Yamauchi's reaction, it seemed her guess was right on the money.

"We couldn't possibly expel a student far superior to you for such a stupid reason. This is precisely why I am nominating you for expulsion," said Horikita.

Horikita wasn't just directing her comment at Yamauchi, but making sure the rest of the class heard, too.

"No one wants to kick one of their own friends out of class. But they hate the idea of betraying your own classmates and colluding with the enemy even more. And you tried to target one of your friends... It's precisely for that reason that *you* are someone we don't need in this class," said Horikita.

"B-But, I..." Yamauchi was frantically trying to come up with something, anything, to turn his situation

around. "Even if... Even if what you're saying right now is true... Why am I the only one getting blamed for it?! I mean, even if I'm working with another class, trying to defend yourself is just legitimate self-defense, right?! I don't wanna get expelled!"

"I see. So, what you're trying to say is, 'What's wrong with protecting yourself?', right?"

It was a pitiful excuse, but Yamauchi stubbornly refused to admit to anything.

"Protecting yourself is certainly important, yes. However, I cannot see any value in a student who would throw one of his friends to the wolves to protect himself, and, moreover, would sell his soul to the enemy," said Horikita.

No matter how much Yamauchi resisted, Horikita wasn't letting up.

"Y-You're just trying to stick up for Ayanokouji because you two are so close!" said Yamauchi.

"No, you're wrong. This is the result of objective, dispassionate judgment. You and Ayanokouji-kun started from the same place. If we examine how the two of you have progressed since then, the difference in the degree that you've contributed to the class is clear. Furthermore, considering your connection with Class A, there's no longer any room for debate," said Horikita.

"I have no objections. I've concluded that it is preferable that we adopt Horikita Girl's idea. I certainly can't be around a student who might betray the class. I say we support her," said Kouenji, the first to voice support for Horikita's proposal.

"Wait! I haven't betrayed anyone! I swear it on my life!" shouted Yamauchi in a last-ditch effort. It was hard to say what effect it had on the rest of the class. "Besides, why the hell would it be Ayanokouji in the first place, anyway?"

"What do you mean?" asked Horikita.

"If I really were working together with Sakayanagi-chan, wouldn't she have me get rid of someone who spelled more trouble for her? Rather than Ayanokouji?" reasoned Yamauchi.

This was probably something Yamauchi had had his own doubts about, back when Sakayanagi approached him. Why Ayanokouji, and not Hirata or Karuizawa, the people most vital to the class, he'd probably wondered?

"I suspect that the answer is, for better or worse, that he doesn't stand out. Even if she wanted to get one of the superior students expelled, she couldn't do so as easily. That's why, quite appropriately, she chose someone inconspicuous. Perhaps the question of who would get expelled from Class C wasn't even that important to

Sakayanagi-san. Maybe what she really wanted was to have a spy that she could manipulate at will, as her pawn," said Horikita.

There was no way someone like Yamauchi could counter such a cunning verbal strategy.

"I'm sure some of you might not like what I'm saying right now. If so, those of you who wish to vote against me may do so. Or if you wish to vote against Yamauchi-kun, do that. Or against Ayanokouji-kun. or anyone else whom you'd rather use your criticism votes on. I just thought that I should give you all my personal opinion on the matter. Please take what I've said into consideration when you make your own decisions," added Horikita, showing that she was fighting with a readiness to be axed herself.

Her strategy was probably going to work. However, Sudou spoke up.

"Wait a minute, Suzune... I understand what you've been sayin' so far. And yeah, I get that Haruki's done some bad stuff." He had a sad expression on his face. This was a desperate show of resistance from Sudou, who always followed Horikita's orders. "But I'm against having Haruki expelled."

"He *is* your friend, after all. I understand very well how much you care for him," said Horikita.

She'd already figured that Sudou would support Yamauchi. But he wasn't going to back down so easily.

"You gotta speak up for your friends. I mean, that's just obvious, isn't it? I mean, I know all that stuff with him workin' with Class A is really bad, but... but he doesn't have to get expelled for that. Isn't it okay if he just takes a hard look at what he did and works hard to contribute to the class from here?" asked Sudou.

"In that case, then there's no reason for Ayanokouji-kun to be expelled, either. He didn't do anything," said Horikita.

"Y-Yeah, but—"

"You know that's not how this works, Sudou-kun," said Horikita.

Horikita let out a deep breath and dug deep, summoning all the courage that she had been saving up. She steeled herself, prepared to be hated by all of her classmates.

"By protecting one person, you're abandoning someone else. That's why this exam cannot be dealt with by using arguments based in emotion. It's something that requires an analytical approach," said Horikita.

"I..."

Sudou went silent. His desire to help Yamauchi was palpable, but to save him, someone else needed to be expelled. The act of forming a group and controlling the vote was wrong. Up until today, the day before the exam, everyone in class had been acting according to their own desires. Their minds were filled with negative thoughts, like, *They should be expelled* or *Well, it's fine even if that person is expelled.*

That was exactly why Horikita said hit so close to home, and why Sudou understood it. Sudou realized that you couldn't serve the class's best interests if you just wanted to save yourself. If Horikita had made this appeal to the class on the same day the exam was announced, it probably wouldn't have been as effective. More importantly, if Horikita had made her appeal before she was ready to confront this test head-on, then her words wouldn't have resonated with the class at all.

But now, everyone in class should understand. They should understand how difficult and how scary it was to take the initiative to expel a classmate.

"Sorry, Haruki... I can't do anythin' for ya..." said Sudou.

To be completely honest, I was amazed at how much Sudou had matured. He still had a tendency to get easily provoked and lose his temper, but he'd been gradually broadening his horizons. Even when forced to choose between a very close friend, Yamauchi, and Horikita and I, someone he wasn't as close to, he remained calm and rational.

"Seems like it's settled, then," said Kouenji. He and the other spectators were ready to render their judgment.

"Wait! Wait! Wait a second!" shouted Yamauchi, trying to stop them from passing their verdict. "It'd just be stupid to use your criticism votes on me!!"

"I've already made up my mind. There is no one more deserving of criticism votes than you," said Horikita.

"Yeah, but that's just *you*! Everyone else has already promised they were gonna vote for Ayanokouji anyway!" shouted Yamauchi.

"...I take it back..." muttered Kushida quietly, still hanging her head low.

"Huh...?" stammered Yamauchi.

"I made a mistake... I didn't see what was happening because I wanted to help Yamauchi-kun. So I take back asking everyone to help..." said Kushida quietly.

At this point, Kushida had no choice but to take Horikita's side if she wanted to keep her reputation intact.

"Wait. What the *hell*?! You're breaking your promise! How low can you get?!" shouted Yamauchi.

"You should talk, Yamauchi-kun... I mean, really... betraying your own classmates..." said Kushida.

And now, Yamauchi was completely alone. He finally understood what it felt like to have the whole class turn against you.

"You are the least competent person in class. Also, you're a traitor," stated Horikita, calmly and diffidently. "That's all I have to say. That's my opinion on the matter," she added, trying to end the discussion there.

No one seemed able to resist her judgment.

"Finally, I would like to hear the opinions of everyone present. What do you all think?" asked Horikita.

But...

"I would like you to wait just a moment, Horikita-san." A solitary male student raised his hand and stood from his seat.

"...What is it?" asked Horikita.

If there was a single thing that Horikita hadn't factored into her calculations, it was the boy named Hirata Yousuke.

"Although I sat and listened quietly to everything you had to say without interrupting, I must say that I object to inciting everyone to vote this way. Friends taking swipes at each other like this is just wrong," said Hirata.

His statement wasn't sentimental, like Sudou's. But it wasn't based in detached theory like Horikita's, either. This was an expression of Hirata's painful resistance, born of his inability to arrive at an answer.

"There is no other way. There are no loopholes. This is an outrageous exam that requires someone in class to be sacrificed. You still haven't accepted that?" asked Horikita.

"There's no way I can accept that. I... I don't want anyone to lose anyone. If it were an expulsion that someone wanted, that would be one thing. But neither Yamauchi-kun nor Ayanokouji-kun want this."

"An expulsion that someone wanted? No one *wants* to get expelled. Okay, then, allow me to go ahead and ask the class a completely pointless question. Would anyone in class please raise their hand if they are okay with getting expelled? If anyone comes forward, we'll have no reason to bicker. We'll just focus all our criticism votes on that person and that'll be the end of it," snapped Horikita.

No one raised their hand. If there actually was such a person, they would've stepped forward already.

"Do you understand now?" added Horikita.

"Still not good enough. There is no way I could accept something so awful," replied Hirata.

The perfect honors student. Someone accomplished both in academics and in sports. And a truly good person. But Hirata Yousuke's weakness was now plain to see. When placed in a situation where he was forced to make a difficult choice, he became overwhelmed and couldn't do anything.

"Regardless of whatever you may think, I will fight for what I believe in. So let's put it to a vote, right here and now," said Horikita.

"There's no point in asking everyone to do that. Even if there's a show of hands right now, there's no guarantee people will actually vote that way tomorrow," replied Hirata.

"That's not true. It's important in the sense that it would help us confirm the voting trends of our classmates," argued Horikita.

"No. Everyone... Everyone is trying to get someone expelled, and I just...!"

Hirata was probably afraid that what Horikita was doing right now would cause friction and infighting, laying bare things existing enmities in the class.

"All right, everyone, let's take the vote," said Horikita, ignoring him to call for a show of hands. No one could stop her now. It was the moment of truth.

"Horikita-san!"

Thud! The loud sound of something toppling over reverberated through the classroom. No one could have anticipated what had just happened: Hirata had unceremoniously kicked his desk over, sending it tumbling forward.

"Hey, wh—H-Hirata-kun?"

Girls cried out in disbelief. I couldn't believe it, either.

I wanted to think he'd just happened to get carried away in his movements and caught his foot on the desk. Chabashira felt the same way, too. This behavior was both completely unexpected and just impossible to believe, coming from him.

"Would you please *stop*, Horikita-san?" snapped Hirata. He lowered his voice, as if trying to scare Horikita into backing off.

"...What do you want me to stop, exactly?" she replied, brushing her bangs aside to hide how shaken she was.

"I'm telling you to stop the vote."

"You have no right..." replied Horikita, her voice trembling slightly at his intimidating words. That was the kind of intensity he was radiating right now.

"This discussion is wrong," said Hirata.

"If it's wrong, then what in the world is the *right* thing for us to do? You don't know that, either. You've been going about your life like normal, doing nothing about this test until today, haven't you?"

"...So what?"

"...So I'm telling you, that's a problem. You're not making a fair assessment."

"Be quiet..." said Hirata.

"No, I will not be quiet. I—" retorted Horikita.

"Horikita... Just shut up for a second," Hirata snapped.

Those were the coldest and most intense words that we had ever heard come out of his mouth. Horikita stopped talking. It was almost like the air itself had frozen, after that.

"Everyone, listen." Hirata changed his tone of voice once again, sounding like an entirely different person as he addressed his classmates. "It doesn't matter whether everything that's been said so far is true or not."

"...It's not true! They're lies, Hirata! I'm the victim here!" shouted Yamauchi, who felt nothing but overbearing pressure in this situation.

"Victim?" Hirata repeated.

"Err..."

Hirata's deep, piercing gaze cut right through Yamauchi. "After everything that's been revealed, there's no way you're blameless."

"But, that's, I mean..."

"The way you think nothing of throwing your friends to the wolves is nauseating." Hirata's anger wasn't just directed at Yamauchi. He was angry at the whole class.

"It's an exam. It's inevitable," argued Horikita.

"Even so, it's wrong to manipulate the vote."

"The exam's tomorrow. If we take this text without a plan in place, that's the same thing as giving our tacit consent to Yamauchi-kun's betrayal."

"And what's wrong with not having a plan for this? We have no right to judge our classmates," said Hirata.

"What are you even saying...? That's what this special exam is asking of us, isn't it? And right now, it's what many students want," said Horikita.

She could see this for herself precisely because she stood up at the podium, under the watchful gaze of the other students in class. But Hirata wasn't going to even try and accept it.

"...Maybe *you're* the one that shouldn't be here anymore?"

His low, intense words carried throughout the classroom. Even now, my brain still refused to register that this cold voice belonged to Hirata.

"It's true that this exam is incredibly cruel and heartless. I'll never be able to accept it. But even if I could somehow come to tolerate it, it would only be in the form of a natural class vote. Not what's happening here, trying to sway others into voting how you want, and dragging each other down," said Hirata.

"That's hopelessly optimistic. Almost everyone in class has already gone behind each other's backs, formed their own groups, and repeatedly discussed who they want to expel and who they want to protect. And Ayanokouji-kun was going to take the brunt of that," said Horikita.

"You're right. That's absolutely awful, too. Still, it's not the same as blatantly calling out everyone in class like this," said Hirata.

"It *is* the same. There's no difference at all. If you're going to be a hypocrite about this, you should have tried to stop them from doing that, too," argued Horikita.

No one could get in the middle of their argument. Hirata was overcome with despair, and Horikita was the only one who could engage with him right now

"Besides, even if we don't take a show of hands right now, I've already shared my thoughts with the class. This 'natural' vote you want is never going to happen. You understand that, right?"

"Yes, you're right... The die has already been cast. You can't take back what's been done."

Hirata took a deep breath and then continued. He'd regained a little bit of his composure, but still seemed as cold as before.

"That's why, I'm going to write your name on the ballot tomorrow, Horikita-san. I will not tolerate you going against the wishes of the class."

He had to be aware of the contradictions inherent in what he was saying. But he was still hurting, because he liked all our classmates and because he valued peace above all else.

"Fine. Do what you will." Horikita didn't seem entirely dissatisfied, as if was saying she'd accept it if people agreed with Hirata. Chabashira, having watched the two of them clash, quietly approached the podium.

"Are you finished, Horikita?" she asked.

"Yes."

Horikita offered the podium to Chabashira, and then returned to her seat. Class had already ended for the day, leaving no role for a teacher to play in this. Even so, she daringly stepped forward to address her students.

"You probably hate the school right now. You probably think this exam is completely outrageous. But when you go out into the world, there will most certainly come a time when you must cut someone loose. And when that time comes, it will be those at the top or in management positions who have to bring down the hammer. You, the students of this school, are being groomed to become meaningful contributors to this country. And you won't grow as long as you see the exams being held here as nothing more than school officials trying to harass you," said Chabashira.

In the real world, people who brought everyone else down would be cut loose to protect the rest of the group. Naturally, this often involved backroom dealings, verbal abuse, and slander of the kind we'd seen here today. It was certainly true that this special exam contained aspects designed to help us mature as people.

But to force students, many of whom were still children in both mind and body, to make that judgment was far from kind. This test might cause lasting emotional damage.

"I have absolutely no intention of taking a side in your discussion today. I believe everyone's comments have been valuable. Moreover, I hope that you think carefully before you cast your votes," she added.

Having listened to our entire discussion and given us those words of advice, Chabashira left the classroom.

So, would it be me? Yamauchi? Horikita? Or Hirata? Or perhaps another student? It wasn't clear at all who'd be voting for whom in tomorrow's poll, which meant people might still change their minds at the very last minute.

You couldn't blame anyone for that, though. That was just the kind of special exam this was.

6.4

HARUKA AND THE REST of the Ayanokouji Group came up to me right away. Horikita and Yamauchi had left the classroom immediately after the discussion.

"Hey, are you free right now?" asked Haruka.

"Hm? Oh, yeah, I am," I replied.

I had actually wanted to talk with Hirata a little bit, but...he'd quietly vacated his seat and left the classroom alone, his face blank. But now that word of what was happening had gotten around, I supposed it wouldn't be a good idea for me to ignore the Ayanokouji Group.

"Let's head over to the café," said Haruka.

Accepting Haruka's invitation, our group exited the classroom, openly clustered together. Even once we were in the hallway, none of us seemed to want to break away and go off on their own.

"Hey, are you okay with this? If you guys aren't careful, you could be targeted by Yamauchi's group," I said aloud.

"Well, if they're comin' after one of us, then I say bring it. I'm *never* going to let someone from our group get expelled." Haruka sounded angry, and she was showing no signs of calming down, unlike usual.

"I agree. There isn't a single reason why Kiyotaka should be expelled," said Keisei, sharing Haruka's thoughts on the matter.

Akito and Airi nodded emphatically to signal their agreement.

"I was just thinking how it was weird we never got any information at all. But I guess it all makes sense now, since it was someone in our group being targeted," said Keisei.

No matter how hard we tried to dig for information, we wouldn't have turned up even a whisper about the target's identity. Now that he'd learned why, Keisei seemed convinced.

Once we arrived at the café and each got our drinks, Haruka spoke up once again.

"I think Yamauchi-kun is a good choice for us to use our criticism votes on. Or rather, I think that's what we should do," she said.

"I have no objections, but what about our other two votes?"

"Can't we just pick the people who're still on Yamauchi-kun's side?"

"But there was a drastic decrease in such people after everyone found out about his connection with Sakayanagi, right? Even Ike and Sudou openly said that they can't support him."

"Yeah, but they're friends. I think they'll still give him a praise vote out of pity," said Haruka.

Her prediction was probably correct. Even though Yamauchi had betrayed everyone, he'd really only acted to save his own skin. To look at the situation from another perspective, you might also say he was just being used by Sakayanagi. There was room for sympathy here.

I suppose it was Horikita who'd incited all of this hate for Yamauchi... Well, no. Actually, it was me. I'd told Horikita's brother the truth about what was going on. That Yamauchi was the one behind it, but Sakayanagi was pulling his strings. And then I'd had him give that information to his sister. In the unlikely event that Horikita did nothing, I would have done the same thing she did myself.

"I wonder how many criticism votes Kiyotaka will actually get, though? I would think that out of the boys in class, there's Yamauchi, of course. Then there's Ike and Sudou. Then there's Hondou, Ijuuin, Miyamoto, and

Sotomura. They're all fairly close to Yamauchi; I think there's a good chance they'll vote in line with him."

That made only seven criticism votes from the guys in class.

"What about the girls?"

"Horikita-san will give Ayanokouji-kun a praise vote, without a doubt, and Yamauchi-kun a criticism vote. But I'm not really sure what the other girls are gonna do... Do you have any ideas, Airi?" asked Haruka.

"...I think Satou-san and Karuizawa-san probably won't give a criticism vote..." said Airi.

"Why do you say that?" asked Akito.

"I dunno, it's just a feeling, I suppose..."

"A woman's intuition," said Haruka.

"We can't rely on that," said Keisei, no doubt thinking these estimates weren't certain.

"No, really, don't be like that. I think she's right on the money. Besides, the fact of the matter is if Airi says it, it's probably true," said Haruka.

"What do you mean, the fact of the matter? Satou aside, what could she know about Karuizawa?" Keisei looked puzzled, his head cocked to one side.

"Come on, just stop questioning it. The point is, I'd say it's safe to rule out those two as people for criticism votes," said Haruka.

"I don't get it..." muttered Keisei.

"But those three aside, we don't really know about the other girls."

"Yeah. But there are a lot of girls who don't really like Yamauchi-kun. Even if they keep their promise to use one vote for Kiyopon, they might still use another criticism vote on Yamauchi-kun."

"Psychologically speaking, that seems likely. The people who want to protect themselves will probably list the students most likely to get expelled and vote for those people, trying to make sure they'll be okay no matter who gets expelled They probably see this as a one-on-one battle between Kiyotaka and Yamauchi. The rest of the votes will probably be scattered," reasoned Keisei, presenting his conclusions.

Kouenji had seemed like the prime target for criticism votes before, but he'd probably gone down a few notches now. To vote against him would be to ignore his abilities. Since there were several other students dragging the class down, Kouenji had probably moved to either the fourth or fifth most likely target.

"I'm sure you'll definitely be okay, Kiyotaka-kun," said Airi.

"Thanks."

I was sure that deep down, Airi was still worried people

might use their remaining criticism votes for her. But she offered me heartfelt words of encouragement all the same, not letting her anxiety show.

"Though I gotta say, you seem like you're the calmest one here, Kiyopon," said Haruka.

"It's just that there's nothing I can really do about this, is all. I'm freaking out on the inside."

"Don't worry. Thanks to Horikita, things don't seem too bad. If anything, it's like she saved you."

If it weren't for what Horikita said, a lot of students would've shown up on the day of the vote oblivious to the true goings-on. And they would've put my name on their ballots without thinking too deeply about it, concerned only with saving themselves. It was pretty easy to imagine such a scenario.

"But... Where did Horikita-san hear about Yamauchi-kun's betrayal, I wonder?" said Airi, the question suddenly spilling from her lips. "We're all close friends with Kiyotaka-kun, so it makes sense that word never reached us, right? I would've thought that Horikita-san would've been in a similar position, but..."

"Yeah, you've got a good point there... Horikita didn't really seem like she tried to form a group herself."

Yamauchi was probably pretty pissed about that right now too, thinking someone in the group he'd worked to put together had betrayed him to Horikita. Not that he had the time or composure to realize that and point it out back then, of course.

"I don't know who, but I'm guessing this means there's someone out there who doesn't want Kiyopon to get expelled, right?" said Haruka.

"Yeah. Can't all be bad apples in our class, then."

They didn't notice that the *someone* they were talking about was, in fact, Kei and me.

6.5

● ●

ON OUR WAY BACK, we saw Hirata sitting on a bench, a totally blank expression on his face. If anyone else saw him looking like this, they'd probably hesitate to approach him—because no one had ever seen him in such a state before.

"He seems so defeated."

"Yeah. He doesn't even look like himself."

Both Haruka and Akito understood the abnormality of the situation immediately.

"I think I'm going to try talking to him a little," I said aloud.

"I'd think twice about that, Kiyotaka. Don't you think it's probably best if we just leave him alone right now?"

"Maybe. But there's something that's been bothering me."

"Something bothering you?"

"Sorry. You guys head on back. I have a feeling he won't be too receptive right now if we try to talk to him as a big group. On the off chance he does get angry, I'd rather it just be at me."

"...All right. But remember, the vote's tomorrow. It's probably a good idea not to get him riled up. To be honest, Hirata's the hardest for me to get a read on right now. I have no clue who he's going to be using his criticism votes on," said Akito.

I nodded in response to Akito's warning and broke away from the group, grateful that everyone in the group understood what I was getting at. They headed on back, but I didn't go over to Hirata right away. Instead, I took a picture of him looking completely depressed and dispirited from a distance, then sent the picture to Kei along with a short text.

"Hirata." Not letting this chance slip by, I called out to Hirata right after.

"...Ayanokouji-kun."

"You got a minute?"

"Yes, I do have time now. Well, um, actually, I wanted to talk to you too anyway."

Hirata might have been waiting for me. If not, there'd be no point in him sitting out in the cold in a place like this. He wasn't sitting in the middle of the bench, but near the edge, which could be taken as a sign that he was leaving a space open for someone.

I sat down in the open space beside him.

"The spring thaw will be here soon," said Hirata.

"Yeah."

"I...was sure we'd all make it to spring together. Well, no. Even now, I still believe that deep in my heart," said Hirata, even though what happened today had nearly brought the whole class down.

Despite exposing the most foolish and unsightly parts of himself in class earlier, he remained unchanged at his core.

"I hate having to lose someone," said Hirata.

"It's a problem we can't solve, though. Whether it's me, Yamauchi, or someone else, a student has to be sacrificed," I told him.

There wasn't any emotion on Hirata's profile.

"Can I leave it to you?" he said.

"Leave what?"

"Class C. I want you to lead the class from here on out instead of me," said Hirata.

"Don't be absurd. I can't do something that big. If you want to protect the people in our class, do it yourself, Hirata."

"It's impossible. I just… It's impossible," he replied.

I was guessing he hated himself for not being able to make a decision. That was almost certainly what was going through his head right now, but it wasn't all there was.

"I made the same mistake again. I was so remorseful, spent so much time reflecting on what happened back then, but still…" said Hirata, his voice trailing off.

I could see his regret in the tears welling up in his eyes. How much was this exam hurting him?

"I feel like I can rest easy and entrust everything to someone as amazing as you," said Hirata.

He let out a sigh, his white breath visible in the cold air. Looking at him now, I saw no trace of the dazzling and enviable leader of our class.

"Hey, for this special exam, it's okay if you use one vote for me, one for Yamauchi, and then one for Horikita," I told him.

"So you're saying to leave the decision to the other students?"

There was no need for Hirata to choose one of the three of us. The other 39 students would do that themselves.

"You really are amazing, Ayanokouji-kun," said Hirata.

"Not really."

"As I was sitting here, I was approached by both Horikita-san and Yamauchi-kun. Horikita-san told me to vote for Yamauchi-kun. Yamauchi-kun told me to vote for you. They each had their own way of arguing their case. But you're the only one not trying to throw someone else to the wolves. That's not something just anyone can do," said Hirata.

That was precisely what my strategy was. I'd simply come to the decision that wasn't a good idea to force Hirata to vote for someone.

"I'm glad we were able to talk. I feel like I might be able to find my answer soon."

"Is that so?"

Hirata stood up. Perhaps he'd found his own way to get through this exam—not that I was going to allow it, though.

"Should we head back?" he suggested.

The two of us headed back to the dormitory, without saying another word.

7 OTHER CLASSES' IDEAS

ON THE SURFACE, Class D had seemed no different than usual all through this exam. That was because about ninety percent of the class had been unified in opinion ever since the supplementary special exam was announced. And that hadn't changed as of Friday, the day before the exam.

Ryuuen Kakeru would be expelled.

A great many of Class D's students had made up their minds about that without even needing to discuss it, or to conspire beforehand. Ryuuen had been a dictator, and no matter how much you tried to sugarcoat it, his leadership hadn't yielded good results. In fact, they'd been demoted from their position as Class C, and were now at the bottom.

More importantly, though, many students had suffered under the violence and intimidation of his rule. He took advantage of the weak-willed, creating a situation where they couldn't talk back to him. He was the root of all evil. If Ryuuen weren't around, then they at least wouldn't have been demoted to Class D, even if they couldn't rise to Class B, either—or so many students thought.

By the time we made it to the third day of the special exam period, many of the students in Class D had already decided to write Ryuuen's name for one of their criticism votes. The remaining two votes should be scattered around so they weren't concentrated on one person. That was the only way to ensure that Ryuuen would get expelled.

Ishizaki didn't really want Ryuuen to be expelled. But matters were complicated by the fact that he was being held up by his peers as a savior—the one who'd supposedly knocked Ryuuen off his pedestal. This left him playing the role of the class's leader, forced to gather criticism votes against Ryuuen.

Ryuuen understood both what Ishizaki was going through and what stance his class was going to take as soon as he heard the rules of the exam. He made the decision not to resist being expelled.

Which was precisely why he intended to enjoy what little time he had left until the supplementary special exam ended. He also needed to think about where he'd go and what he'd do after leaving school. There was no greater waste of his time right now than to just sit around in the classroom, so Ryuuen immediately left when class ended.

Ibuki watched him go, quietly thinking about how to kill time after class. Ryuuen often invited her to join him, but he hadn't been doing so of late.

Then, a figure appeared before Ibuki.

"Well, don't you look sad. What, do you hate the idea of Ryuuen getting expelled that badly?"

"*Sigh*... You again? Do you enjoy messing with me that much?" Ibuki replied.

"Not really. I'm talking to you because I've been worried, is all. Since Ryuuen-kun's been gone, it seems like you've become more and more invisible in class, you know?"

The speaker—the one currently provoking Ibuki—was her classmate: Manabe Shiho. She was the person the rest of the girls in class followed, and she and Ibuki had never gotten along ever since they started school here. They'd clashed more than a few times, but since Ibuki had Ryuuen's support, Manabe couldn't really complain about her out loud.

It had to have made her really upset, deep down. What she was doing now, provoking Ibuki, was her way of finally releasing all the anger she'd been holding onto.

"You're going to use a criticism vote on me, aren't you, Ibuki-san?" asked Manabe.

"Dunno."

"Go ahead. I'm going to vote for you. It'd be mutual."

"...Is that so?"

Ibuki's unenthusiastic reply irritated Manabe. She wanted to see Ibuki angrier and more upset.

"Aren't you just relieved that you're not going to be expelled, Ibuki-san? Even if a few people give Ryuuen praise votes, it still looks like he's going to get thirty or more criticism votes," she said.

Manabe might have been acting tough because Ryuuen wasn't around, but she was far from the only one doing so. The supplementary special exam was tomorrow. Once it started, there was nothing more they could do.

Ishizaki rose from his seat.

"Hey Ibuki, come with me for a sec," he said, approaching the two girls, who were glaring at one another.

"...Sure, whatever."

Though Ibuki looked depressed, she took Ishizaki's suggestion and left the classroom with him. If it meant being able to get away from Manabe, then going with him was a good idea.

"You can go ahead and act all cool and composed, fine. But once Ryuuen-kun is expelled, you're next," Manabe said, a strongly worded parting shot. It was almost as if she was implying Ibuki was another person the class needed to be concerned about.

"Okay, so where are we going?" asked Ibuki, once she and Ishizaki were in the hall and out of Manabe's sight.

"Nowhere, really. I just wanted to chat with you a bit, is all... about the private points Ryuuen-san has. What happened to 'em?" asked Ishizaki.

"What do you mean what happened to them? He's still got them," said Ibuki.

"You still haven't collected them? The exam's tomorrow, remember? If he gets expelled, they're all gone," said Ishizaki.

"Oh, and who was the one who got all worked up and said we weren't going to take those points, earlier?"

"Well, that's... At the time, I wasn't really thinkin' much about private points and all, and..."

"If you want to get those points so badly, why don't you just go beg him for them in person? Collect them yourself?" said Ibuki.

"I can't do that," said Ishizaki.

Ibuki knew that already, which was precisely why she'd said something so cruel.

"Look, as far as the rest of our class is concerned, you're the guy who took Ryuuen down. So if they catch you talking to him, they'll get suspicious. And then they'll wonder if you're going to betray them," she said.

That was exactly what Ishizaki wanted, though, considering his desire to stop Ryuuen's expulsion. But if he did that, he'd risk getting expelled himself next time. More importantly, the truth that Ishizaki was only pretending to be the person who'd brought Ryuuen down would be exposed. There was no way he could go through with it.

He wanted to save Ryuuen, but he also wanted to save himself. He was stuck between those two conflicting desires.

"I... Ugh, damn it! What do I do...?"

"The best thing is for Ryuuen to get expelled. You know that too, don't you?" said Ibuki.

"Is that really what's best? Do you really think we can win at all in the future without Ryuuen-san?"

"He had us put him up on a pedestal, even though he never really produced results. And his behavior was totally incomprehensible. Honestly, the future wasn't looking bright with him around, anyway," said Ibuki.

"It's definitely a gamble, having him around. But without him, Class A might as well be a pipe dream for us," said Ishizaki.

There was Sakayanagi in Class A, who wielded such complete and total power that even Ryuuen was wary of her. Then there was Ichinose in Class B, with superior team unity at her disposal and consistently good grades. And there was Ayanokouji in Class C, who not only had the kind of physical strength capable of overwhelming Ryuuen, but also possessed unfathomable ingenuity.

The difference in power between their class and the others was clear. Ishizaki was solidly convinced that if they intended to compete with such monsters, Class D needed a monster of their own to match them. Ryuuen Kakeru wasn't the student they should be losing right now.

"Well, I do admit that Ryuuen's not exactly normal," replied Ibuki.

She had her own thoughts on the matter. Strangely enough, her opinion of Ryuuen hadn't been affected by his defeat at Ayanokouji's hands. There was something that only Ryuuen possessed, something that Sakayanagi and Ichinose didn't. It might even be something that could reach Ayanokouji. She found herself thinking about that.

"Damn it..." huffed Ishizaki, irritated.

Ibuki gave Ishizaki a sidelong glance, wondering what she could do, herself. Even Ishizaki, a hothead, was trying his hardest to push through this exam. And here Ibuki was, thinking about saving herself by letting Ryuuen fall.

That was right. Ibuki didn't have the kind of leeway Ishizaki did.

She was very aware that she was, without a doubt, someone the rest of her class hated. In fact, if Ryuuen disappeared, Ibuki would be the next target. Manabe's parting words hadn't been mere harassment.

Still, if Ibuki just stayed quiet, she'd survive this time. She might even find a different path in the days ahead. That was the main thing stopping her from doing anything.

Ibuki thought back to what *that* guy had said.

"This exam isn't easy enough that you can save someone just because you want to."

That guy understood what Ibuki was feeling, the way she thought. That was why she hadn't seriously considered doing this.

"Hey, Ishizaki."

"What...?"

"You don't want Ryuuen to get expelled. Is that really how you feel, deep down?"

"...Yeah. I ain't lyin'."

"I see."

There was absolutely no way anyone would get more criticism votes than Ryuuen.

"I don't want to admit it, but I feel the same way. Just remember this, though. When Ryuuen's gone, I'm the next to go," said Ibuki.

Once Ryuuen was out of the picture, she was next. She laid out that truth for Ishizaki to see.

"I'm going to go meet with Ryuuen tonight and recover those private points. I'm probably the only one who can," she added.

That way, they'd keep those points around to be used in Class D's best interests. They would inherit Ryuuen's regrets and use them to sustain the class.

"So there's really no other way, is there...?"

"It's just about all we can do," said Ibuki.

She had come to a decision. She would take all the remaining private points from Ryuuen. If it was for the good of Class D, then they were assets that needed to be seized.

7.1

• •

IBUKI PAID RYUUEN a visit in the middle of the night and without asking him first. The dry sound of her fist knocking lightly against his door resounded through the cold hallway. Moments later, the door opened.

"So, it's you, huh?" Ryuuen answered the door half-naked, wearing only a pair of boxers.

"...What are you doing?" asked Ibuki.

"If it was something indecent, would that scare you off?"

"I'd just kick you square in the balls and head back to my room."

"Heh heh. I just got out of the bath. Come on in," said Ryuuen.

His hair was definitely still wet, so it looked like he was telling the truth about having just finished bathing. Though still wary of Ryuuen's teasing and his word games,

Ibuki entered his room. It was the first time she'd been here this whole year. There were more knick-knacks scattered around the room than she had expected. It felt different from *that* guy's room.

"You're not here because you wanted to spend the night with me before I get expelled, are you?"

Ibuki had no intention of drawing this out by playing games with Ryuuen. She cut straight to the heart of the matter.

"Your private points. Give them to me. All of them," said Ibuki.

"Huh? Didn't you turn me down before? Said you didn't need 'em?"

Drying his hair with a bath towel, Ryuuen took a plastic bottle from the refrigerator. He opened the cap and started pouring the contents of the bottle down his throat without offering any to Ibuki.

"You have no way out of this exam. Which means that money is going to go to waste," said Ibuki.

"Yeah, that's right. If I get booted out while holding onto those points, they'll just vanish into thin air," said Ryuuen. His secret contract with Class A would be null and void, leaving Class D with nothing.

"So I'll take them and put them to good use," said Ibuki.

"That's pretty audacious of you."

"This is what you wanted, isn't it? If you didn't want to hand them over, you might've wound up squandering them all before the end. But there's no sign you did anything of the sort. It's like you've been telling us to come and get them from you," said Ibuki.

Ryuuen had been keeping pretty quiet over the past few days. It was clear he'd only used a few hundred or a few thousand points, at most.

"Heh heh. Well now, *that* is interesting. Okay, fine, take 'em. They're useless to me anyway," said Ryuuen, smiling at Ibuki.

He took out his cell phone and started fiddling with it. A minute later, all of Ryuuen's assets were transferred over to Ibuki.

"Okay, I've got them. That means our business is settled, Ryuuen," said Ibuki.

Just as she moved to put her phone back into her pocket, Ryuuen grabbed her arm. Then, he slammed Ibuki against the wall.

"Hey, what're you doing?!"

Ibuki immediately tried to kick him, but he grabbed her leg with his other arm and stopped her without much effort.

"You know, I never disliked your belligerent personality," said Ryuuen.

"Huh?!"

Ibuki looked back at him with hostility, as if ready to retaliate. But Ryuuen quickly smiled and let go of her. It was his way of giving her a final farewell.

"You're strong. But if you ask me, you leave yourself wide open. You can't win against Suzune," he said.

"That's none of your business," said Ibuki.

"See ya later, Ibuki."

Ryuuen looked away from Ibuki, disinterested. He walked over to the front door, as if he were trying to get her to leave. There was a short silence as Ibuki put on her shoes.

"Did you have fun, being here at this school?" asked Ibuki, with her back still to Ryuuen.

"Huh?"

"Nothing."

If you knew what Ryuuen was normally like, then you knew he couldn't be satisfied by this. He was going to quietly leave the school, still dissatisfied. When Ibuki stood up and opened the door, a cold wind blew in.

"Goodbye," she said, leaving behind those parting words as she closed the door behind her.

Ibuki stood in an empty hallway in the middle of the night. A huge number of private points was reflected in her balance on her phone's screen, but all she felt was empty. She exited the screen.

She immediately placed a call as she began walking down the hallway. The person she was calling might have already been asleep, in which case she planned to leave a voicemail. But the person on the other end picked up just before the second ring.

"It's me. I've collected all of Ryuuen's private points."

Once she'd given her report to the person she was supposed to contact, Ibuki's work was done. Over the phone, *that* guy had said he wanted to meet with her in person.

"Sure. That's fine, I guess..."

She was already out, anyway. Agreeing to his request, Ibuki headed toward his room.

7.2

● ●

IT WAS FRIDAY, the day before the supplementary special exam, and the students of Class B were still hanging around in the classroom after school. Every single student was there. Not a single one was missing. The person standing up at the podium wasn't their homeroom instructor, Hoshinomiya, but rather, Ichinose Honami.

"Hello, everyone. Thank you all for carrying on as usual this week. I'm honestly really grateful to you for indulging my selfish request," said Ichinose.

After the supplementary special exam was announced, Ichinose had said just one thing to her classmates.

"I want you all to continue as normal, and get along, until after class on the day before the exam."

That was all. That was all she'd said—no mention of more detailed strategies. The fact that someone would have to be expelled in this exam was clear, but they would gain nothing from being on edge or getting into heated arguments with each other. You might have expected the students of Class B to be anxious nonetheless, but they had faith in Ichinose, who had proved to them over the past year that whatever she did, she did for the good of their class. They did as she had said.

Their homeroom teacher, Hoshinomiya, felt a hint of uneasiness as she listened to Ichinose speak. As one of the instructors who found this special exam entirely outrageous, she felt incredibly sorry for Class B, who was being forced to suffer through it. The class was strong precisely because they had managed to become a united front, without anyone getting expelled. They were dazzling. And if they were to lose anyone now, it would surely dim their light.

"I know I've worried you all... a lot. But I want you to rest easy. I won't let anyone from our class get expelled," Ichinose asserted forcefully, reassuring them despite the anxiety apparent in their eyes. What she said was good news, but also raised some questions.

"Is that really okay, Ichinose? To say that for sure?" asked Kanzaki.

This was his way of extending her his consideration, suggesting that she needn't lie for the sake of her classmates.

"It's okay, Ichinose. We can prepare ourselves for this," said Shibata, implying that he wouldn't blame Ichinose, even if she didn't come up with a plan.

But Ichinose spoke up once more, still sounding certain.

"Don't worry. Kanzaki-kun, you taught me something. You told me that only a fool holds power but doesn't use it. That's exactly why I've been thinking long and hard on this, until I could come up with a solution myself," said Ichinose.

No one here was going to get expelled. She was sure of it.

"...Okay then, please tell us. How do we stop someone from getting expelled?"

But if she couldn't present her classmates with proof of her plan, it might be nothing more than her fantasy.

"You know there's only one way for everyone to survive this supplementary exam, right?" asked Ichinose.

"Yeah. The only way to do it is to nullify the expulsion by using twenty million points."

"Which is why I want everyone here to entrust me with all of the points you currently have. You won't have any points to use until April, but that way, we can make sure everyone is safe," said Ichinose.

"I thought it still wouldn't add up to twenty million, even if we pool all of our points together?" said Shibata, surveying everyone else in class as he spoke.

They'd already discussed this at length, but it wasn't like you could use what you didn't have. They were still millions of points short, a gap that couldn't be bridged.

"So what? Honami-chan is the one asking. I'll hand mine over," said one of the girls in class.

Some of the girls immediately began to transfer their points over to Ichinose, not asking for any further details. Since the whole class sent her points every month anyway, the process felt familiar.

"Well, yeah, I suppose you're right," replied Shibata, immediately feeling convinced himself.

He took out his phone, too. Ichinose, whom her classmates trusted implicitly, had been given the responsibility of guarding all the private points that they had on hand. The final balance displayed on her phone was just a little shy of 16 million points.

"Okay. We're basically 4 million points short, just as I calculated," said Ichinose.

"How are you going to make up those points? I can't imagine that the other classes in our grade level or the ones above will give us that kind of money," said Kanzaki, prompting Ichinose for more details as he calmly sent over his points.

When Nagumo made the offer to lend private points to Ichinose, she promised not to say anything about it to anyone. But she couldn't keep it from her friends after coming this far. Which was why Ichinose had gotten permission from Nagumo before today to reveal the details of the deal—*except* the part where dating him was one of his conditions.

"Student Council President Nagumo is going to help. I talked to him about our situation, and he said he would help me cover what we're short," said Ichinose.

"The student council president? Can he even give us that many points?"

"Yes. In fact, he even went ahead and showed me how many points he has." She'd gotten proof that what he'd showed here was correct, later. "We'll have to pay him back eventually, of course."

"What is the repayment plan like? And how much interest will President Nagumo be charging us?" asked Kanzaki.

"Would the answer to that question affect what we're going to do?" asked Ichinose.

"No, I suppose not. No matter how high the interest rate, I don't think we can ever replace one of our friends," said Kanzaki, who was of the same mind as Ichinose on that point.

He still considered it important to understand the details of this deal, which was why he was taking the responsibility of asking the questions that other students couldn't. Ichinose was very grateful for that. Kanzaki was a valuable partner, aiding her by speaking for the rest of the class to represent their feelings.

"The repayment period is three months, and there is no interest," said Ichinose.

"Wait, he's okay with us not paying interest, even though we're borrowing that much...?"

Given the complexity of the situation, no one would have been surprised if Nagumo had imposed an interest rate on the loan. The president, who was willing to lend Class B money without interest, seemed like their savior.

"I'm sure this will inconvenience you all for a while, but... Are you okay with this plan?" asked Ichinose.

"Amazi—I knew you could do it, Ichinose! Heck yeah, we're all for it!"

Her classmates were all on board.

This was exactly why Ichinose Honami would never let anyone get expelled. This was the reason for her resolve to protect her friends.

● ●

THAT NIGHT, Ichinose called Nagumo on the phone to finally confirm the arrangements for tomorrow's exam.

"Nagumo-senpai. It's Ichinose."

"Oh, Ichinose? If you're calling me, I'm guessing it must be about our deal, right?"

"Yes. I talked to everyone in Class B today. So, I thought I'd check with you just one more time and confirm everything."

"My conditions haven't changed. Gather as many private points from your classmates as you possibly can. Don't leave even a single point unaccounted for. We can't have you getting off the hook without each member of your class sharing in the pain and suffering, after all," said Nagumo.

"I suppose so. I think so, too."

Nagumo wasn't going to hand over the points necessary for Ichinose to save everyone while the other students in her class still had pocket money left over. That was one of his conditions. He had a massive number of private points saved up—nearly ten million, in fact—but obviously couldn't lend out all of them.

Even if Nagumo hadn't said anything, though, Ichinose would have done all she could to reduce the amount she needed to borrow. Even if it was just by one point.

"How many points are you short?" asked Nagumo.

"Four million, forty-three thousand and nineteen points."

"I see. Welp, I can cover that. That's keeping the strain on my account to a minimum, really. Still, there's no getting around the fact I'll be at a considerable disadvantage in the upcoming exams."

"Yes..."

The burden that Nagumo was taking on was significant. If anyone from his own class were to get expelled in the next exam, he'd have to take action to compensate for that. When that time came, it was possible he might fall short because of the four million points he was lending out now. Ichinose was painfully aware of how fortunate she was to be offered this.

"I'm terribly sorry for making such a selfish request," she said.

"Nah, it's fine. Not leaving anyone behind is definitely a 'you' kind of plan, I gotta say. Oh, just one more thing. You *do* remember the other condition I have for lending you those points, right?" asked Nagumo.

"...Yes. You mean that I, um, that we would start going out, right...?"

"Yep. I'm prepared to transfer you those private points right now, if you agree to those terms," said Nagumo.

"...The deadline to decide is at midnight, right?" asked Ichinose.

"You're still hesitating? Isn't having someone from your class be sacrificed the thing you want to avoid most?"

"Yes, of course I want to avoid that. It's just, well, I'm feeling a little anxious."

"Anxious?"

The words were almost painful to get out. Ichinose swallowed them, but then strained once more to get them out.

"Senpai, do you... Well, um, do you like me?" she asked.

"What?"

"O-oh, nothing. I'm sorry. That was a rude thing to ask... It's just that, well, I thought that was what dating was all about. That it stemmed from those feelings..." said Ichinose.

"If I *dis*liked you, I wouldn't have put that condition on our deal," answered Nagumo without missing a beat.

Ichinose was happy to hear him say that, but still couldn't hide her anxiety.

"If you accept that, then I'll send you the points right now," said Nagumo.

"Please wait. I...want to keep trying my best. Until the last minute."

"Haven't you been doing just that these past few days?"

With every second that passed, Nagumo's deadline was getting closer and closer.

"You couldn't borrow any points from the other second-years, or from the third-years, right? And it's even less likely that you'd be able to get any from other first-years, since they're your enemies," he said.

Nagumo was well aware he was the only person who could afford to lend her over four million points. Still, he didn't press Ichinose too harshly. After all, it was clear it was only a matter of time before she came to him for help.

"Be careful. I'm the kind of guy who is *very* picky about his time."

"I understand. I will most definitely contact you later."

Ichinose ended the call. She leaned up against the wall, letting out a deep sigh.

Protecting her classmates was her first and foremost priority. And if Nagumo could help her do that, then she felt like she should accept his conditions. However, Ichinose had no experience when it came to romance. She couldn't imagine it was normal to start a relationship with someone this way.

More importantly, though...her heart told her this would be a mistake. That there was no point to dating someone unless you both liked each other. If the feelings were one-sided, it was meaningless. And once you *did* start dating, you couldn't break up that easily.

"*Sigh*... I should have already made up my mind about this, but..."

It was a little after nine at night. Ichinose would have to give her answer in less than three hours.

She let out another heavy sigh. If she persevered, she could save her classmates. If that was the best and only option available, then...

But even so, even at the very last possible moment, her heart was telling her to pump the brakes. She had an ominous premonition that she would cease to be herself if she accepted such a condition.

"No. Come on, Ichinose," she said to herself.

Why bother trying to change your mind once again after coming this far? If she didn't reach an agreement with Nagumo right here and now, someone from Class B would get expelled.

"...All right," said Ichinose, lightly smacking both of her cheeks at once to psych herself up. "I'm... going to protect everyone."

Having found her resolve once more, she smiled quietly to herself.

7.4

● ●

LET'S REWIND to a few days before Ichinose came to a decision about accepting Nagumo's conditions. Back to the day the supplementary special exam was announced.

Class A, unlike the other classes, had welcomed this exam with open arms. This was because they'd come to a clear conclusion faster than any other class.

"The rest is for you to discuss among yourselves. Please come to a conclusion on the day of the exam," said their homeroom instructor, Mashima, once he was done explaining the rules.

He gave them the rest of the period to discuss. Sakayanagi began to speak, still seated.

"I think I would like Katsuragi-kun to make his exit in this exam," she said, nominating Katsuragi without hesitation.

Katsuragi, eyes closed and arms crossed, remained completely still.

"Wh-What the heck is that?! That's totally unfair!" Totsuka Yahiko, loyal to Katsuragi, was the only person to show any resistance to Sakayanagi's proposal.

"Stop, Yahiko." However, Katsuragi flatly brushed Yahiko aside, asking him to stand down.

"B-But, Katsuragi-san!"

"I intend to accept whatever happens," said Katsuragi.

"It would appear there are no objections. Or rather, that there's no room for any objections," said Sakayanagi.

The majority of Class A was already part of Sakayanagi's faction. Some students were uncomfortable with the situation, but not enough so to rebel. In the interests of making sure they could graduate safely and securely, they still fell in line with Sakayanagi. The only person who resisted was Totsuka, who had blind faith in Katsuragi. But Katsuragi himself understood better than anyone how pointless resistance was.

"Well then, let's decide via a show of hands. Those of you who don't mind having Katsuragi-kun be the one we sacrifice in this supplementary special exam, kindly raise your hands," said Sakayanagi.

All their classmates raised their hands at once. Excluding Totsuka, Katsuragi, and Sakayanagi, all 37 other students agreed with the motion. Mashima quietly averted his eyes, as if he had expected things were going to turn out this way.

"Well then, it would appear that discussion of this test is at an end," he said.

"Are you really going to take this?!" shouted Yahiko.

"It's fine, Yahiko."

Totsuka resisted until the very end, but Katsuragi didn't even try to argue with Sakayanagi.

"The contract I entered into is still valid, even now. It's because of that contract that Class A has been pointlessly funneling private points to Ryuuen in Class D. I accept full responsibility," said Katsuragi.

"B-But we got Class Points because of it, right?! It's not like we're really losing anything, then! Besides, if anyone's getting expelled from Class D, chances are it'll be Ryuuen! If that happens, the contract will become null and void even without your expulsion, Katsuragi-san!" yelled Totsuka, frantically doing his best to piece together an argument. "Don't think you can do anything you want just because you're the class leader!" he added, snapping at Sakayanagi.

"Enough, Yahiko."

Totsuka was the only one getting heated, so Katsuragi once again reeled him back in. He spoke in a much firmer tone than before.

"Katsuragi-san...!"

Even though this situation had to be hitting Katsuragi harder than anyone else, he worked hard to maintain composure. Totsuka, moved, sat back down in his chair and hung his head low.

"Well, personally speaking, I wouldn't have minded if he kept going. It was a rather interesting speech," said Sakayanagi.

"It's fine. I have no objections to the plan to expel me."

"Is that so? I suppose we should act in accordance with your wishes then, Katsuragi-kun," said Sakayanagi.

With less than five minutes of discussion, Class A had reached a decision about the supplementary exam. The students resumed their normal activities, passing the time as if there had never been a test at all. Katsuragi got up from his seat and walked out into the hallway to be alone. Naturally, Totsuka came running after him.

"Katsuragi-san, do you really not have any objections to being expelled?!"

"...There's nothing that can be done. Students with influence have an overwhelming advantage in this test. No matter how hard I fight back, there is no way I can counter the number of criticism votes Sakayanagi's faction wields," said Katsuragi.

"B-But, I'm sure there are students out there who aren't happy with Sakayanagi. If we get them together, then—"

"You've helped me many, many times before today, and I am grateful for that," said Katsuragi.

"Katsuragi-san..."

"But, after I've been expelled, follow Sakayanagi. If you foolishly oppose her, then you will be her next target, Yahiko."

It was precisely because Katsuragi knew that that he'd wanted to avoid letting Totsuka clash with Sakayanagi earlier.

"Those are my final instructions for you," said Katsuragi.

"...D-damn...!"

His face contorted with frustration, Totsuka could only manage to nod in response.

7.5

"SHALL WE BE GOING, Masumi-san?" said Sakayanagi after class, that same day, calling over to Kamuro as she stood up from her seat.

"...Sure," replied Kamuro.

"I've heard there's a new drink being served at the café in Keyaki Mall. How about we go get one on our way?"

This weekend, one of their classmates would be expelled. A student whom Sakayanagi had nominated herself, no less. And yet, even so, she was acting the same as usual.

"Hey."

"What is it?"

"...Nothing."

Kamuro changed her mind, deciding it would be pointless to even ask. Sakayanagi's cold-blooded decision might seem inhuman, but Kamuro was a similar kind of person, which was precisely why she felt it might be absurd for her to point that out.

A phone call broke the silence between the two of them. Sakayanagi took her phone out of her pocket and answered it with a thin, happy smile on her lips. "Good day to you, Yamauchi-kun. I was hoping that I would get a call from you about now."

"You've sure got strange taste in guys…" muttered Kamuro.

Seeing Sakayanagi talking to Yamauchi wasn't exactly an unusual sight these days. They would call each other on the phone almost daily, chatting away about trivial things.

"Today? Not at all, I don't mind. Let's meet. I'm afraid that I do have a minor prior engagement first, so I'll have to meet you after that," said Sakayanagi.

Based on the content of their conversation, Kamuro immediately understood that this was yet another lovey-dovey phone call from Yamauchi.

"I'm walking right now, though, so I'll have to get back to you later," she added, ending her call just a few seconds later. "Well, then. It's been decided that I'll be meeting with Yamauchi-kun tonight."

"Seems like you've been talking to him a lot lately. What are you planning?" asked Kamuro.

"He's caught my interest," said Sakayanagi.

"Caught your interest? Meaning you like him?"

"Would it be strange if I did?"

Kamuro pictured Yamauchi and just shook her head. "You're joking, right?"

"Yes. I'm joking."

"Jeez..."

"I'm training him. To see if I can use him to spy on Class C," said Sakayanagi.

"Training him...? It can't be that simple, can it?"

"Actually, in his case, it is that simple. Also, since a rather interesting exam has just been announced, I was thinking of using him as a test subject," said Sakayanagi.

Her words were half-true, half-lies. Even though Kamuro was part of her entourage, Sakayanagi didn't trust her completely, so she hid what she needed to when she spoke to her.

"Let's meet with him today. You'll have some idea of what my goals are, after that."

Sakayanagi smiled happily as she imagined what was about to happen.

7.6

THAT NIGHT, Sakayanagi and Kamuro met up with Yamauchi at the Keyaki Mall. They used the karaoke room as their meeting spot, so they wouldn't be seen by anyone else.

"So, uh... I see Kamuro-chan is with you again today," said Yamauchi.

"I'm sorry. I'm still kind of shy about going out on a date with just the two of us..." replied Sakayanagi.

"N-No, it's fine! Totally fine! Seriously, I'm just happy to be able to even go on a date like this!"

Yamauchi, who wanted desperately to be liked, did his best to put on a smile. In truth, if it'd just been the two of them alone tonight, he would've confessed his feelings and asked her out. He wanted to make things official, be her boyfriend for real—but he pushed that down, trying as hard as he could to just grin and bear it.

"Yamauchi-kun. Will you be all right in this special exam?"

"Huh?"

"If you're going to be all right, then it's fine. I was just..." said Sakayanagi, intentionally leaving a pause before speaking again. "If you do get expelled, we won't be able to meet like this anymore, Yamauchi-kun. That's...the last thing I want to happen."

Even though Sakayanagi's cute and innocent act made Kamuro feel sick to her stomach, she didn't let it show on her face. This was, at best, Sakayanagi just toying with him. Besides, Kamuro thought, if she let every single thing Sakayanagi did get to her, she'd have a breakdown before long.

"I-I don't want that, either!" shouted Yamauchi.

"So we both feel the same?" Sakayanagi patted her chest lightly and breathed a sigh of relief. "If there's something troubling you, you can talk to me."

"But—"

"It's true that you and I are technically enemies, Yamauchi-kun. But this test is a different matter. There's no reason to compete with the other classes, is there?" said Sakayanagi.

"Yeah, you've got a point there..."

"It might be possible for us to cooperate, instead."

"Cooperate...?"

That was an idea that had crossed Yamauchi's mind, as well.

"This is just an example, but...I could use my praise vote for you, Yamauchi-kun," said Sakayanagi.

Hearing that, Yamauchi gulped. People wanted as many praise votes as they could get from the other classes. Students at real risk of expulsion needed them so desperately they could practically taste it.

"Y-you're seriously going to help me?" he said.

"If you are in trouble, I will gladly cooperate," said Sakayanagi.

Although Yamauchi looked calm and composed on the outside, internally, he was jumping for joy. Her kind words left him elated. He'd never had such a warm conversation with a girl in his life. It would have been mortifying for him if Sakayanagi found out how inexperienced he was when it came to love.

"I... To tell you the truth, people in my class seem like they're kinda jealous of me. So, uh, well, I'm worried that those people are gonna use their criticism votes on me," said Yamauchi.

"Jealous?"

"Because I'm the only one who can meet with you like this, Sakayanagi-chan."

"I see. I have absolutely no interest in other boys."

He couldn't possibly, under any circumstance, bring himself to say he was a potential candidate for expulsion because his grades were bad. Yamauchi wanted to make himself look good, so that Sakayanagi would like him.

"But I understand. So I'm going to teach you a secret plan to save you, Yamauchi-kun."

"S-Secret plan?"

"Yes. Please find and persuade potential allies to join you. Roughly half of the people in your class. Then, target one specific person and have that person expelled," said Sakayanagi.

"Wait... But, if I do that, then they might come after me...!" said Yamauchi.

"Yes, you're right. Anyone would be afraid of being seen as a ringleader, in this situation. After all, if you end up carelessly hurting the wrong person as a result, you might end up getting criticism votes instead."

Yamauchi nodded.

"Which is why I'll help you."

"H-how?"

"I have about 20 allies in Class A who follow me. I will call on all of them to use their praise votes on you, Yamauchi-kun."

"Huh?!"

"Besides, I'm sure you have more than few class-mates who are going to give you praise votes too, right, Yamauchi-kun? If you include those people, then supposing even if you do get thirty criticism votes or more, we'll be able to offset those votes. It is unlikely that you will be expelled," said Sakayanagi.

"A-Are you being serious?"

"Of course. But, even if you do gather 20 votes, we cannot say for certain that you will be absolutely safe. Which is precisely why I'd like you to take the lead and go after one specific student," said Sakayanagi.

"...Who?"

"Yes, that is a good question... Obviously, we cannot eliminate anyone who would be useful to Class C. Masumi-san, can you think of any suitable candidates?"

"...What about someone like Ayanokouji?"

"Ayanokouji-kun, hm? I've heard that name before, but..."

"Oh, uh, well, he's the kinda guy who just blends into the background. How do I explain it...?" said Yamauchi.

"That's quite all right. No need for details. It sounds as though he might be the perfect candidate. You're not particularly close with him though, are you?"

"Oh no, not at all! We're just classmates!"

"In that case, let's make him the sacrifice," said Sakayanagi.

"But..."

Yamauchi's desire to save himself clashed with his inability to sacrifice one of his classmates. But it went without saying that his desire to protect himself was far, far stronger.

"I think it would be truly painful to cut ties with a classmate, no matter what kind of relationship you have. So let's not dwell on that too much, hm? I think we've chosen an appropriate target. All we need to do is follow through," said Sakayanagi.

Her smile seemed to say that if it wouldn't hurt as much if they did that.

"Next week on Monday, after the exam is over, would you meet with me? Just the two of us? There's something I'd like to tell you then, Yamauchi-kun. Something very important," said Sakayanagi.

"Wha—?!"

Sakayanagi had delivered the final coup de grâce, ensuring that Yamauchi was hooked. His delusional fantasies ran wild, interpreting what she said as a sign of a confession of love. Yamauchi would do whatever he could to prevent his expulsion, no matter the cost, if it could turn those fantasies into reality.

More importantly, if he didn't successfully carry out the strategy Sakayanagi had proposed, it might sour her opinion of him. That thought, too, had occurred to him.

"Then let's begin by identifying the people who seem to be close to Ayanokouji-kun. It would be best if we can get him expelled quietly, without him hearing anything about it."

"G-got it."

"However, before that, a word of warning, Yamauchi-kun."

"Warning..."

"Please do not tell anyone that I and the other students in Class A will be using our praise votes on you. If we carelessly let that slip, then we run the risk of you being resented by your classmates."

"Oh yeah, that's true..." It was clear as day that the other students would grow jealous and hostile if they found out Yamauchi was the only one home safe. "Got it. I promise I won't say anything."

"Thank you."

"But... u-um, well..."

"What is it?"

"Well, it's not like I'm, you know, doubting you at all or anything, but... Are you really going to use your praise votes on me?"

"Are you saying you'd like it in writing, then?"

"It's just that I'm really worried, and..."

Yamauchi's anxiety was to be expected. A verbal promise wasn't iron-clad.

"Do you think I'll betray you, Yamauchi-kun? There'd be no benefit to me, even if I did that. But if you're saying you can't believe me, then...let's just pretend this conversation didn't happen. If you can't trust my word on this, then I suppose I need to reconsider meeting with you next week, too," said Sakayanagi.

"W-wait! I believe you, I do!" As Sakayanagi attempted to pull out, Yamauchi frantically tried to keep things together. "I'm sorry for doubting you..."

"It's all right. I understand you're feeling anxious."

Sakayanagi, smiling gently, gave Yamauchi one final warning.

"And also... Yamauchi-kun, if you ever happen to do something like secretly record our conversations or take pictures on the sly, our relationship will be over that very instant. You and I will become enemies."

"D-don't worry. I'd never do anything like that!"

"Good. Well then, Masumi-san, please perform a body search."

"Wait, me?"

"If you please."

"...Fine."

Despite sounding reluctant, Kamuro proceeded to pat Yamauchi-kun down.

"Things are getting quite interesting," said Sakayanagi.

This was nothing more than a game to her. As far as she was concerned, the outcome had already been decided long ago.

After Yamauchi left, Sakayanagi stayed behind in the karaoke room with Kamuro.

"You're still not headed back?"

It was now a little after eight o'clock. Students could only come in until nine. Stores were going to close soon.

"What do you think of my strategy, Masumi-san?"

"What do I think...?"

"Ayanokouji-kun is no ordinary person. You understand that too, don't you?"

"Well, I know that you're extremely interested in him," said Kamuro.

"But that's not all, right? You've seen him up close before, Masumi-san. I'm sure you sensed it."

Kamuro couldn't put her finger on it, exactly. The impression she had of him was of someone enigmatic, but also unpleasant.

"Don't you think he's strong?" asked Sakayanagi.

"...How strong?" asked Kamuro in return.

"The likes of Katsuragi-kun, Ryuuen-kun, and Ichinose-san are no match for him," said Sakayanagi.

"Huh? Wait, then what about you?"

"Who can say? I have to wonder."

"...You sound like you're serious. I can't believe you're saying this."

Kamuro was shocked. She'd been sure Sakayanagi would immediately say she could beat Ayanokouji.

"I can beat him, of course. But it's also true that I can't see the full extent of his abilities. Well... No, I suppose that's not quite right. Maybe there's a part of me that *wants* Ayanokouji-kun to be an opponent even I can't hope to compete with."

A mysterious feeling, that. One she'd never felt before.

"I hope to see him get serious before he is expelled by my hand," she added.

That was what she wished for, from the bottom of her heart.

• •

SAKAYANAGI AND YAMAUCHI came to their agreement on Tuesday. Starting the next day, Sakayanagi continued to receive reports from Yamauchi. While moving around chess pieces that she had placed on the board before her in her room, she kindly instructed Yamauchi on what to do and how to make it through this exam.

"I see. That many people will be using their criticism votes on Ayanokouji-kun then, hm?" asked Sakayanagi.

Twenty-one people, in total. Yamauchi had gathered more supporters than Sakayanagi had expected. She was impressed. Things probably wouldn't have gone so well if he'd been acting alone, though.

"Yamauchi-kun."

"Wh-What is it?"

"It looks as though asking Kushida-san to act as the

intermediary was the correct decision after all," said Sakayanagi. Kushida was the kind of person who kept her classmates in mind when choosing her next move.

"Well, yeah. It's just like you said, Sakayanagi-chan."

Sakayanagi had determined that if Kushida couldn't easily turn down Yamauchi if he went to help. More importantly, she'd also learned a few interesting tidbits of information regarding Kushida.

"When you asked her to help you, did you cry your eyes out to persuade her?" asked Sakayanagi.

"I-I didn't do anything that uncool!" shouted Yamauchi.

Sakayanagi and Kamuro had a conversation with just their eyes, both of them concluding that yes, Yamauchi had probably begun bawling to convince Kushida to help him.

"It would appear that your negotiation skills are exemplary, then," said Sakayanagi.

"Well, yeah..."

"At any rate, I'll contact you again tomorrow regarding who you should draw in."

"Got it."

Crucially, tomorrow was Thursday. Sakayanagi decided the real question, now, was how Yamauchi could expand his reach to win more of his classmates to his side. When she ended the call, Kamuro spoke up.

"Do you really think Kushida would help get someone kicked out of school?"

"If someone comes crying to her, there's no way she won't try to help them. And you have to be a good talker if you're going to draw in this many students. This student, Kushida-san, appears to have quite the silver tongue."

Sakayanagi, holding her queen, looked at Kamuro.

"What do you think will happen next?" she asked.

"At this rate, Ayanokouji will get enough criticism votes to be expelled... But, if he's as powerful a foe as you say, won't he try and do something about it?"

"Even if he doesn't know that he's being targeted?" asked Sakayanagi.

"He doesn't know the method, though."

"He is always wary. Even if he doesn't know that he's being targeted now, considering the nature of the exam, he won't rule out the possibility of getting some criticism votes. Given that, he'll think of countermeasures ahead of time."

"...What kind of countermeasures?"

"Like proving in front of everyone that there's a student who's holding the class back. It could be for any reason, but the more incompetent the student, the more immediately effective the method would be."

Sakayanagi could imagine a scenario that might play out in Class C a little further into the future.

"Take for example, Yamauchi-kun. He's working with me to eliminate a friend, Ayanokouji-kun. If something like that were to come to light, then he'd be the ideal candidate for such a countermeasure."

"So, you're saying that it doesn't matter to you whether it's Ayanokouji or Yamauchi who gets expelled."

Sakayanagi took the opposing king with her free hand.

"No. You need to save the king for last," she said.

She controlled every single move made in this game.

7.8

IT WAS FRIDAY NIGHT, the day before the exam, and Sakayanagi was in the karaoke room, preparing for tomorrow's test.

"What's the situation?"

There was a total of four people there, including Sakayanagi. The other three were Kamuro, Hashimoto, and Kitou.

"It would appear everything was brought into the open today. Horikita-san got wind of what was going on and revealed that I was working with Yamauchi-kun. I wonder where in the world this leak could have been?" said Sakayanagi, grabbing a single French fry and popping it into her mouth.

One of the students watching spoke up. "Sakayanagi, the leak came from Karuizawa. I said it before, didn't I?

I said that if you really wanted to make sure that Ayanokouji would get kicked outta school, Karuizawa shouldn't be brought into Yamauchi's group."

Hashimoto Masayoshi. He was one of Sakayanagi's close followers, and a student who had developed suspicions about Ayanokouji completely on his own. While in the process of tailing Ayanokouji, he'd seen him meet with Karuizawa in secret. And so, Hashimoto had advised Sakayanagi not to include Karuizawa in Yamauchi's group. At first, Sakayanagi had agreed. But on Thursday, she changed her mind. And now, the truth had gotten out.

"Wouldn't the best strategy be to make sure Ayanokouji didn't know he was being targeted until the exam was over? Didn't I say that?" said Hashimoto.

"Yes. I remember your advice quite well. You said that Ayanokouji-kun and Karuizawa-san might have some kind of unusual relationship. In other words, if she found out, chances were high that word would inevitably reach Ayanokouji-kun."

That was exactly why Sakayanagi had decided to postpone putting Karuizawa in Yamauchi's group. She purposefully waited until Tuesday and Wednesday had passed, and then did so on Thursday. Given what had happened today, she could conclude it was highly likely Karuizawa had leaked information to Ayanokouji.

"You made a bad move, huh, Sakayanagi?" said Kamuro, who had been listening to the conversation so far.

Hashimoto offered his analysis of why Sakayanagi had made such a poor move.

"If we managed to rope in Karuizawa, the leader of the girls in her class, we could have rained down criticism votes on Ayanokouji from all sides. It's possible we could've exceeded our goal of 20 votes and gotten closer to 30. You got a little greedy," he said.

"I knew they were going to have a class trial. It was only a matter of time."

"But if this hadn't come to light, Yamauchi might have had a way out."

Having heard all their theories, Sakayanagi couldn't help but be amused.

"Herbivores will make one final show of resistance when they know they're about to fall prey to a predator. But that's exactly why I find it interesting. Don't you want to see what he'll do with the time he has left? How he'll struggle?"

"Is that why you deliberately gave this information to Karuizawa? Because you wanted to see that?"

"It also let me confirm that your tip was correct."

"But Ayanokouji consulted with Horikita about it, and in the process, she revealed that information to their classmates. Now we don't know what's going on. Even if Yamauchi doesn't get expelled because of the praise votes he'll be getting from us, there's no way that Ayanokouji will be getting expelled, either. I don't even know *who's* going to get expelled anymore," said Hashimoto.

"Also, wasn't it a mistake to limit things to spoken promises, rather than written contracts, when it came to people casting criticism votes for Ayanokouji? I have to wonder how many are going to change their minds after learning what came out today..." said Kamuro.

Criticism votes for Ayanokouji would fall dramatically, while criticism votes for Yamauchi would increase. However, Yamauchi would be getting 20 praise votes from Class A, so he'd make it out of this. Given that, it was hard to tell who'd be getting the most criticism votes in the end.

Hearing Hashimoto and Kamuro's analyses, Sakayanagi smiled. She could already see the outcome, she thought. The outcome that still wasn't visible to Kamuro, Hashimoto, Yamauchi, or the others.

She took out her cell phone, which had been turned off. When she turned it back on, she found innumerable missed calls and messages from Yamauchi. He was wondering where the many praise votes from Class A would be going to. He wondered if they were really going to vote for him.

Well, it was only to be expected that he'd be this anxious.

"Oh, there's something I forgot to tell you, everyone. Something very important regarding Yamauchi-kun," said Sakayanagi, who then proceeded to tell everyone what she had apparently not felt bad about forgetting whatsoever.

8 THE EXPELLED STUDENTS

SATURDAY MORNING had come. Finally, it was the day of the exam.

It seemed nearly every class had come to a consensus. For Class A, it would be Katsuragi. For Class D, it would be Ryuuen Kakeru. And Class B still believed no one would be expelled from their class.

Of course, there was the possibility that none of these students would be expelled. Or that all of them would. No one could know for sure until the results were announced. Even if you tried to eliminate someone, your plans could be foiled by that person getting praise votes from the other classes.

All that mattered was what happened now, from this moment onward. It wasn't like I was 100% in the clear myself, either. There were no absolute guarantees in this exam.

We still gathered in the classroom at the usual time, but the exam didn't start until nine. It was now around eight-thirty. I wondered if the school had scheduled the test slightly later out of consideration—or if it was for a much worse reason. A trick to keep the students mired in doubt, jumping at shadows until the very end.

"So, in the end, you really didn't do anything?" asked Horikita.

"What?"

"I'm asking if you just stayed on the sidelines, even though you're in danger."

"Do I look like I've done anything?"

"...On the surface, no, I can't see that you've done anything."

"Well, there's your answer. I didn't do anything this time. If anything, you're the one who saved me."

"Then it won't be funny if you get expelled after all that."

"I don't think I'd find it funny even if I got expelled despite fighting back, like you did."

This might be the last conversation that we would have, as desk neighbors.

"I suppose," replied Horikita shortly.

I thought we were all just going to quietly start the exam. At least, that was what I thought...but at the very last minute, the situation had changed yet again.

"Everyone, please listen to me."

It was Hirata. He'd had a shouting match with Horikita the other day, but it wasn't like he had actually *done* anything. He'd just said he'd be voting for Horikita. Of course, some of the students who worshipped Hirata might go along with what he did, but that probably wouldn't become a deciding factor. Horikita's standing within Class C was relatively high. Her blunt and unreserved manner might come off as prickly, but at the same time, people felt like they could count on her.

"After listening to what Horikita-san said yesterday, as well as what everyone else had said, I've come to one conclusion. And that's, well...the main focus of this exam is who to use our criticism votes on, right?" said Hirata, calm and collected.

"He still has something to say?" said Horikita.

"Looks like it," I replied. If not, he wouldn't be bringing this up at the last minute like this.

"This is pointless. He doesn't have a plan. All he can do is talk and try and delay the inevitable."

I wasn't not so sure about that. I could see something like a kind of determination in Hirata's eyes.

"First of all, I would like to apologize for yesterday, when I said that I would use my criticism vote on you, Horikita-san."

Just as I thought, Hirata had bowed to Horikita, apologizing to her for his rudeness.

"There's no need to apologize. What in the world are you trying to do here?" said Horikita.

"I've just decided that you are necessary to this class," said Hirata.

"Can I interpret that to mean you've thought of someone who is unnecessary?"

"Yes. I have," replied Hirata definitively, causing Horikita to swallow her words and stumble a bit.

"...Can you tell us who it is you've thought of?" she asked.

"Yes, I'll tell you now."

Hirata slowly rose from his seat and went over to stand behind the podium. Just like how Horikita had done yesterday.

"I love this class. I think all of you are necessary. No matter what anyone says, I won't change my mind on that. However, I know that won't solve the problem here," said Hirata.

After much agonizing, this was the answer Hirata had arrived at. I doubted it had changed from what I heard yesterday.

"I would like you...to use your criticism votes on me."

...or he was going to say what I'd thought he might end up saying.

"Th-there's no way we could do that!" shouted Mii-chan.

Other girls spoke up afterward in quick succession, saying similar things.

"I don't mind if I get expelled. I'm prepared to do at least that much right now. I intend to."

"Think about what you're saying... Have you lost your mind?" snapped Horikita.

It would've been fine if she'd let Hirata say whatever he wanted to. And yet, Horikita unconsciously raised her voice at him.

"You plan on sacrificing yourself because you can't pick someone else to expel?" she demanded.

"You said it yourself, Horikita-san. You said that if a student wanted to get expelled, then discussion would be over," said Hirata.

"But—"

"So, I'm volunteering," said Hirata.

"There isn't a single person in this class who seriously wants you to be expelled. You act as the class mediator, you resolve conflicts. This is absolutely ridiculous."

"Even so, I don't mind."

It was safe to say that Class C had already become a total mess. At this point, anyone might get kicked out without it being total surprise. The issue was no longer one of who would get criticism votes, but of who would get praise votes.

Without Hirata, the hurdles in our path would get significantly higher. Passing the special exams to come would probably be much harder. We risked losing one of the central figures of our class.

"There's no way I'm voting against Hirata-kun! No way!" shouted Shinohara, speaking up for Hirata, along with several other girls.

Each time they spoke up to defend him had to hurt him even more.

"There's nothing to be gained by defending me. I've already come to hate all of you," said Hirata. He had the same tone of voice as usual, but his words were harsh. "So, please, just make this easier on me."

"I... I'll vote for you, Hirata!" shouted Yamauchi. "If Hirata's asking, then I think we should all do like he says!"

"I see. So this is Yamauchi-kun's last stand..." said Horikita.

Yamauchi had probably gone to Hirata sometime yesterday. He must have begged and pleaded for help, telling Hirata that he didn't want to get expelled. That might have be one of the reasons why Hirata had steeled his resolve to accept expulsion himself.

Then, after a long period of silence, Chabashira came into the classroom.

"We will now begin the class poll. Students will head over to the voting room in the order that their names are called."

Apparently, we weren't all going to be voting at the same time in the classroom. I supposed it wasn't necessarily impossible to sneak a peek at people's votes if we did it that way. It sounded like this meant the school was doing what it could to keep the vote anonymous.

Well, I wonder what the results will be...?

8.1

••

EVERYONE IN CLASS A calmly waited for the results to be announced on Saturday. The question of who was going to be expelled had been settled right when the supplementary exam had been announced, with no one raising any objections. When the bell rang, signaling that the poll results were going to be announced, Mashima strode into the classroom.

He was calm and collected, as always. No matter what lay ahead today, it seemed he wasn't thinking too hard about it—or rather, that he was *trying* not to think about it. This was his fourth year teaching at the Advanced Nurturing High School. He had seen many students get expelled.

"I will now announce the results of the supplementary special exam. First, the student with the most praise votes is...Sakayanagi. You've come in first place, with thirty-six votes," said Mashima.

"I never imagined that you would all pick me. Thank you very much," said Sakayanagi diplomatically, paying the class an empty compliment for politeness' sake. She had gotten praise votes from almost every single person in class.

"Next... I'll announce the student who had received the most criticism votes in class. I'm sure that you're already aware of this, but the student whose name is called will be expelled. Afterward, that student will be asked to pack their things and come with me to the faculty lounge."

There was no commotion whatsoever. No one made the slightest sound. The students of Class A just quietly, solemnly waited for the name of the student who would be expelled.

"The student in last place, with the most criticism votes, a total of thirty-six, is..."

There was a brief moment of silence. And then...

"Totsuka Yahiko."

A name was called. The name that Mashima spoke clearly reverberated throughout the dead-silent classroom.

"This is ridiculous! What is the meaning of this?!" shouted Katsuragi immediately, raising his voice and standing up from his seat.

"K-Katsuragi-san... Wh-Why...?"

Totsuka looked at Katsuragi in complete disbelief. The results showed that Totsuka had gotten the over- whelming majority of criticism votes. A total of thirty-six, ensuring his expulsion. Mashima went on to announce how many praise and criticism votes the rest of the stu- dents in class had received. Katsuragi had come in just before Totsuka in terms of number of criticism votes, with a total of thirty.

"What is the meaning of this, sensei? I'm the one who should have been expelled, not—"

"The results are correct," answered Mashima calmly.

One girl opened her mouth to speak, as if she trying to explain how such an incomprehensible situation had come about.

"Katsuragi-kun, it would seem you got some praise votes. I'm so glad."

When Katsuragi heard that, he understood what had happened. This wasn't some kind of slip-up. This was exactly as planned.

"Wait, Sakayanagi! Wasn't *I* the one who was supposed to have been expelled?!" shouted Katsuragi.

"Expelled? You, Katsuragi-kun? You were never the target from the beginning," said Sakayanagi flatly and decisively.

"Enough with the jokes. You definitely said it yourself! You talked about getting rid of me!"

"Come to think of it, yes, I suppose I did, didn't I? Well, what I said about getting rid of you... That was a lie."

There wasn't even the slightest trace of guilt in Sakayanagi's gentle, broad smile.

"Why...? Why?!"

"The answer is quite simple. It's because Totsuka-kun does nothing to benefit Class A. On the other hand, you, Katsuragi-kun, are quick-witted and your athleticism is nothing to scoff at. That, combined with your calm, composed attitude makes you quite useful, in your own way. This exam is meant to dispose of unnecessary people. Only an idiot would eliminate someone of superior stock."

"Grr!"

That wasn't Sakayanagi's only goal, either. Totsuka wasn't the only student who'd been following Katsuragi from the start. His expulsion would probably have a significant impact on Class A in the sense that it would serve as an example, showing traitors would be punished without mercy. It planted the idea in people's minds that if they were to cooperate with Katsuragi, they, too, would be punished straight away.

"Why would you do something like this? In such a roundabout way...?"

"Isn't it only natural to try avoid risk as much as possible? The other classes had quite a few praise votes at their disposal in this exam. If Totsuka-kun had collected praise votes from them on his own, then I can't imagine we would've been able to get him expelled, no matter how hard we tried," said Sakayanagi.

It was impossible to completely rule out the possibility that the other classes wouldn't try to save Totsuka on a whim. Openly naming Katsuragi the target meant no one was going to waste their praise votes on Totsuka.

"Thank you for all of your hard work, Totsuka-kun. Please take care, even after you've left this school."

"U-ugh, da... Damn it! Damn it...!" shouted Totsuka, hunching forward, looking as though he were about to collapse on the spot.

Katsuragi was unable to go over and say anything to him. Normally, Totsuka would have probably been overjoyed to find that Katsuragi wasn't going to be expelled. However, now that he was going to be expelled himself, that no longer mattered anymore. If anything, he felt resentful, wondering why it was him and not Katsuragi.

If Katsuragi had been expelled, Totsuka Yahiko could have remained in Class A. While he wouldn't have liked it, he could have followed Sakayanagi, graduated, and had a successful life. Although he felt bad about it, he had begun to vaguely envision that future for himself. But this unforeseen attack had taken everything from him.

"We probably can't...save him by using twenty million points, right?"

"Yes. Unfortunately, even if you add up all of our points, we can't reach that number."

"Totsuka, there...is no way to overturn this decision," said the homeroom teacher, Mashima, also hiding the pain he felt.

"............"

Totsuka was at a loss for words. All he could do was slowly nod.

"Come with me to the faculty lounge for the time being. We'll collect your things later," said Mashima, urging Totsuka to leave the classroom out of consideration for his feelings. It would only hurt him more to stay in the classroom after his expulsion had been decided.

"By the way, Mashima-sensei... I would like to ask you just one question," asked Sakayanagi, stopping Mashima just as he was about to leave the classroom with Totsuka.

"What is it, Sakayanagi?" replied Mashima, instructing Totsuka to go ahead and wait for him in the hallway.

"While it is sad that Totsuka-kun was sacrificed in this exam... It has already been decided who will be expelled from the other classes, correct?" asked Sakayanagi.

"Tentatively. As soon as the results are confirmed, they will be posted on the bulletin board on the first floor."

"So, isn't it possible that Katsuragi-kun might still be affected, depending on the results?" said Sakayanagi.

"What are you saying, Sakayanagi?" said Katsuragi.

"I'm just trying to confirm something."

For a few moments, both Mashima and Katsuragi didn't seem to understand what Sakayanagi was saying. Mashima hadn't considered the possibility that she might be referencing one particular issue. After seeing the unsettling smile on her face, however, it occurred to him.

"...No matter who gets expelled, there will be no such repercussions, no. The thing you're thinking of isn't going to happen, and even if it did, you probably couldn't get someone expelled quite that easily," said Mashima.

"Yes, I suppose you're absolutely right. Thank you very much."

After Mashima left the classroom, Katsuragi quietly approached Sakayanagi. Hashimoto and Kitou hurriedly stood up and blocked his path to Sakayanagi, probably to keep anything violent from happening in the unlikely chance that things got heated. But before Katsuragi could even say a word, Sakayanagi went first.

"It would be entirely unreasonable for you to hold a grudge against me, Katsuragi-kun. This is an exam where someone had to be expelled. Whether it was you or Totsuka-kun, we must come to grips with the result. The fact is that it was the students of Class A who voted. Not anyone else," said Sakayanagi.

"...I understand."

Katsuragi had never planned to do anything violent in the first place. He was only planning on airing his displeasure, but Sakayanagi had stopped him from even doing that.

"That's good. I would much prefer if you didn't fall into despair and drag Class A down. However, on the off chance that you do anything to harm Class A, then..."

"I already told you that I understand. Don't go after any more students."

"I'm glad we could conclude this conversation so quickly," said Sakayanagi.

If Katsuragi had bared his teeth at Sakayanagi in resentment over Totsuka's expulsion, then she would have someone else from Class A eliminated. That was the threat she was making. Sakayanagi was well aware of the fact that, as long as Katsuragi followed her obediently, he could contribute greatly to Class A. Now, Katsuragi had given up completely. He had no choice but to raise the white flag.

"Now then... I wonder how the other classes are doing right about now?" Sakayanagi mused aloud.

Of course, she didn't care whatsoever about Class B or Class D. She only wanted to hear the results from Class C, the one that Ayanokouji was in. She couldn't help but look forward to it.

● ●

THE SOUND OF YAMAUCHI restlessly fidgeting and rattling was extremely annoying to listen to.

"Hey... Quiet down a little, Haruki," whispered Ike in warning.

"Sh-shut it. I know."

"Heh heh heh. At any rate, it would seem the matter of your defeat has been decided. Am I wrong?" said Kouenji.

"The hell are you on about, Kouenji? I ain't getting expelled," replied Yamauchi, slowly turning and looking back with an unsettling smile on his face.

"I'm sure quite a few students in our class have voted against you," said Kouenji.

Ike and Sudou could do nothing to help Yamauchi as he was being poked and prodded by Kouenji.

"That's not true. I'm the one who will be expelled," said Hirata.

"You're still saying such nonsense? You really don't see what's going on?" replied Kouenji.

"...What do you mean?" asked Hirata.

Kouenji took out his phone, with an audacious grin on his face.

"I received this message from several of the girls in our class. It reads, '*I think Hirata-kun is intending to sacrifice himself tomorrow and will volunteer to be expelled. He might say terrible things or act cruel toward everyone, but those won't be his true feelings. Please have faith in him and only give him praise votes*.' It would seem this message made its way to everyone save for you and Yamauchi-kun, no?"

Hirata approached Kouenji and looked at the message displayed on his phone's screen.

"Most students would feel sympathy for you after seeing a message like this. It's not as though the fact you've worked hard for the class's sake this past year has been a dream, is it? Don't you think it makes more sense for you to get all the more praise votes?" said Kouenji.

"But, I..."

The notion of Hirata getting the most criticism votes went up in smoke. The ones who were upset about this, of course, were the students in danger of being expelled.

"You seem calm. It's almost like you already knew what was going to happen," said Hirata.

"You probably knew, too."

"Even if I did, I still wouldn't just sit back and wait so calmly. As long as there's room for doubt, there's still room to worry."

"*He's* the only one who should be shivering in his boots," said Kouenji.

The eyes of almost every student in class were piercing Yamauchi's back. How would he answer, after hearing all of that? Yamauchi slowly stood up and turned to look at Kouenji. The look on his face seemed to suggest that he was confident he was going to come out of this on top.

"...Heh," he said, letting out a scornful chuckle in response. "Fine, whatever. Go ahead and say what you like... But *I'm* not the one who'll get expelled."

"Oh? Let's hear the reason why," said Kouenji.

"Fine. I'll tell you."

It seemed Yamauchi was done letting Kouenji say whatever he liked.

"How many of you here are going to use a criticism vote on me? Twenty of you? Thirty? I didn't even really betray any of you, but you're all being so horrible to me. Seriously! But it's fine. I'll forgive you," said Yamauchi, smiling thoughtlessly, slapping Ike on the shoulder. "I'm sorry, Kanji. For making you worry so much."

"U-Uh, okay." Ike, not understanding what Yamauchi was trying to say at all, could only nod in response.

"I mean, there are a few people who could possibly get expelled from our class, right? It could be me, or Kanji, or Sudou, or Kouenji, or Ayanokouji. But you know, I'm not so sure how many praise votes you guys are gonna get. I'm just *oh so worried*," said Yamauchi.

"Based on the way you phrased that, it sounds as though you're expecting to get a lot of praise votes yourself," said Kouenji.

"Yeah, that's right. Truth is, I will be getting a lot."

"Even if you get praise votes out of pity from your close friends, that would, at most, be four or five votes. You can hardly say that puts you in the clear, can you?"

"It's okay. Even if that's all I got, that would be plenty. Hah hah hah... Yeah, that's right! Pointless! This is all pointless!" shouted Yamauchi, throwing his arms dramatically in the air in. "Sakayanagi-chan promised that she'd get me twenty praise votes. Which means that even if most of the class used their criticism votes on me, I still won't get expelled!"

Realizing there was no point in hiding it any longer, he revealed his hand.

"That's why it doesn't matter how many of you vote against me... I'm protected by Class A!" he added.

The votes had already been cast. It was probably true that Sakayanagi had made Yamauchi such a promise. If he received five praise votes from Class C and twenty from Class A, then his final tally, even in the worst-case scenario, would still leave him with about nine criticism votes. Which meant he wouldn't be getting expelled.

It would be me or Kouenji. Or possibly Sudou or Ike. The runners-up would be in danger.

"Then why do you seem so anxious? There shouldn't be any need to be, no?" replied Kouenji.

Yamauchi wasn't calm. He was trembling in fear, clearly under a great deal of psychological stress.

"That's..."

"Since you made a deal with the enemy, I assume you procured a proper written contract, yes? That is one of the fundamentals of negotiation, wouldn't you say?"

"N-no, but we..."

"A verbal promise is bound to be broken. That little girl isn't that kind."

"I know already, I know! But it'll be fine!" shouted Yamauchi.

Kouenji's words weren't getting through to him. Yamauchi could no longer do anything *but* believe that he was going to get those praise votes. He had to have checked with Sakayanagi many, many times last night to make sure.

"Well then, I suppose you have nothing to worry about. The criticism vote I cast for you would be meaningless then, hm?" said Kouenji.

"That's right! Meaningless! Totally meaningless!"

"Be quiet, Yamauchi. We can hear your shouting all the way out in the hallway," said Chabashira, who had just come into the classroom. "Sorry to have kept you all waiting. I will now announce the results for Class C. Everyone, please take your seats."

Finally, judgment time had come. Soon, one student would be expelled from our class. It could be Yamauchi, who was trying to tell himself that everything would be fine. Or it could be Sudou or Ike, who'd been told they were next in line as potential candidates. Or it could be Hirata, who was calmly waiting for the results to be announced. Or Kouenji, who was acting the same as he always was. Or Horikita or me, who were quietly observing the situation. Or would it be someone else?

"First, I will announce the names of the three students with the highest number of praise votes. In third place is... Kushida Kikyou," said Chabashira.

Kushida let out a sigh of relief at hearing herself named

as one of the students at the top. Even though Yamauchi had targeted her yesterday, she'd ended up getting praise votes instead as a result, huh? If you considered how she was idolized by her classmates, it made sense.

"Next...in second place..." said Chabashira, reading the results a little slower. Even I couldn't predict what she was going to say. "Hirata Yousuke."

"Wh—!"

The moment that his name was called, Hirata closed his eyes and looked up. His shameful behavior earlier had led to no major negative consequences. It just went to show how much hard work he'd put in over the past year for the class's sake. He'd earned a tremendous degree of trust, especially from the girls. Even if I hadn't moved behind the scenes to have Kei circulate that message, the results probably wouldn't have been much different.

"B-But, if Hirata is in second... then who is in first?"

Everyone had expected Hirata or Kushida to take the top spot all along. While it was still within expectations for them to have placed second and third, that meant that there was one person who had surpassed them.

"In first place is..."

A smile appeared on Chabashira's face before she read the name. I shut my eyes.

"Ayanokouji Kiyotaka."

"So that was the end result after all, huh?"

"H-how?!" shouted Yamauchi, the first to respond to the announcement. We were supposed to have been fighting for the bottom. "Sensei, don't you mean he's first in terms of most criticism votes?!"

"No. He is unquestionably ranked first in terms of praise votes. A truly superb result. Forty-two votes," replied Chabashira.

More praise votes than there were people in our class. Everyone present had to be stunned to hear this.

"What did you do...?" asked my neighbor Horikita, unable to hide her shock.

"I already told you, didn't I? I didn't do anything."

Sakayanagi was the one who did everything.

"And now, for the student with the most criticism votes, with a total of thirty-three. Unfortunately, it's you, Yamauchi Haruki," said Chabashira, her words hitting him like a slap in the face, pushing him over the edge.

Before Yamauchi could even understand what was going on, he'd been told he was going to be expelled.

"Th-thirty-three votes?!" he shouted.

That pretty much proved he'd gotten no praise votes from Class A. Sudou came in second in terms of criticism votes, with twenty-one. Ike was in third, with twenty.

Yamauchi's friends understood that they were by no means in the clear themselves.

"No! Why?! Why do I have to be expelled?!" shouted Yamauchi.

Chabashira approached Yamauchi and stretched out her arm to support him, but he shook her off.

"...Haruki..." she said quietly.

Ike and Sudou, his friends, could only look at the floor. While they'd been hoping to make it through this, they'd also just been waiting for the results to arrive. And now that those results were here, they were become painfully aware of the reality of the situation. If Yamauchi hadn't gotten expelled, who knew what might have happened to them?

"Why?! Why, why?! WHY?! This stupid-ass test! Stupid-ass exam!" shouted Yamauchi.

"You are free to think whatever you wish about it, but this decision can't be reversed, Yamauchi," said Chabashira.

"SHUT UP!!" Yamauchi howled with everything he had, railing at the cruel reality he couldn't bring himself to accept. "That's right. Sakayanagi. Please, just go talk to Sakayanagi! She said they were going to use praise votes on me! She broke her promise! Can she be allowed to just do that?!"

"Do you have anything that clearly shows such a promise was made?" asked Chabashira.

"She promised! At the karaoke place! I *heard* her!" shouted Yamauchi.

"While I would like to believe you, that doesn't prove anything."

"This sucks! This is the worst thing ever...!"

"It's time to go, Yamauchi," said Chabashira.

Despite her telling him it was time to leave, he didn't budge.

"Hurry up and get out of the classroom. You have already been deleted," said Kouenji.

"I don't accept this!" shouted Yamauchi.

"So even at the very end, you're still a miserable, ugly, hopeless waste, hm?"

As a result of Kouenji's persistent, prodding provocation, Yamauchi snapped.

"AAAAAAAAHHH!!" he screamed.

He picked up the chair he'd just been sitting on, charged right at Kouenji, and swung it with both arms, aiming for Kouenji's head. A direct hit would have hurt quite a bit. Of course, Kouenji wasn't soft enough to let himself be hit by such an obvious attack. He casually grabbed the leg of the chair, stopping Yamauchi's swing, and then forcefully pulled the chair from his hands.

"You came at me with murderous intent. Surely, you can't complain if I do something about that, hm?" said Kouenji.

Yamauchi's face stiffened.

"That's enough," said Chabashira, understanding the signs of danger in Kouenji's words and moving to intervene.

In response, Kouenji promptly let go of the chair.

"Yamauchi, for your own sake, don't do anything else," said Chabashira.

Yamauchi's classmates were looking at him, their gazes filled with heartbreak. Filled with pity.

Then, something broke inside of Yamauchi.

"W-waaah!"

He collapsed right then and there, letting out a sound that was like both a loud wail and a scream.

"...Outside," said Chabashira.

Being told it was time to go once more, Yamauchi lost the last ounce of resistance he had.

●●

ONE PERSON WAS MISSING from the classroom. It was the same classroom, but it now it felt completely different. The atmosphere was heavy; the inhabitants were disheartened.

It'd probably have been like this no matter who was expelled. Even so, considering that *someone* had to go, it was only natural that we'd had to consider the pros and cons. Which students were necessary to the class? Which students were unnecessary? That was what we'd had to decide.

One person got up from their seat. Once they did that, everyone else got up and left one by one, too, without saying much of anything. We had one day off. Come Monday, we'd be seeing each other's faces in this classroom again. And when that time came, there would be no Yamauchi.

"He's more seriously messed up than I thought."

The 'he' Horikita was referring to was Hirata, of course, who'd been in a daze since Yamauchi left. He remained sitting at his desk, completely motionless, looking blankly ahead.

"Hirata-kun... um..." said Mii-chan in concern, calling out to him timidly.

But Hirata only shifted his gaze slightly to look at her, saying nothing. What did he think of our class right now? Only he knew the answer to that. But he had no choice but to keep moving forward.

The other students, unable to watch Hirata in such a state, slowly left to return to the dorms. Sudou and Ike quietly left the classroom, too.

"Let's just quietly head back to the dorms by ourselves today."

Everyone else in the Ayanokouji Group agreed with what Haruka posted in the chat.

"Guess I'll head on back, then," I said aloud.

Bag in hand, I went to leave the classroom. Before doing so though, I stopped in front of Kouenji, who was still hanging back.

"What is it, Ayanokouji Boy?" he asked.

"I never thought you'd take action for the class's sake," I told him.

"Of course. Even I would cooperate with Horikita Girl to avoid getting expelled."

"That's not what I mean. You incessantly goaded Yamauchi because you were trying to have the thankless job of being the sole recipient of his hate."

Yamauchi was going to hate his classmates if he got expelled—but Kouenji had made himself Yamauchi's sole focus by continually goading him more than anyone else. When Yamauchi was told he'd been expelled and clearly lost all sense of reason, Kouenji had taken matters into his own hands and personally dealt with him. To the eyes of everyone around him, though, he might have just seemed like a jerk.

"Hm, I have no memory of such a thing. I simply wanted a front row seat to his pathetic disintegration," said Kouenji.

"I see. We'll leave it at that, then."

When I stepped out of the classroom, Horikita immediately ran after me. She grabbed my arm.

"Ayanokouji-kun. You... How much of this did you anticipate ahead of time? And when?"

When Sakayanagi offered a truce for this exam, I was more than ninety percent certain I wouldn't have to worry about getting expelled. It was obvious that she didn't want to beat me via a pointless sneak attack. She wouldn't be satisfied by lying about a truce just to chase me out of school.

On the other hand, she *had* been using Yamauchi to try get me expelled. A clear violation of our truce—or at least, it wouldn't be strange to think of it as such. Which meant there was a contradiction in terms. To eliminate that contradiction, Sakayanagi had to do whatever she could to nullify the criticism votes that I would be getting.

In other words, she was going to use most of Class A's praise votes on me. That way, even if I got twenty or thirty criticism votes from Class C, I'd still be in the clear. My safety was absolutely guaranteed.

Then why did she do this? It was probably to get Yamauchi Haruki expelled. By making him play the part of the villain, she had lowered his standing within Class C.

Of course, I couldn't say I was one-hundred-percent certain about all this. I couldn't completely eliminate the possibility that Sakayanagi *was* trying to get me expelled through underhanded means, which was why I'd lit a fire under Horikita and used her to bury Yamauchi. And, by letting everyone in class know that Yamauchi was trying to get rid of someone harmless like me, I was able to get some votes out of sympathy or because people wanted to protect me. Although ending up with the most praise votes might have been a little much, honestly.

"Didn't I tell you before? I didn't participate in this exam at all, in the clearest sense."

"...But..."

"Well, I'm headed back."

"Ayanokouji-kun!!" shouted Horikita, standing stock still. "It was you, wasn't it...? The one who told my brother about the connection between Yamauchi-kun and Sakayanagi-san."

I descended the stairs without giving her an answer, and took a peek at the bulletin board on the first floor. On it was a notice showing how the other classes had fared in this exam.

In-Class Voting Results

EXPELLED STUDENTS

Class A = Totsuka Yahiko

Class B = N/A

Class C = Yamauchi Haruki

Class D = Manabe Shiho

Only those three students will be expelled. There will be no changes to Class Points because of this test.

"Yahiko, huh... I guess all that talk about getting Katsuragi expelled was just a fake-out after all," I said aloud.

The praise vote totals had been posted in addition to the criticism ones. Sakayanagi had ranked first in Class A, Ichinose ranked first in Class B, and Kaneda ranked in Class D. Of those three, Kaneda had the least number of praise votes while still being number one for his class, with twenty-seven. On the other end, Ichinose got a stunning 98 votes. Considering the fact that most of the students in Class A had given me their praise vote, that just made it clear how many students valued Ichinose.

Other students showed up as well, perhaps wanting to confirm the test results themselves. Katsuragi and Ryuuen showed up at almost the exact same time.

"I see you didn't get expelled either, Katsuragi."

"...You took the words out of my mouth. I thought for sure you would have been the one to disappear," he replied.

"Heh heh. Apparently, I have the Grim Reaper on my side," said Ryuuen.

"Grim Reaper?" asked Katsuragi.

"Don't worry 'bout it. It's not like you'd be able to see him anyway," said Ryuuen, looking at the results with a smile. "Though, I gotta say, looks like that Sakayanagi chick did something pretty interesting. Man, I can't *believe* she deliberately tossed your only ally to the wolves, man."

Though Ryuuen sounded amused, Katsuragi, beside him, had a remorseful expression on his face.

"She completely robbed you of your fighting spirit, huh?" Ryuuen added.

"I have absolutely nothing to gain by acting out any more than I already have," replied Katsuragi.

"So, what, you're just gonna quietly follow Sakayanagi until graduation? That's hilarious."

"........."

There was a brief silence. However, there was something almost dreadful about the look on Katsuragi's face. Yahiko, who had always been devoted to him, was gone. At the same time, what this meant for Katsuragi was nothing more than the absence of anyone he needed to protect.

"What, Katsuragi? I didn't know you could make a face like that." Ryuuen might have gotten the same impression I had. "As you are right now, you look like you could even dupe Sakayanagi."

"...Enough jokes. More importantly, what are *you* planning on doing now? So, your life was spared by the Grim Reaper, hm? Are you going to challenge Sakayanagi, Ichinose, and Horikita again?" asked Katsuragi.

"I ain't interested," spat Ryuuen, almost immediately. "The contract I have with you Class A folks is still valid.

I'll just casually continue to bleed you dry while I hang back and play around for a while. Just thought I'd thank you for that, today."

Apparently, that was why he'd come here. After all, from Ryuuen's perspective, Katsuragi's expulsion would have probably resulted in his contract being annulled.

Katsuragi went ahead and headed back to the dorms ahead of us. Now it was just Ryuuen and me.

"Come over here for a sec," said Ryuuen.

Without refusing, I followed Ryuuen as he led me around to the back of the school building.

"Since when did you turn into such a saint, huh, Ayanokouji?" he asked.

"I had nothing to do with it. Of course, even if I say that, it doesn't seem like you'll believe me." But I knew Ryuuen had to have a clear idea of exactly what I'd done. "It's not like I did this. The people who adore you were the ones who did."

I looked up at the sky as I recalled what had happened over the past few days.

8.4

As THE TEST RESULTS SHOWED, no one had been expelled from Class B, and Ryuuen got to stay. I'd been involved in both these major events behind the scenes, starting with the day I'd met Hiyori in the library and had invited Ichinose to my room.

My doorbell rang at around ten o'clock that night. I only had a few friends who'd come visit me in my room—Horikita, Kushida, or the members of the Ayanokouji Group. But they usually sent me a chat message or a text beforehand, and I hadn't gotten any calls or texts or anything this time. Which meant it wasn't that kind of guest. Who in the world was paying me a visit?

"...Well, this is a first," I said aloud to myself.

On the intercom monitor were two people I hadn't expected to see. They looked chilly, waiting for me to answer the door.

"Well, I guess...that curfew is only for the upper levels," I muttered to myself.

It was forbidden to enter the girls' floors after eight o'clock at night, but even if you did break that rule, it was fine as long as you didn't get caught. And if you *did* get caught, you wouldn't be punished too severely the first couple times. Regardless, it was fine if a girl came to visit *you*, though.

"Yes?" I didn't give them much of a welcome, but decided to at least respond to them in my usual fashion.

"...We want to talk to you," said the boy, speaking up first. He peered into the camera, a close-up of his pupil appearing on the screen. It seemed this wasn't the kind of conversation that could be had over the intercom.

"Wait a second," I replied.

I walked over and unlocked my front door. When I did so, the person on the other side swung it open with great force. Ishizaki, from Class D, entered. He'd pushed the door open so hard that it would have smacked me if I hadn't been careful.

"Sorry for bargin' in. Hey, get in, quick. It's cold out there," said Ishizaki.

"Jeez, why do I even have to be here...?" grumbled the other person as they came into view. It was Ibuki, another Class D student.

"Come on already, just get in," snapped Ishizaki.

"Whatever."

At Ishizaki's urging, Ibuki came into my room. It was true there was a chill blowing in from the hallway, so I quickly closed the door behind them. Thinking there would still be a draft if we hung around by the front door, I ushered everyone into my room.

"So, what business do you have with me this late at night?"

When Ishizaki heard me ask that, he quickly brought his hands together.

"Please, Ayanokouji! Tell us how to stop Ryuuen-san from getting expelled!!" he pleaded.

"...What?" Apparently, these two had come barging into my room in the middle of the night to ask me a completely ridiculous favor. "Did I hear you wrong? Can you repeat that?"

"I asked you to please tell us how to stop Ryuuen-san from getting expelled!" he repeated.

So I hadn't misheard him, after all.

"Just stop, Ishizaki. It's not like Ayanokouji would help us anyway," said Ibuki. From the looks of things, she wasn't here to ask me for anything, unlike Ishizaki.

"Well, yeah, you're probably right, but Ayanokouji's the only one I could think of," said Ishizaki.

"Whatever. I don't care. I only came here because Ishizaki dragged me along with him. And he called me like a million times..." said Ibuki, letting out an exasperated sigh as she showed me her phone's screen. Her call history had at least fifty incoming calls from Ishizaki.

"It wasn't like I could just ask him by myself! He's our enemy, man!"

"And he's still our enemy, even if I'm here with you. You really are a moron," said Ibuki.

"Ugh, just shut up..." snapped Ishizaki.

They grumbled at one another.

"Well, I suppose it's not like you're assassins sent here by Ryuuen," I told him. If they were putting on an act, then it was a pretty impressive one. But I doubted that was the case.

"Of course we're not. There's no way...that Ryuuen-san would ask us to do something like that. You know that."

"Yeah, I guess."

Ryuuen had already shown that he was bowing out, by way of telling everyone that he had been defeated by Ishizaki. In fact, he seemed fully determined to leave the school. Even if he wasn't planning on dropping out, he wouldn't be seeking my help. He'd never be okay with something so pitiful as coming to me.

"You seriously don't want Ryuuen to get expelled? Aren't you thinking about all the messed up things he did?" said Ibuki.

"...Well... yeah, he did do lots of bad stuff. But it's different now."

"What is?"

"Huh? What is what?"

"I'm asking you what's different now."

"I guess it's like, I understand now that Ryuuen-san is someone Class D needs," said Ishizaki.

"I don't understand you. Do you have any clue how much trouble we've had just because of him?" snapped Ibuki.

Apparently, they'd paid me a visit without first making sure they were both on the same page. It was like they were incapable of mutual understanding.

"If you're going to fight, do it later," I told them. When I did so, they stopped glaring at one another.

"Ugh, I wanna go back to my room," muttered Ibuki.

They didn't seem to be in agreement at all. Ibuki's face was particularly grim.

"Don't say you wanna go back. You gotta help me convince Ayanokouji."

"Don't wanna."

"If you're going to fight, do it somewhere else."

Since the conversation was going nowhere, I decided to ask them something myself.

"Ryuuen's entire class hates him. At least, it looks that way from the outside. That's not wrong though, is it?" I asked.

"Well, I guess... He is kinda hated, yeah."

"Kinda? I think you mean by almost everyone. There's no point in lying about that," said Ibuki.

"Shut it! What I said was fine!"

"Ugh, god, you're so annoying. Also, stop shouting. You're getting spit everywhere."

"Look, I told you already, if you're going to fight, do it later," I reminded them.

If they created a commotion in my small room, it would carry over into the rooms next door. They seemed to finally calm down a little when I reprimanded them with a hint of anger. I wondered if they understood that they'd come in uninvited? If so, we could proceed with the conversation.

"Stopping Ryuuen from being expelled would be fool-hardy." I didn't beat around the bush, but directly stated the truth, thinking they'd understand better that way.

"You've got that right," said Ibuki, nodding in under-standing.

However, it didn't seem Ishizaki was going to be so

easily convinced. "Isn't there *anything* we can do?!" he shouted.

His motivation, at least, was genuine. There seemed to be no doubt that he really wanted to save Ryuuen.

"You really want to stop Ryuuen from getting expelled, huh?" I asked him.

"...Yeah."

With the exception of me, Ibuki, and a few others, most students seemed to hate Ryuuen. Of course, this was because of what had happened between Ryuuen and I. Even so, Ishizaki had been on the receiving end of Ryuuen's abuse many times. Did he really want to save Ryuuen badly enough that he would reluctantly force himself come beg for my help? I supposed it all came down to the emotions he'd cultivated over the course of the past year.

But if emotions alone could deal with this test, then no one would be struggling. I was going to have to explain this test's complexity to Ishizaki in a manner easy enough for him to understand.

"There are two main reasons why I think saving Ryuuen is foolhardy. This supplementary exam will be decided by the number of criticism votes your class has. Even if you, Ibuki, and two or three other people use praise votes on Ryuuen instead of criticism votes, it's very likely he'll get over thirty criticism votes. And besides, no one else would want to get expelled themselves," I reasoned.

"B-but...there aren't that many people in our class who think that we can actually get to the top without Ryuuen-san's abilities!" replied Ishizaki.

It was probably true that some members of Class D acknowledged Ryuuen's abilities. However, that wasn't good enough. Such students couldn't overlook the risk of being expelled themselves.

"Going after Ryuuen, the most hated person in class, would cause students the least amount of heartache," said Ibuki.

She was exactly right.

"Even if the worst-case scenario happens and we don't move up to the higher-level classes, we'd still want to make it to graduation safely, right? Everyone wants to avoid being stuck with the label of high school dropout," she added.

Ishizaki's face told me their class had already had this discussion.

"Since you're being treated as the person who spearheaded the revolt against Ryuuen, I'm sure you've already heard all this, haven't you?" I asked.

Ishizaki nodded. He'd probably had to at least ostensibly voice his approval of Ryuuen's expulsion, because of the position he was in.

"I think everyone in class is in favor of Ryuuen-san's expulsion except for Ibuki, Albert, and Shiina," said Ishizaki.

"So, he's screwed no matter how you look at it, right?" said Ibuki.

"Yeah, he is," I replied.

He was completely screwed.

"That's why I came to you for help. You were the one who beat Ryuuen-san, so..." said Ishizaki.

"You're asking me if there's any way for him to avoid expulsion. Before we get to that, I want to ask you something."

"What...?"

"Saving Ryuuen means that one of your other classmates will be expelled. Do you understand that?"

That was a crucial aspect of this test. I needed to ask him that.

"Well, yeah, but..."

"If you really do understand, then do you have anyone else in mind to get rid of, instead?" I asked.

"N-no, I don't. I don't want to get rid of any of my classmates."

"Then we already have a problem. This test is designed to ensure someone is sacrificed." This wasn't a situation where you could blithely talk about wanting to save someone and leave it at that.

"Come on, you know Ayanokouji is right, don't you? If you were really serious about saving Ryuuen, then why don't you go ahead and just volunteer to get kicked out yourself? If you ask for everyone to give you criticism votes, then maybe you can save him that way," said Ibuki.

A cold statement. She was basically suggesting Ishizaki be cast aside, but in truth, it was probably the most effective option available. Ryuuen had earned a lot of hatred from his classmates. Even if he was a talented person who could devise outlandish schemes and had the kind of nerves ordinary people didn't, once you considered the fact that the class had been demoted to bottom place, it was inevitable that he'd be cut.

"So, there's...no way to avoid someone being expelled?" asked Ishizaki.

"That's what everyone has been thinking about, obviously. And we've all given up on the idea," I replied.

"...Right," said Ibuki, letting out a short, exasperated sigh. She hadn't wanted to reach out to me for help because she knew this was absurd from the very beginning. "This is a complete waste of time. There's no changing the fact that Ryuuen is getting expelled."

"Damn it...!"

Ishizaki pounded the wall in apparent frustration.

"I think Ryuuen was planning to spend the next three years without taking action—but he immediately changed his mind when he heard the rules of this supplementary special exam. He probably knows there's no way for him to avoid being expelled, which is why he didn't say anything, but decided to just quietly wait for the exam to be over," I reasoned.

Ishizaki probably didn't consider Ryuuen's self-sacrifice some kind of beautiful, noble act, either. He simply wasn't resisting. That was all.

"I, I..."

Ishizaki clenched his fists tight, clear frustrated. He really wanted to save Ryuuen, huh? No matter how many enemies you had, it wasn't a bad thing to have friends who'd follow you. Ryuuen might not admit this, himself, but he had some good friends.

An idea began to form in my mind. However, we were missing some things we'd need to make it work.

"If there's any advice I can give you, it would be..."

"What? Whatever it is, just tell me!" shouted Ishizaki, pitching forward. He must really have been clinging desperately to hope. Unfortunately, that hope was going to be dashed.

"It would be a shame to let Ryuuen's private points just go to waste. If he's been continuously receiving kickbacks from Class A, then he must have accumulated millions of points. Right?" I asked.

"Yeah. He does have about that much. If he hasn't spent them," said Ibuki.

"There's no guarantee that those private points will be transferred or disseminated if he's still holding them once he's expelled. Given that, you should probably transfer all of them before his expulsion is set in stone. They'll be useful to Class D later," I reasoned.

If those points were distributed among everyone, they wouldn't be one big lump sum anymore. It was better for them to have someone pocket them for themselves now. I was sure Ryuuen would at least agree to that.

"Th-that's not what I was askin' for! I wanted to know how to *save* Ryuuen-san!" shouted Ishizaki.

"Knock it off, Ishizaki. There's no point in pressing this," said Ibuki, reprimanding Ishizaki with a light kick. "That being said, I have no intention of picking up those points that Ryuuen has saved up, Ayanokouji."

She said that assertively and with force. She was serious about letting those points go rather than begging Ryuuen for them.

"I see. What about you, Ishizaki?" I asked.

"No way!" he shouted.

Despite their different thoughts on the matter, they

were apparently in accord on this. They were determined to let those private points go if Ryuuen was expelled. No...I supposed it wasn't anything quite so noble as determination.

"Unfortunately, there's no way you can save Ryuuen."

"Wh—!"

Ishizaki looked at me, the expression on his face somewhere between anger and frustration.

"Listen. The *only* thing you can do right now is collect those points. This test isn't simple enough to let you save someone just because you want to," I replied.

"That's bullshit! So, what, I'm supposed to just get those points from Ryuuen-san and be like, 'see ya later'? Ain't no *way* I could do that!" snapped Ishizaki.

He raised his fist, but Ibuki immediately grabbed it and stopped him.

"It's pointless. Just stop. He might look like a normal person, but he's a monster," said Ibuki.

"Even if I'm no match for 'im, I can least get one hit in!" shouted Ishizaki.

"I told you, enough already!" Ibuki promptly smacked him over the head. "Look, we just waltzed over here and made this completely crazy request. And what Ayanokouji is saying isn't wrong—you're just completely lashing out over it. This is just pathetic, so can you *stop*?"

"Ugh..."

The blood had completely rushed to Ishizaki's head. It seemed he just couldn't keep his cool when it came to Ryuuen.

And apparently, neither of them intended to do anything about the millions of points that were going to disappear into the ether. Those points should *definitely* be collected if they were thinking about Class D's future. If Ibuki and Ishizaki—Ryuuen's friends—didn't want to take them, then that was that, but...

"Actually, I was really hoping to see a little more of your resolve," I told him.

"...Huh? What? Resolve?" asked Ishizaki.

"If you can't even collect those private points from Ryuuen, this has nothing to do with you anymore."

With that, I brought our conversation to an end. But I was halfway convinced that Ibuki and Ishizaki *would* still go collect those private points from Ryuuen.

8.5

• •

AT JUST PAST TEN O'CLOCK on the night before the test, my phone rang.

"It's me. I've collected all of Ryuuen's private points." Ibuki cut straight to the chase, stating just the facts.

"Good job finding my contact info," I replied, trying to prod her for information, but she said nothing in return. I was betting Shiina had given her my number. That was probably how she got it. "Okay, so you got the points, huh?"

I'd figured she was going to make a move, but this was cutting it pretty close.

"Can you get Ishizaki and come to my room right now?" I asked.

"Huh? Right now?"

"Is there a problem? I need to talk to you about those points that you recovered."

"No, it's not really a problem... All right."

Ibuki quickly agreed to my request and said that she would get in touch with Ishizaki before ending the call. Perhaps because they had a hunch about what was to come, both of them showed up at my door about ten minutes later. I immediately let them in.

"How many points did Ryuuen have?" I asked.

"A little over five million."

"That's plenty. If it wasn't enough, we would've needed to do some scrambling." As I'd expected, there was no indication Ryuuen had spent any of the points.

"What do you mean? What are you going to do?" asked Ishizaki, unable to see where I was going with this.

Ibuki, on the other hand, already looked determined. So she was following along.

"You're going to use them to do something, aren't you?" asked Ibuki.

"Correct," I replied.

"To do what...?" asked Ishizaki.

"We're using them to do just one thing. To save Ryuuen."

"H-hold on, wait a second. Didn't they say we needed twenty million to do that?" asked Ishizaki.

It was true. We didn't have nearly that many points.

"Before we do this, I have something to ask you, Ishizaki. Are you prepared to shoulder this burden? Do you have the resolve to do that?" I asked.

"Wh-what are you talkin' about all of a sudden? Resolve for what now? Burden...?"

"Keeping Ryuuen around means someone else will be cut loose. I told you that before, didn't I?"

"...Yeah." Ishizaki nodded, despite looking flustered. "Yeah, I'm resolved."

"I see. That's good, then. So who's going to get expelled?" I asked.

"Who's going to get expelled...?" repeated Ishizaki. Apparently, he hadn't yet decided on a person yet.

"If you can't decide, then I can choose for you. If that'll make you feel less guilty, it's easy enough to do. Of course, if you think I might carelessly get rid of a key person in your class, you don't have to go along with my decision," I told him.

"W-wait, hold on. Just let me think for a second..."

"We don't have time."

"I-I'll have an answer in just a second."

So he said, but if he could come to a decision that quickly, he wouldn't be struggling in the first place.

"Wait a second. I don't really care who we get rid of, but the real question is, what's our plan here? If you say we're going to save him with those points, aren't we short by fifteen million?" asked Ibuki.

Her irritation was understandable. That being said, there were other circumstances to consider.

"If you want to stop Ryuuen from being expelled, then I'd like you to decide who to target instead," I told her.

We would discuss the finer details of the strategy once that was settled. Though I felt bad for not answering Ibuki, since she was clearly disgruntled, I moved the conversation forward.

"For example, are there any troublemakers in your class?"

"Troublemakers, huh...? Well, I guess me and Komiya, probably. For girls, Nishino or Manabe, I'd say," said Ishizaki.

"If we're keeping Ryuuen around, then I honestly don't think it's a good idea to get rid of someone like you, who understands his importance to the class. If there's another test like this, there's no guarantee he'll be safe the next time," said Ibuki.

"Which means Nishino or Manabe..." Ishizaki said.

So those were the names that came to his mind after what I'd said. I remembered hearing both those names before. Manabe, in particular, was someone I'd thought about getting expelled. That being said, it was Ishizaki and Ibuki who had the right to choose. I would ask them for the name of the student they wanted to get rid of, and honor their decision.

"So, expel one of those two. Or someone else. It's up to you," I told them.

Ishizaki also knew about the incident with Manabe and Kei during the cruise ship exam. If that knowledge had even the slightest impact on his thought process, then Manabe would most likely be the student he decided to get rid of.

He was trying to think of Manabe's flaws. He was searching for things that would basically give him a way out, to let him say that he had no choice but to pick her. Manabe had brought all this trouble upon herself by putting her hands on Kei. Even if she got expelled, there was nothing she could do to stop it. Such were the thoughts currently running through Ishizaki's mind.

Also, though Kei had already put the incident behind her, there was no changing the fact that Manabe's very presence made her uneasy. Having one less thing to worry about would give Kei some peace of mind. And if I insinuated to her that I'd been the one to get Manabe eliminated, then she would trust me even more.

However, someone unexpected piped up first.

"Is it okay if I decide?" asked Ibuki.

"Huh? You?" asked Ishizaki.

"Yeah. There's someone I want to have expelled."

"Who?" I asked, without waiting for Ishizaki to answer yes or no.

"I want to have Manabe expelled. That's just my personal preference, though," said Ibuki.

"Are you sure you're okay with deciding that way?" I asked.

"It should be fine. Right?" asked Ibuki.

There was no hesitation in her eyes. I understood right away.

"If Ishizaki has no objections, then Manabe it is. Even though we've come to that decision, though, we have no way to guarantee it. We can only ensure that Ryuuen won't be expelled. In other words, the person who gets the most criticism votes will still be expelled. Our goal is to reduce the possibility that either of you could be that person. We don't have much time left," I reasoned.

"Got it... Okay, I'll tell the guys that there's been some changes, and they should use their votes on Manabe. I think they'll be on board if I tell them the plan is to just to scare her by giving her the second-most criticism votes in class, after Ryuuen," said Ishizaki.

"Not a bad idea," I replied, approving of the plan.

As long as the students thought Ryuuen's fate was sealed and he was bound to get the most criticism votes, they wouldn't think it mattered who they used their other votes on.

"...Well, I think I might be in trouble, though," said Ibuki.

"Huh? Whaddya mean, Ibuki?" asked Ishizaki.

"Manabe and her friends are probably going to vote for Ryuuen and me. Which means I'll be in a tight spot."

"W-wait, are you serious?"

"Dude, even you know that Manabe and I don't get along, right?" said Ibuki.

"Well, yeah, but..." Ishizaki sounded shaken, unable to keep up with what was going on.

"That just means that Ibuki's made up her mind, too," I said.

Of course, if someone other than Manabe got expelled, then Ibuki would have no choice but to give up.

"Well, it might be a good idea for the girls to talk to Hiyori."

"To Shiina?"

"She might be able to help you out with this. You could get in touch with her and say you want to focus criticism votes on Manabe in order to save Ryuuen."

"...Okay," replied Ibuki, nodding, before sending a message to Hiyori. "So, wait, you've talked to Shiina? I really can't imagine she'd be on board with getting Manabe kicked out."

"We've talked a little about this exam," I replied.

While Hiyori was a pacifist, her resolve was strong when it came to respecting the wishes of her class.

"She said she would help if it was for the good of the class. I'm sure she'll lend you a hand, since she concluded herself that it would be in Class D's best interest for Ryuuen to stay," I added.

We would control the boys' and girls' votes as much as possible. We would reduce the number of praise votes used on Manabe and increase the number of criticism votes coming her way. On the other hand, we'd increase the number of praise votes Ibuki got, while decreasing the number of criticism votes cast for her. That alone would likely dramatically reduce the huge initial gap in one fell swoop.

"Okay then, tell me what your strategy is. How are you going to save him with only five million points?" asked Ibuki.

Her eyes were telling me to hurry up and spit it out. I picked up my cell phone and sent a text to a certain person. My message was marked as read almost immediately, followed by the recipient responding that they'd come to my room at once, since the time limit was only two hours away. We were fortunate this person was patient.

"What're you doing?" asked Ibuki.

"Someone's going to come and visit. They're the secret weapon that's going to stop Ryuuen from getting expelled," I replied.

"Secret weapon to...stop Ryuuen from getting expelled?"

They probably couldn't believe it. A few minutes later, my doorbell rang. Ibuki and Ishizaki were even more guarded than before.

"Are you sure it's okay for someone to see us together?" asked Ibuki.

"Don't worry about that. But I am going to ask you to make sure we all get our stories straight."

In the brief window of time before the visitor arrived, I told the two of them what to say.

● ●

"PARDON THE INTRUSION."

Naturally, Ibuki and Ishizaki were shocked when they saw who'd come to visit. I doubted they'd ever imagined this was who I was talking about.

"Seriously...?"

"Whoa."

"Oh! I had thought there might be other people here... Good evening."

"G-good evening," replied Ishizaki. For some reason, he sounded a little shy.

The person who'd just showed up at my room was none other than Ichinose Honami, currently seated alongside Ibuki and Ishizaki from Class D. After seeing Ichinose, Ibuki finally started to piece together what was happening.

"It looks like we've got a common interest, huh?" said Ibuki.

"Huh? Whaddya mean?" asked Ishizaki, cocking his head to the side in apparent confusion.

"Yes, it would seem we do, Ibuki-san," replied Ichinose.

"No one out there actually *wants* to save Ryuuen. Even if, hypothetically, someone showed up saying that they'd get him praise votes, we wouldn't know if they were really telling the truth. But...there are some exceptions," said Ibuki.

"O-Oh, I gotcha. So, does that mean Ichinose is gonna get everyone in Class B together and...?!" exclaimed Ishizaki.

It seemed he was finally beginning to understand as well.

"Yes. I'll talk to everyone and ask them to please use their praise votes—all forty of Class B's praise votes—on Ryuuen-kun. In exchange, Ibuki-san will help us make up the private points we're missing," explained Ichinose.

This was a strategy that could only work once. Ichinose had been moving to collect private points from her class-mates since school started, while Ryuuen had made a deal with Class A and continued to amass private points that way. The two of them were the only students capable of executing this power play.

"If you two work together, no one will get expelled from Class B, and Ryuuen will get to stay in Class D," I told them.

No matter how many students in Class D voted against him, Ryuuen could only get a maximum of 39 criticism votes. With Class B's support, all the votes against him would be cancelled out, pushing him into the green.

Ibuki and Ichinose looked one another in the eyes. People who rarely interacted with one another just as rarely had a relationship of trust. But looking into another person's eyes allowed you to judge, to some extent, whether or not they could be trusted.

Ichinose shifted her gaze briefly away from Ibuki and looked me in the eyes as well.

"So... by using twenty million points, I can save one of my classmates from getting expelled, right?" said Ichinose, before looking back at Ibuki.

"What do you think? Are you going to take the deal or not? It's up to you to decide, Ichinose," I told her.

Ichinose had the right to choose. She did still have the option of rejecting Ibuki and Ishizaki's offer and asking for Nagumo's help instead.

"I've made up my mind. As long as Ibuki-san and Ishizaki-kun are okay with it, I would like to go ahead and work together," said Ichinose.

"Are you really okay with this?" I asked.

"Yes. I can tell their feelings are genuine," replied Ichinose.

"You're an idiot, aren't you, Ichinose?" said Ibuki.

"Huh?" asked Ichinose.

"Even though all those nasty rumors about you were going around, you still collected and saved up those points from everyone. And now you're going to blow them all on something like this?" asked Ibuki.

"Well, we can always just start saving up all over again. We know now that it's not entirely impossible to save up close to twenty million points in just a year. Besides, I don't know if you can really point that finger at me right now, Ibuki-san. I mean, you could keep those five million points for yourself, but you've decided to spend them all on Ryuuen-kun," answered Ichinose.

Ibuki averted her eyes, without answering.

"I'm not like you... Besides, someone else from our class is going to end up going home in tears in Ryuuen's place. It could very well be me," she said.

"Even so, you're going to save Ryuuen-kun, aren't you?" asked Ichinose.

"He's... I just don't like the thought of me ending up owing him a weird debt is all."

Ibuki offered Ichinose salvation, prepared to earn the

resentment of her peers in return. She sent the designated number of private points to Ichinose via her phone.

"Check it," said Ibuki.

"Okay." Ichinose immediately took out her own phone and checked her own point balance to see if it now displayed twenty million. "Thank you. Looks like it was sent over successfully."

She showed us her phone, proving that she did indeed have the twenty million points.

"I'll act as your witness in these negotiations. I've also been recording this conversation," I said, pulling out my own phone, for the sake of fairness. "Ibuki offered roughly four million points. In return, Ichinose will ensure that all forty praise votes from her class go to Ryuuen. If there's any breach of this agreement, then—"

"If I think that I haven't fulfilled my end of the bargain, I will voluntarily drop out of school," said Ichinose.

Of course, none of us actually thought Ichinose would ever go back on her word. In fact, an exchange involving such a huge sum would be kept in the school's records. It wouldn't even be surprising if they flagged it as a fraudulent transaction. But it was precisely because this was Ichinose Honami we were dealing with that Ibuki and Ishizaki felt like they could rest easy and let her handle it.

And that was the story of what happened between me, Ichinose, Ibuki, and Ishizaki.

• •

THE BACK OF THE SCHOOL building was quiet.

"You asserted that if you took this seriously, you could've gotten through this test without getting expelled. You were thinking of the same method too, I'm guessing?" I asked.

"Yeah. I knew that Ichinose chick was saving up points. And besides, she's a goody two-shoes. I knew there was room to negotiate, even if she didn't like me. But I didn't think Ibuki had the wits or the skill to negotiate using private points. So, I was just planning on resting easy, and letting her have 'em... I didn't think you'd get involved, though," said Ryuuen.

"Ibuki and Ishizaki just happened to ask me for a favor. I took advantage of that opportunity and made good use of them. As far as I'm concerned, it was an excellent opportunity for me to build trust with Ichinose, so I'm grateful for that. If I'd come to you directly, you would've seen through my plans and refused to hand over the points. Right?" I asked.

"You made the right call not explaining anything to Ibuki," he replied.

If I had done that, Ryuuen would have grown suspicious. He would have seen what was going on and noticed me acting behind the scenes.

"So, were you the one who targeted Manabe?" he asked.

It was only natural he'd think I'd targeted her, I supposed, given the fact that Manabe had bullied Kei.

"No, that was simply a coincidence. You do know that Ibuki and Manabe weren't on good terms with each other either, right?"

"Ah, I gotcha. That was pretty gutsy of her. Manabe was crying her eyes out."

I could vaguely imagine how she had reacted when her name was called in the classroom.

"This means I got saved by Ishizaki and Ibuki then, huh? Talk about unwelcome favors, man."

"Yeah, I guess." I deliberately held back from delving into the matter any further.

If Ibuki and Ishizaki hadn't paid me a visit in my room that day, I would probably have broached the subject with Hiyori, then had her collect the private points in the same fashion. I'd done it so Ichinose would owe me a debt of gratitude. At the same time, I didn't want to let Ryuuen be expelled, for some reason. Those thoughts were swirling around in my head as I went through this exam.

"What are you doing to do if the next exam is like this one?" I asked.

"Heh heh. Who knows?" he replied.

He didn't say he wouldn't do anything. I supposed that might mean Ryuuen felt at least something for Ibuki and Ishizaki, deep down. Things might get interesting if he returned to the fold in the not-too-distant future.

Of course, whether or not that happened was entirely up to him.

My cell phone rang. Ichinose's name was displayed on the screen. When Ryuuen saw me getting a call from someone, he headed back into the school building without saying another word.

"Seems like Class B made it through without anyone getting expelled," I said on the phone.

"Yes. Kanzaki volunteered to be the one to be expelled, so everyone focused their criticism votes on him. Then I paid the twenty million points to prevent his expulsion. Everything came together at the very last minute, but all of Class B managed to make it through safely, without any expulsions," said Ichinose.

"I see. But the price you paid wasn't cheap," I answered.

Thanks to this, Class B was now even poorer than Class D, albeit temporarily. Even though they'd see points deposited in April, they were probably facing some rough times ahead. Besides, we were about to be starting our second year. We might need private points right away. Though I supposed I didn't need to confirm any of that right now.

"If we lose our private points, we can always get them back. But if we lose even one precious friend, there's no getting them back," said Ichinose.

I might've said too much. Ichinose spoke without hesitation. I could tell that she was firmly determined to make sure everyone in Class B made it to graduation.

"Ryuuen-kun might not like this result, though. It seems Manabe-san was the one who got expelled, in the end," said Ichinose.

I decided to not comment on the fact that I'd just met up with Ryuuen a second ago.

"Were you close to Manabe, Ichinose?" I asked.

"Not really. I think we've only spoken a couple of times. But even so, it's still sad. Totsuka-kun from Class A and Yamauchi-kun from Class C are gone, too..." said Ichinose.

She sounded like she still couldn't believe it had really happened.

"I wonder if someone else is going to disappear like this again, somewhere down the line?" asked Ichinose, clearly uneasy.

"Maybe," I replied. A student you'd thought you were going to see every day might suddenly be gone. "But even so, you're going to continue to fight it, right?"

"Yes. I'm going to move up to Class A with all of my friends and we'll graduate together," said Ichinose.

Before today, there might have been some people who would've branded Ichinose a hypocrite. But now any notions of her being a hypocrite would have been completely swept away. No matter what, Ichinose would fight to protect her class until the very end.

"...Thank you so much, Ayanokouji-kun. If you weren't here, I..." said Ichinose, trailing off.

"Would have started going out with Nagumo?" I replied, finishing her sentence.

"...Yeah," she answered, confirming it. "I know it's stupid. I was trying to convince myself that it would be a small price to pay if it was for the sake of saving my classmates. But...I was deeply relieved to know I didn't have to choose that route, after all."

She must have been patting her chest. I heard her let out a deep sigh of relief on the other end of the line.

"I think I definitely would've regretted that decision eventually," she added, letting out a laugh afterward.

"If neither the student council president nor I were around, what would you have done?" I asked.

"...Do you have to ask?" she replied.

"Just curious. I mean, it's not like you didn't come up with something, right?"

"Yeah, I had two plans. One option was for me to quit school myself," she replied.

Just as I thought. Ichinose had been considering sacrificing herself too, huh?

"But I had a feeling that wasn't quite the right choice. I thought that as a student at this school, I should be willing to fight until the end," she added.

Which meant her other plan would've been her real choice, I supposed.

"And the other plan was...was to draw straws."

"I see..."

The strategy seemed simple enough that anyone could've come up with it. But it wasn't something you could pull off without everyone's consent.

"Was everyone in Class B prepared to start drawing straws?" I asked.

"Yeah. We discussed it and decided that if we couldn't come up with a way to avoid expulsion by the day of the poll, we would draw straws and use criticism votes on the three people who pulled the short straws. We didn't discuss who would get praise votes, though—we decided to just let people pick those themselves and see how it went."

I supposed there was probably no other way to judge students equally, without paying mind to who was superior or inferior. Even if Ichinose had ended up pulling a short straw in that scenario, I was sure it would've been offset by the praise votes she would get—and sure everyone would have been fine with that.

"That's probably the fairest way you could have handled the situation. But that method definitely wouldn't have worked in the other classes," I replied. The more gifted the student, the intensely they would reject such an idea.

"No one wanted to get expelled, but no one wanted to see their friends go away, either. Once I explained things properly to everyone, they understood," said Ichinose.

That was precisely because they were so completely united under a leader like Ichinose.

"I'm impressed," I told her.

Even though it couldn't be conveyed over the phone, I bowed my head, expressing my respect for Ichinose.

The strategy by itself wasn't all that great. But the fact that she was in a position to actually execute it was amazing.

"Well, I'll talk to you later. Really, thank you so much, Ayanokouji-kun."

"I was just the middleman. If you're going to thank anyone, thank Ryuuen and his pals."

8.8

• •

AFTERWARD, I SAW that I had received another message.

"Sakayanagi, huh."

I didn't know where she got my contact information, but I figured I might as well meet with her. I'd been expecting her to come check out the bulletin board herself, but...

As per Sakayanagi's message, I made my way over to the special building, where she said she would be waiting. Even though it was already past the time she had asked to meet in her message, I figured I could still catch her if I left now. Once at the special building, I went immediately to the spot where we'd talked last time.

"I'm ever so glad you came," said Sakayanagi.

"If you have my e-mail address, doesn't that mean you also have my phone number?"

"Even if I couldn't meet you in person, I wouldn't have minded," she replied.

"What did you want to talk about?"

"I was just thinking I would explain things to you, more or less," she replied.

As Sakayanagi spoke, she held onto her cane, moving forward and slightly closing the distance between us.

"I was afraid I might have made you uneasy by causing something of a disturbance. But I suppose such concerns were unnecessary on my part," she added.

Of course, she was referring to the fact that she'd used Yamauchi to gather criticism votes and focus them on me.

"Back when we had our talk about wanting to postpone our contest, I was about ninety percent certain that you were being truthful. But I couldn't trust you completely. So, I made a couple of moves myself, just to be safe," I replied.

"I know. However, you do agree this doesn't mean that I've broken our promise, hm?" she replied.

"You didn't do anything to impede me. Besides, you didn't lie."

Setting aside the mental strain of recent events, the end result was that I'd gotten an overwhelming number of praise votes. I hadn't even the slightest reason to hold a grudge against Sakayanagi.

"Thank you ever so much," said Sakayanagi, showing her gratitude by bowing lightly. "By the way... Totsuka-kun should have gotten a total of thirty-eight criticism votes, but he only got thirty-six. Did you give him a praise vote?"

"I wasn't entirely sure. But when you talked about having Katsuragi expelled, I thought you might be bluffing," I told her.

If that was true, I felt it was more likely that she was going after Yahiko, Katsuragi's follower. So I voted for him, even though it was only one vote and it wasn't going to change anything.

"Wonderful. I knew you were the opponent I needed to defeat, after all."

"So? Was this all just because you wanted to mess with me?" I asked.

"Well...I'd be lying if I said that wasn't part of it. But there's a reason why I wished to postpone our contest. I mentioned something along these lines a short time ago, but this supplementary special exam was undoubtedly arranged by a certain someone just so that they could get you expelled. In fact, this certain someone sent me an e-mail, specifically asking me to have you expelled," said Sakayanagi.

"An e-mail?"

"Yes. I'm sure the sender was the person who had my father suspended from his position. It would seem they originally intended to only allow students to cast criticism votes for students from other classes. But that would've been far too outrageous of an exam, wouldn't you say?" said Sakayanagi.

"If that rule had been put in place, it wouldn't matter what kind of student you were. If classes colluded, they could get anyone expelled."

It would've been an entirely ridiculous exam. One where people could even take down the likes of Sakayanagi and Ichinose, if they wanted to.

"Yes. The current staff were vehemently opposed, and it seems they were able to prevent that rule from being put in place. At any rate, cooperating with this individual to get you expelled that way would be the dullest possible thing. I decided to allocate every praise vote from Class A to you, in order to protect you no matter what. That way, even if someone was acting in secret to get you expelled, it wouldn't work," said Sakayanagi.

"In that case, why Yamauchi? Did he just happen to be the one you picked to use?"

"Do you not recall? When we were at the school camp, he bumped into me. He was quite rude," she answered.

Come to think of it, yeah. That had happened.

"It was retribution for that," she added.

So that was all it took for Sakayanagi to make him a target, huh? Well, I supposed that was more than enough reason for her.

"However, I only created the opportunity. In the end, he was eliminated because he was unnecessary to your class."

"Yeah, that's true."

Even if Sakayanagi hadn't gotten involved in this test, the end result would probably have been almost the same.

"So there you have it. That's the main reason why I asked we not have our contest this time around. Now, while I would love for my father to be reinstated to his position as soon as possible, and for school management to be returned to a state of normalcy..."

There was no one else in the special building. It had only been the two of us. But suddenly, a figure appeared, casting a shadow in the space between Sakayanagi and me.

"Oh, hello."

It was a man clad in a suit.

"This is my first time at this school. Do you happen to know where the faculty lounge is?" he asked.

"My, my. I must say, if you're looking for the faculty lounge, then you're looking in entirely the wrong place. Oh, by the way—please excuse my rudeness, but who are you?" asked Sakayanagi.

"My name is Tsukishiro. I'm the new acting director," he replied, giving us a gentle smile and a kind, polite wave.

He was probably in his forties, about the same age as Sakayanagi's father. A young director.

"Heh heh. Is that so? Well, I must say, our new acting director must be *quite* directionally challenged, if he just so happened to get lost and accidentally came all the way here. Or perhaps... I wonder if he spotted us on the security cameras and came here to check on us? This is the place Ayanokouji-kun and I used to hold our secret meetings during the exam. If the director was always watching, it would be rather easy for him to come pay us a visit," said Sakayanagi.

As Sakayanagi spoke, I recalled the strange look she'd given the cameras earlier. If someone had been watching us meet here, she might have done that to lure them out. That had been Sakayanagi's plan. And it would appear that this person had fallen for it.

Director Tsukishiro avoided her implications with a smile.

"You're a girl who says very interesting things. Well, I *have* heard this is an exceedingly delightful school. I wonder if all of the students are like you, hm? If you'll excuse me..." He moved forward, as if he intended to walk between us.

"If you're looking for the faculty lounge, shouldn't you to turn around and go the other way? You're in the wrong building."

As Sakayanagi gave him that polite advice, Tsukishiro, still smiling, kicked her cane out of her hands. The unexpected action naturally left Sakayanagi unable to react, and she started to fall.

"Whoa!"

I rushed over and grabbed her to keep her from falling. In the next instant, a large arm came swinging right at me. Since I was holding Sakayanagi, unable to dodge, I took the hit, doing my best to absorb the impact. I set Sakayanagi down on the floor and he followed immediately with another swing, catching me by the neck and pinning me against the wall with monstrous force.

"You're not as good as the rumors say, Ayanokouji Kiyotaka-kun."

He was pressing so hard on my throat that I couldn't make a sound. His strength was almost impossible to comprehend, given how he looked. It seemed it was going to be difficult for me to shake him off.

"...Well, you've gone and done something quite contemptible, haven't you, Acting Director?" said Sakayanagi.

"I was sure you were given orders. To have him expelled."

"Oh, that e-mail was from one of your people, hm?

I suppose it's understandable that you'd want to rely upon someone like me, since school officials can't just blatantly have a student expelled," she replied with a smile, while slowly getting back up. "Thank you for helping me, Ayanokouji-kun."

I couldn't possibly have told Sakayanagi, with her disability, to dodge the attack. She might have done more than just fall.

"Don't you think there might be a problem with the acting director getting violent with students?" she asked.

"There's no need to worry. The surveillance cameras have already been rigged to show dummy footage."

Meaning, no matter what happened, there would be no record of it.

"Now then, I have a message from your father. He says, 'I'm not playing these childish games anymore. Come home at once.' How about you blink twice for yes?" said Tsukishiro.

He didn't let me speak, and didn't even give me the option of saying no. This was certainly something *that* man would do. I didn't answer, but simply remained silent.

"So you have no intention of leaving this school voluntarily, huh," muttered the acting director, sounding bored. "Aren't you going to at least *try* to resist? Show me that you're not just some normal kid."

He started applying more force on my throat. This wasn't an opponent an ordinary student could handle. He was a well-trained foe.

"You have more than just observational skills, right? I want to see what you can do," he goaded me once again. But I still wasn't showing the slightest sign of resistance.

Finally, realizing that I had no intention of fighting back, Tsukishiro let me go.

"I officially start work at this school in April. I sincerely hope you're looking forward to it."

And with those parting words, he left the special building.

"You made a wise choice, Ayanokouji-kun," said Sakayanagi, praising my decision to not resist.

"He's the acting director. Had I carelessly decided to fight back, I don't know what he might have used against me," I replied.

He'd said the security cameras were showing dummy footage, but there was no guarantee he wasn't still recording what was happening here. It would've been checkmate if he had cut the footage to just show me being violent with the acting director.

"Are you all right?" she asked.

"Don't worry. I'm used to this kind of thing. More importantly, Sakayanagi?"

"Yes? What is it?"

"Let's officially have our contest in the next exam."

Sakayanagi's eyes widened in apparent surprise. "I never thought you'd say that directly to my face."

"If Tsukishiro's going to be involved come April, we're not going to have time for me to deal with you much longer. I'd like to make things explicitly clear. I want to end this."

"I do not mind. There won't need to be a second or third time. I will happily be your opponent," said Sakayanagi.

The final exam of our first year was about to begin. And I was going to bring an end to the confrontation Sakayanagi was hoping for.

8.9

• •

MONDAY.

I was sure some of the students in our class were wondering where Yamauchi was. Wondering if all that talk of getting expelled in the last test was just meant to scare us. But reality was cruel. After that weekend, the number of desks in the classroom had decreased by one. Yamauchi Haruki's place was already nowhere to be found.

Hirata's smile was gone. Kushida's smile was gone, too. Neither Sudou nor Ike looked like they had any energy at all.

"...Now then. I will announce the final exam of your first year."

And so we, the students of first-year Class C, advanced toward the final special exam of our first year.

POSTSCRIPT

Yooo, how're y'all doing? Happy New Year! This is the postscript that I wrote in the middle of the night for no reason at all, and here's Kinugasa, all super fired up!

Yep. Every year that goes by, I find it harder and harder to stay awake until the middle of the night. Back in my teens, I'd boast about trivial things like, "Hey, I can stay up for two whole days (48 hours) in a row!" But now that feels like a lie. Now, it's like, I've only been awake this long (20 hours), and it feels like I'm gonna die. When did this happen?

Make sure you get at least six hours of sleep a day, at minimum.

Yes. Well, okay, so yeah, in this volume, we're finally getting to the end of the first year...

The end...is NOT here! Even though I said something

in the previous postscript about how it seemed like it was going to end in the next volume, it's actually not ending! In truth, I had originally planned to incorporate both the "supplementary special exam" and the "Year 1 final exam" in volume 10, but I ended up spending over half the book on the former. There was no way I could cram both parts into the same book, so this is how it turned out.

While this book did turn out to be thicker than I had expected, the next volume will most definitely mark the end of the first year. After that, I'm planning for there to be another book in the interval between the end of the first year and the start of the second year (following the established [?] convention of 0.5 numbering).

Still, my plans seem to go awry after I write these postscripts, so I'm a little anxious.

...I'm going to try not to think about that.

Anyway, unlike in my books, the year in real life goes by so fast! I really can't believe that it's already 2019 now (at the time of this book's release), when I was just thinking that 2018 had only just started. Despite the fact that I've been wanting to move from releasing a book once every four months to once every three months, I haven't been able to actually make that happen over these past few years. But I'm always aiming to get things done in a three-month span, you know?

My illustrator, Tomoseshunsaku-san, and my editor have been an immense help to me in 2018, just like always. I'll be counting on you again in 2019, so please continue to take care of me!

Anyhow, I sincerely hope that you, the reader, will continue to enjoy my works in 2019 as well.

Let your imagination take flight with Seven Seas' light novel imprint: Airship

Discover your next great read at www.airshipnovels.com

Airship

Experience all that SEVEN SEAS has to offer!

SEVENSEASENTERTAINMENT.COM
Visit and follow us on Twitter at twitter.com/gomanga/